Trouble
Down Mexico Way

"I was a girl walking in a world of colors,
of clear and tangible shapes.
Everything was mysterious
and something was hiding;
guessing its nature was a game for me."

—The Mexican artist, Frida Kahlo (1907-1954)

Trouble

Down Mexico Way

A Blanche Murninghan Mystery

Nancy Nau Sullivan

Light Messages

Durham, NC

Copyright © 2021, Nancy Nau Sullivan
Trouble Down Mexico Way
Nancy Nau Sullivan
www.nancynausullivan.com

Published 2021, by Light Messages
www.lightmessages.com
Durham, NC 27713 USA
SAN: 920-9298

Paperback ISBN: 978-1-61153-375-0
Ebook ISBN: 978-1-61153-376-7
Library of Congress Control Number: 2021932340

To my students in Mexico,
and for the missing

Chapter One

DOWN

It was a good day for taking in the ancient Mayan exhibit but not so much for finding that dead body.

Blanche Murninghan didn't know what she was walking into. Besides, she wasn't walking; she was practically running through the streets of Mexico City.

Blanche was exhilarated after the flight from Tampa to Mexico, toting a backpack full of T-shirts, underwear, and books. She and Haasi had checked into their hotel and then set out at a fast pace for the Zocalo, the main plaza in one of the largest cities in the world. First up was a visit to a rare exhibit at the Palacio Nacional. Blanche was anxious to see the thousand-year-old art objects. But the city! She was inside a kaleidoscope. The people, the cosmopolitan women in tight dresses and high heels and men in suits and the indigenous people in native dress, the mariachi music pouring out of restaurants, the smell of roasted corn and traffic fumes, the balloons and bubbles and mimes painted gold. She was an island girl and more accustomed to the sounds of birds and waves and the wind in the pine trees. Her head was spinning.

"Jeez, Blanche, slow down." Haasi laughed. "That old Mayan stuff isn't going anywhere."

"Just look at this place. It's hoppin'."

At the edge of the Zocalo, they dodged traffic. Blanche could hardly see across the huge plaza. People swarmed out of the Metro stop. Cars and bikes and all sorts of wheeled vehicles zoomed past. She and Haasi joined the chaos. They had a long list of places to visit and only a couple weeks to absorb it all.

They stopped under Diego Rivera's wide swath of brilliant turquoise and red and gold murals at the Palacio. The wall in the stairwell all the way to the second floor blazed with Mexican history from ancient to modern times: a black-haired woman wearing a mantel of white lilies, a stepped pyramid hovering in the distance. Kings and revolutionaries on horseback, Moctezuma and Frida Kahlo.

"You have to wonder how he came up with all this!" Blanche said. The topknot of black curls wobbled and came loose.

Haasi aimed her camera at the murals. "Seriously. He didn't exactly have photos to work from."

"But there were cave paintings and art…"

Haasi nodded, clicking away. Inside the Palacio, soft lighting gilded the ancient pottery and figures in the glass cases. The unique Mayan collection included hundreds of artifacts assembled from digs in the Yucatan, Belize, Honduras, and Guatemala.

Blanche peered at the first display. "Hey, Haas, look at this. Organized games." Sure enough, the players were lined up on a field, kicking around a ball. Or a skull? In the next display, a crocodile and dog were laughing together.

The adjoining room was quiet, and crowded, the walls bare except for posters of the clay masks and native costumes.

"Kinda crowded in there," said Haasi. "Maybe check it out later?"

Blanche backed up against a wall and shivered. "Did you feel that?"

"No, what?"

"Well, it's not the air conditioning kicking in."

Haasi knew that look, one of trepidation and curiosity. "Don't be silly, Blanche. You afraid of ghosts or something?"

"Something."

"Let's have a look." Haasi linked her arm through Blanche's, and they squeezed in among the visitors.

Everyone seemed to be staring down at the floor where a wide expanse of polished glass stretched from wall to wall. The light under the glass cast a greenish glow on the faces of the people jostling each other. Blanche and Haasi pushed ahead and looked into a pit of ancient bodies dressed in tattered fabric. Mummies! Mounds of earth and broken wood and stone surrounded the dead in the macabre arrangement in the floor, a drape of black fabric and a Spanish cross finished it off. The eyes were nothing but sunken, shriveled spots — just a touch of ghoulishness that made Blanche's stomach churn.

She couldn't tear away. "This is just plain *eerie*."

There were four. A mother cradled an infant in dusty, pitiful love. Next to them were two adults with bony fingers crossed on their chests. The skin on one was bronze, another chalky white. The bodies were straight and stiff, as brittle as ancient bark, with ragged wrappings, some of it strips of disintegrating cloth, or cloaks, that once tightly bound the bodies.

"Poster says they're adults. They're so small. How could they know they're adults?" Blanche looked at Haasi for an answer.

"They're not all adults. Look at that baby. Hard to tell if it's even human. It's just creepy, but I guess we end up looking like that. A pile of dark leather and bones." She squinted at the signage. "They were found in some vein of minerals. Preserved them some. But not much, if you ask me."

"Says they're only a couple hundred years old."

"Only?"

Haasi shrugged. "They could be descendants of the Maya. Or Aztec." Her arms shot out and nearly knocked off the baseball hat of the man next to her. "They're on loan from a museum complex outside Mexico City."

The poster detailed the discovery of the long-lost mummies among bones in a crypt. Blanche leaned closer to the floor. She didn't move for several minutes.

"Really, Blanche. Don't be pressing your nose up against the glass. Bad luck."

"For someone," she almost whispered.

Haasi did not like the sound of that. "What is it?"

"Don't think this one's been dead hundreds of years. He, or she, or whatever, might've bought it not too long ago."

"What are you talking about?" Haasi peered into the floor.

"See that pink plastic thing above its right ear? They didn't wear pink plastic hair clips back then."

On closer inspection, Blanche noted the difference in the texture of skin between the One of Pink Plastic and the other mummies. "The face is shrunken to beef jerky like the rest, but it appears to have a newer sheen."

"As if the dead could look fresh," said Haasi. "Maybe, the exhibitors decided to do its hair up with that clip." But there was no conviction in her voice.

"Oh, right, and why not do the nails, too. They sure do need it." The fists curled on this one, and the nails were short or missing on the others.

Blanche stood up, and now several in the crowd were pressing in. A woman with large teeth and bright eyes screeched. "*¿Es posible?*"

Haasi smiled. A nervous smile. "So the wild ride begins," she murmured.

Blanche had a slightly crazed expression for which Haasi often forgave her. That was Blanche. But among her many physical attributes was an eagle eye. She stood straight, hands on her hips. "I'd swear. This one is different. It's not like the others!" Blanche frowned. "This mummy is a new one?"

Chapter Two

AND DEAD

THE BUZZING STARTED UP BEHIND BLANCHE. "What's going on, Haasi?"

"I don't know. Curiosity? What have you started?" Haasi turned to see people jamming into the room with the ancient bodies. She tugged at the back of Blanche's denim jacket. "Now what? Any ideas?"

"I think we should find somebody in charge," said Blanche.

"Right. But I think he's found us." The two stood close together, pressed against the sign that touted the origins of the exhibit.

"*¿Qué pasa?*" The small man dressed in black jacket and trousers, his clothes painted on, hurried toward the crowd. His long thin fingers waved people out of the way. His voice hit a high note that did nothing to calm the group. "*Por. Favor.*"

The toothy woman pointed at Blanche. "*¡Es ella!*"

The black-clad man ignored the gesticulating and bowed to Blanche. "Raúl López, assistant to the director of the Palacio Nacional." He extended his hand. "The pleasure is mine."

At little more than five feet, Blanche was almost eye level with *Señor* López. She shook his hand. Gravely. "Blanche Murningham, and Haasi Hakla, my cousin. We're visiting from Florida…" The two waited for a response, but all they got was a rather forced smile and another peremptory bow.

Señor López scanned the room and smoothed a hank of hair off his forehead. He had remarkable eyebrows that skittered up and down while the hairpiece didn't move. "*Bienvenido. Encantado,*" he said, but he looked far from enchanted. "What seems to be the … issue?" His clipped English was impeccable. He lowered the volume and tried to corral the discussion to just the three of them.

"This person. This very dead person…," Blanche began. "Are you sure he, or she, is *ancient,* like the others? It would appear to be, well, newer." Blanche scratched her head. She had no idea how long it took to make a mummy, but she would hazard a guess. "Maybe only a few weeks, a couple of months dead. Tops."

"That's preposterous," said *Señor* López. His eyes darted over the crowd. Blanche took his arm and steered him gently in the direction of the glass enclosure in the floor. "Look. Pink plastic? Do you see it? Above the ear? Don't think that hair clip was around back then. *Plastic* wasn't around back then. And the skin. It's *visibly* different than the others."

No question. To discern that the object in all that tangled, dry black hair was a pink hair clip was one thing, and to further speculate about the skin was another. *Doesn't López know this?* The thought that he might know it was frightening.

The man leaned over the glass. For one second. "Again, preposterous."

The crowd didn't agree. "*¡Lo veo!*" Someone, and then another, seemed to confirm Blanche's discovery.

Raúl waved people out of the sala. He looked at his watch. "We will indeed look into it," he said. "*Pero, ahorita. ¡Vámonos!* It's almost closing time."

Haasi had been oddly quiet, scanning the crowd. Blanche could sense Haasi's radar even as the tension ramped up. Nonchalantly she broke away and meandered around the edges while Blanche stood firm, determined not to give in to the blustering López.

Haasi was back, whispering in Blanche's ear. "Give me a minute. I'll catch up to you."

"Now what?" Blanche watched Haasi's black braid disappear among the shoulders and heads of the visitors.

Blanche set her lips in a thin straight line, the one a person did not cross. "*Señor* López, it's not anywhere near closing time."

For response, Raúl took Blanche's arm and nudged her toward the door. "*Señorita*, look what you've started!"

"I haven't started anything." Her irritation began to bubble up.

"Perhaps they didn't prepare the exhibit properly. Perhaps that hair clip was dropped into the case accidentally," he said, all the while hustling her along.

"Well, in *that* case, I don't think the piece would be *embedded* above the ear." She shook his hand off her arm, firmly, and stopped in the doorway. "By the way, is the person a man or woman?"

He sighed, visibly relieved the topic had shifted. "It says, right here on the sign, the person is a woman." He looked Blanche up and down. "Approximately, someone of your age and height." His voice took on an even frostier tone.

Haasi appeared. "Come on, B, let's go." She jerked her head slightly. *And winked?* Haasi had found out something, some little tidbit that would add to the whole drama. Blanche read it in her expression.

Blanche turned to Raúl. "I think someone should inspect this mummy, or corpse, or whatever it is," she said. "And report it to the authorities. The police, maybe. Something's not right."

At this suggestion, Raúl's face drained. "You continue to press this. Forgive me, but who are you?"

"A concerned citizen?" *No, not really. A concerned tourist?*

"Your claim will be investigated. To disprove such a thing, I'm sure." Raúl tossed his head. "In any event, it is not our responsibility. The mummies are on loan to us, and we will advise our partners at the cultural center who arranged the exhibit."

The matter seemed settled, but Blanche wouldn't let go, even while Haasi tugged at her sleeve. "You do that," said Blanche. "Clearly, the textures, the nails, the hair, all of it. This one is different from the others. You must see it."

Several people hung on. Eyes were on them. The toothy woman yelled. Again. "*Tell him, tell him, señorita!*" She turned to her groupies who were nodding furiously. "*¡Verguenza!*"

"Yes, a shame," said Raúl, eyes cast to the ceiling. "This is exasperating! Such a ridiculous fuss."

Haasi scooted around in front of Blanche, teeth clenched. "Time to go, *señorita*. Show's over."

Raúl's face was red, and he was seething. The long, white fingers waved like direction signals, shooing them out the door. It was time to go. *Everyone.*

His jaw tight, he spoke pointedly to Blanche. "*¡Adiós!*"

"To be continued, *señor*," she said.

Haasi hovered over Blanche's ear. "More later. Come on."

They joined the crowd and shuffled out the door in one large clump.

A tall, bulky man stood off in the corner of the exhibit, casually leaning away from the crowd. At first he turned to watch Blanche, then the black-clad man, and finally Haasi. He didn't react, except for his eyes, and his ears, that seemed to follow every nuance on the faces and every word of the conversations and exclamations exploding around him.

Haasi held tightly to Blanche's arm as they hurried down the stairs. Blanche couldn't tell if she was cursing or praying. Blanche felt a sudden need to pray for the dead.

Chapter Three

SOME VACATION

"BLANCHE. LET'S TRY TO RELAX." Haasi let out a deep breath. Her voice rose above the crowd rushing out of the subway, but it was the distracted tone that caught Blanche's attention.

She eyed the agitated expression on Haasi's face. "What's wrong?"

"I'll tell you later. Let's find a place to sit. And eat."

The two crossed the Zocalo in front of the Palacio. They gawked at a military display of vehicles and equipment. Large tents were set up. It was a curious contrast to the vendors selling embroidered linen and carvings and toys from carts.

"Where should we go? Looks like the universe showed up here." Haasi still held tightly to Blanche's arm.

"Dunno, but I'm all for sitting. I didn't exactly expect to go to the Palacio and find a newly dead body," said Blanche.

"Newly dead? Really, Blanche, I'm just not sure what you mean by that."

"You tell me. That is not a real mummy. As advertised."

"Maybe not, but what can we do about it? The poor soul!"

Blanche bumped into a dancing man wearing a feathered headdress and clackers like walnuts on his ankles. "Excuse me, sir." Blanche was chagrined; it was his plaza, not hers. He gave her a wide berth and a forgiving smile and didn't seem to miss a beat.

They ran-walked, arminarm, Haasi steering, Blanche trying not to run into anyone again. They cruised along the arcade that bordered the Zocalo, past jewelry stores and narrow entrances that led to homes and businesses overlooking the plaza.

"I'm starving," said Haasi. "And we have to talk."

"Talk about? Vacation? Food? Dead bodies?"

"All of the above."

Blanche was hungry, too, but where Haasi was concerned, they did not put off meals. She was a machine, the smallest eating machine Blanche had ever met, and it needed to be fed.

Haasi again looked over her shoulder as they circled the plaza. Blanche nudged her. "What is up with you?"

Haasi shook her head.

A small sign on the sidewalk advertised a restaurant, and they ducked up a flight of stairs. A young boy produced enormous menus and seated them in the long dining room with a high ceiling, white tablecloths, and red leatherette chairs. They sat in a window with a view of the crowd rushing back and forth across the Zocalo.

Two frosty Tecates appeared on the table. Haasi lifted her beer, a look of relief in her dark eyes. "To vacation. But I have a feeling it's already screwed up. Blanche, you are not going to save the mummies of the world."

"I hear you. But that dead...? Person? Come on, Haas. We can't let this go. What if there is something going on over there? We *saw* it."

"You think so, don't you."

"I think so," said Blanche. "We have to deal with it."

"Blanche, we don't have to deal with it."

Blanche did not seem to hear her; her eyes glazed over with a faraway look. "You might be right, but we'll see." She sighed. "We *do* have to get that work done for Clint. One way or the other." This was the actual purpose of their visit to Mexico City. She had an assignment for the *Island Times*, the newspaper on Santa Maria Island, to write stories about Mexico City, the Mayan exhibit, and the amazing Aztec Temple in the city center. Haasi was in charge of photography for the stories. An advertiser, The SunStream Travel Agency, was paying the newspaper for the photos and articles, and the trip was handsomely covered. Blanche's boss, Editor and Publisher Clint Wilkinson, grumbled and huffed about editorial and advertising crossing boundaries, but then he decided it was a sort of bonus assignment. It hadn't taken much for him to relent as a rare wave of gratitude washed over him. Blanche and Haasi were alive and well, after helping crack the murder case of a local realtor. They deserved a break.

"That said, I know this 'dead body' thing is going to drive you crazy," Haasi said. "I just get the feeling we're off to a shaky start here. Can't help it."

"Guess we have a knack for it."

"Uh-huh." Haasi took a long pull of the beer and stared out at the plaza. Blanche was struck once again by the strength of that gaze. She was leery, too, about the start of this Mexican adventure, but they were together, and for that she was thankful. They were so different, and at once, blood—distant cousins connected through the same great-grandmother who'd had a Miccosukee lover. Blanche knew she wouldn't be sitting here if it weren't for Haasi, who'd saved her from a kidnapper. They were a good team. Now, it was just the two of them. Sister-cousins. Stuck with each other and loving it.

"Haas, I don't think we're the only ones on to something." She leaned over, dipping a sleeve in salsa. "That guy, Raúl López, acted really weird. He got crazy when I came up with the pink plastic clip and the skin on that mummy. Did you get that?"

Haasi raised an eyebrow. "Do you hear yourself? Yeah, I got it."

"We have to find out what he's hiding."

"Blanche! I don't know."

"Might be a murder there."

It wouldn't do any good to argue the matter. It was apparent something weird was going on at the Palacio.

Haasi studied Blanche and hesitated.

"What?" Blanche said, waiting for the shoe to drop right on top of her enchilada.

Haasi glanced around. "Now, don't get all excited, Bang." The old nickname stuck. Blanche "Bang" Murninghan had a tendency to shoot from the hip. Or, as she readily admitted, shoot off her mouth.

"*What?*"

Haasi winced. "Did you notice the suspicious, tall guy at the exhibit? The one standing in the corner near the mummies? Seemed to be listening to everyone."

"Haasi, there were dozens of people. Is that what all that drama was back there? After you disappeared? You've been acting kind of funny ever since we left the exhibit."

"The guy. Tall and wide as a door. I checked him out, watched him for a bit. He wasn't a tourist." Haasi jabbed a poblano with her fork and stuck a huge bite of the cheese-stuffed pepper into her mouth.

"Big guy would be unusual, I guess. Most of the people here are more our size. But why not a tourist? Could be security, or an official of some sort for the Palacio."

"Don't think so. He looked fierce, and cagey, secretly writing a bunch of notes."

Blanche considered this bit of news, while she sucked on a wedge of lime and stared out at the plaza. The food was delicious, and now a wave of fatigue washed over her. They'd been up most of the night, hustling to the airport and customs, catching the bus from the air terminal to their hotel. They'd been so anxious to get going and see the city. And now this. It frazzled her. Gave her a raw edge.

Blanche frowned. "What do you think?"

"I think we should lay low. Not get entangled in something that is…well, too creepy for words. And maybe just plain dangerous. In any case, it's not our business. Our business is *travel writing*. And eating." The last observation was delivered with a huge smile, and a helping of quesadilla off a plate they were sharing.

Blanche picked at a tortilla and chewed thoughtfully. "Speaking of notes, I didn't get a whole lot of them, with the mummy and such. What am I going to write about? Headline: Dead Body Found in the Palacio Nacional of Mexico City. Don't think so. We have to go back."

"You are changing the tune."

"Maybe."

"We need to be careful, Blanche. I mean it. This is *not* Santa Maria Island." She went at the chips and salsa with a vengeance.

Blanche put her fists under her chin. *No, this is not anything like our sleepy little hometown of Santa Maria Island.*

Blanche stared a hole right through sister-cousin. "They do have police here."

"True. Let that crew at the Palacio check it out, now that you've stirred it up," said Haasi. "Wow, this is soooo good." A salsa-verde-covered chip disappeared.

Chapter Four

BEWARE OF THE SNAKE

BLANCHE AND HAASI HEADED TOWARD THEIR HOTEL on Calle Donceles where they'd dropped off their things that morning. For now, all Blanche could picture were those crisp white sheets and the cool room, a single window between the twin beds. It was a long way from Santa Maria Island and her cabin on the beach, and even farther from Haasi's abandoned boat in Sarasota Bay, which she was "renting" from a ninety-two-year-old fisherman. They had traveled to another world. It was 2002, but she felt out of time. They were in the land of the Aztecs, in Mexico City founded upon lakes and lagoons; a grand city on a plateau mostly surrounded by mountains and hills. Indeed, they were a long way from home, and Blanche was feeling it. She needed to recharge after that visit to the Palacio exhibit, and *think*.

"You tired? I need a short nap," she said. "You must be tired, too, after eating everything in that restaurant."

Haasi laughed and fell in step. "I'm good."

"Haas, you don't look it. Why are you so jumpy? Maybe you need dessert, or something."

"No, I'm OK. But dessert sounds good!" She glanced over her shoulder. They kept walking. "Blanche. That guy. The big one I was telling you about in the restaurant. I think he's following us."

"You're imagining things. You need some sleep."

"Blanche, I'm serious. You can't miss him. Why would *they*, whoever they are, send an elephant when they could send a cat."

"O-M-G. What are you talking about?" Blanche hurried to catch up to Haasi who walked even faster. They threaded through the crowd on the narrow sidewalk—past a red-painted devil, a couple of clowns, and a newspaper vendor.

"I'm sure it's him. We need to lose him."

"Haasi, you don't even know…" She didn't finish. Haasi had hold of Blanche's arm. The two ducked behind a kiosk selling corn on the cob slathered in mayo and chili powder. For a second, Blanche's mouth watered, but then her thoughts leapt to survival.

"In here." Haasi yanked her into a recessed entry. The door was open. At the top of the stairs, an old woman was silhouetted under a sky light. Her silvery hair shined like a halo, her full skirt was wider than an overstuffed chair. In fact, Blanche's first impression was one of comfort. The kind that she could sink into. To hide.

"*Ven.*" The woman beckoned to them.

Blanche and Haasi stared up the narrow, rickety stairwell. "I guess that means come up," Blanche whispered.

Haasi nodded and called up, "*Gracias.*"

"*Peligro,*" the woman said. The waving became a bit more insistent.

"Danger, Haas. She says, *danger.*" Blanche stumbled against the door and it banged shut. She followed Haasi up the stairs. *How did an innocent visit to an exhibit turn into…this.* She considered grabbing Haasi and backing out into the street and sneaking away, but they were into it now, and Blanche was curious as all get out.

"I saw you," the woman said in halting English. "At the kiosk. Hiding. No?"

"Someone was following us," Haasi said.

"Not unusual. Two beautiful young *señoritas* in a big city."

"Haasi Hakla." She thrust her hand toward the old woman in greeting. "My cousin, Blanche Murninghan."

"María Obregon Villamajor." The hint of a curtsy.

The woman showed them into a large room off the stairwell. It was dim, and crowded with furniture and other trappings of rugs, pillows, draperies, cloths that covered tables—including an altar with flowers and candles and old, curling photos.

"Sit. Don't worry. *Tranquila*." Their host directed them to two ladder-backs with intricate carving and small cushions.

Blanche was relieved to be in a quiet place after their adventure thus far, but she didn't feel so tranquil. She was not tired anymore, with that spike of adrenalin, and she was confused. She wasn't afraid. If anything, she was annoyed that someone might be following them. Haasi had the same sort of reservation, and confusion, written all over her face.

"*Un momento, por favor*." María clasped her hands together, looked Blanche and Haasi over, and disappeared into the back of the flat. The light shifted on the sunbeams speckling the floor through the lace curtains. It was a comfortable living room, and cool with a cross-draft passing through the front windows to back.

María shuffled toward them with a pitcher of red liquid and three glasses. She set the tray on the table. "Jamaica. Drink." They drank. Blanche didn't realize how thirsty she was.

"You like it?" María refilled their glasses.

"Yes!" said Blanche, Haasi nodded. "What is it?"

"You say, hibiscus."

Blanche thought of the huge bright flowers on the bushes that ringed her patio back in Florida. She'd never thought to drink them. But the beverage was delicious, a flowery, tart taste that cut her thirst.

María sat and crossed her arms over the generous folds of her skirt. "Lowers cholesterol and fever. Good for digestion. Very good for you."

"We are grateful. ¡*Gracias!*" Blanche hesitated, unsure of how to approach the subject. She wasn't shy. "*Señora*, I'm not sure why anyone would follow us."

María shrugged. "Do not worry so much. Be careful, stay to yourselves. Take a minute now to relax."

Blanche and Haasi exchanged a look of relief, but Haasi turned to María. "Will you tell us about the police here?"

"They are police. What can I say?" She turned her palms up, resigned. "Sometimes they are friends, sometimes not so much. In Mexico, prepare for the surprise. But maybe there is no one. Maybe you see people and imagine danger... It does happen here."

Blanche didn't want to seem abrupt, but she could hardly help herself. "What does that mean?"

"We are complicated. Our history is a good example."

"We're learning," said Blanche. "We just visited the Mayan exhibit at the Palacio... In fact..."

Haasi crossed her leg under the table and nudged Blanche.

"In fact, it was very memorable," said Blanche.

"The Mayans. And the Aztecs. There are many indigenous peoples, of many names." The woman's thin lips curled into a smile. "You have an interest in the history of Mexico?"

Blanche leaned forward. "Very much."

Haasi seemed guarded.

María's pensive look drifted toward the window. Her high cheekbones and hooded eyes glowed, an imposing figure with thick black and silver hair and a face straight out of the exhibit they'd just left.

"I have a story." María's voice was firm, almost demanding their attention. "Do you know Coatlicue?"

Blanche shook her head. Haasi's fingers drummed the side of her chair.

"A strange woman. She is an important goddess here in Mexico," María said. "In mythology, Coatlicue gave birth to four hundred children."

"Whoa." Haasi looked skeptical.

María walked to the window and looked down into the street. She seemed satisfied with what she saw. She turned to Haasi. "*Claro*," María said. "I do not believe Coatlicue gave birth to so many children. But it is part of the story. *Our* story. The myths, the contrasts of life and death. True, we take many lives away, but we celebrate birth and new beginnings." She smiled again, flashing large white teeth. "New life is hope."

Blanche was thrown a thousand years back in time as she looked into María's eyes. But what she'd heard, and seen, since arriving seemed new. She remembered the ride from the airport, the children in beautiful clothes, the little ones in strollers, the older ones running through clouds of bubbles, bunches of balloons—their parents and grandparents, sitting on benches, smiling and watching the antics. Her friend Pilar had told her: *Proud of appearances, and proud of their children.* Blanche patted her hair back in place and pulled at her T-shirt and shorts, probably the best of her ratty island wardrobe.

"There are many stories about Coatlicue, the earth mother." María smiled. "She is fierce and constant, sometimes deadly. Her head is two vipers squirting blood."

Blanche shivered. "Really? That doesn't sound very motherly."

"True. But the history of Mexico is one of contrasts, the good and the evil. The story of Coatlicue begins simply, like many stories." Maria nodded with a wry grin. She settled herself back in the chair and began…

"One day, Coatlicue was sweeping the temple floor. She was a goddess but she believed in the value of hard work and small tasks. The work is needed to keep order. It's a quality of the mother to see the need, and it is a quality of our people. Coatlicue swept and cleaned and prayed for her children.

"While she worked, the sky opened up. Lightning blazed above the dark hills, and a dagger of fire struck near the stones where she swept. It tore into the earth and burned the spot. Coatlicue did not move. She did not speak. Then she saw near the scorched ground a ball of feathers. She stared at the strange appearance—a beautiful and perfectly round shape of black and white feathers, hundreds of them, moving with life." María paused, her dark eyes shining.

"Coatlicue picked up the feathers. They seemed to have a strange energy. She cradled the ball of feathers and put it on her belt. She held it close. And in the moment she accepted it, she became pregnant."

"Was this baby number four hundred and one?" Blanche murmured. Haasi raised her eyebrows and poked Blanche.

María's stolid expression broke into a smile. "This child, this one. Four hundred and one. He was *muy importante*. The most important of all the gods.

"The earth was at war. Fighting and jealousy were everywhere. The children of Coatlicue tore at each other. Her daughter, Coyolxauhqui, wanted control of the power and the influence of her mother, and she incited a battle. The daughter decided to kill the mother to take over her powers.

"Coyo went to Coatlicue in the middle of the night with the weapon of a fire serpent. But Coatlicue was ready. The daughter forgot many things in her blind fury and rage, and one very important thing she forgot: A mother sleeps lightly. She must be ready to care for her children. Coyo also forgot that Coatlicue, her mother, was full of life. Blessed with a gift of the gods.

"And so, a miracle happened to save Coatlicue. Her son, Huitzilopochtli, burst from her womb, fully grown and armed as a great warrior. He stood by his mother, ready for battle. The god of war and the sun. Coatlicue had nurtured and carried him, her safeguard against jealousy and greed and the forces that would destroy her. Coatlicue's full power as earth mother came to life.

"Huitzil decapitated his sister Coyo and her blood spilled down and poisoned the corn and all of the harvest. It withered and died away, and the greed and jealousy of Coyo was a poison that covered the earth.

"Killing, jealousy, and greed are hateful crimes. Still, there is much generosity and goodness in our history. To a fault. Even the worst ones provide for each other. It comes from the power of the mother. She gives birth and new beginnings at the worst of times. But she is also the snake, the viper. Deadly and diverse, and a cunning survivor. Coatlicue is all of that."

"Why are you telling us this, María?" Blanche frowned. "Sounds like a warning."

Maria's expression was like stone. "Be aware," she said, "of the goodness, the giving side. It can save you." She got up and poured more jamaica into their glasses. "And be aware of the snake."

Chapter Five

THE GUY AS BIG
AS A DOOR

THE THREE WOMEN SAT, EACH WITH HER OWN THOUGHTS: María in an armchair, Blanche and Haasi at the small table in the window. But the moment didn't last long.

The curtain waved like a ghost at their backs. Blanche had absentmindedly braided the fringe on the tablecloth as she listened to María talk about a goddess with four hundred and one babies, and now she glanced around the room. Woven rugs criss-crossed each other on the polished, dark red concrete floor. The sepia photos of stiffly dressed men and women, small votives and mums, were neatly arranged on an altar with a two-foot-high statue of the Virgin of Guadalupe, the gold rays radiating from her blue robe. Blanche wanted to ask about the photos, but there seemed to be sadness in the room, as if it were a private place that strangers shouldn't touch. Yet, she felt welcome here. It was hard for her to hold back, but she determined to keep her mouth shut. For once.

María slipped off to the kitchen again and now she offered them empanadas. Their host was definitely an earth mother, warm and encouraging, but a mystery. Their savior? Maybe, and maybe not. Blanche did not want to dwell on the negative aspects of this visit. She was glad for the invite, to get safely off the street and calm down, for the moment. But it was definitely time to go.

They'd only sat quietly for a minute or two when the banging started up. Blanche jumped. She'd been lulled by the snacks and María's voice, carried away on the story of the earth mother. Blanche's imagination was like a boat; once she climbed into it, she sailed away. But now she was back and disturbed plenty by the constant beating on the door that echoed up the stairwell. She shot Haasi a look. Sister-cousin had an implacable expression, but her eyes squinted in alarm.

The hammering was steady, and it seemed whoever was at it had no intention of giving up. Haasi leapt to her feet. María stopped moving about the room with the tray. She signaled them to be quiet. "You stay. I go."

She dropped the tray on the table with a clatter. Her footsteps creaked down the stairs. "*Momento, momento, por favor.*"

"*¡Señora!*" A loud male voice boomed.

Blanche stood up, but Haasi didn't move. She put a finger to her lips. "We may need to bolt out the back. Or out a window," said Haasi.

"What is up with you? I'm not jumping out a window." Blanche looked dubious, considering all possibilities.

"I'm just saying. You know, the guy who was following us. It might be *him*. Someone did not like your little discovery among the Mayans. I'm sure of it."

Blanche didn't want to believe it, but she knew Haasi might be right.

María's voice rose and fell with a sing-song quality. "She could soothe any beast," Blanche said. She gave Haasi a thumbs-up. "Maybe she's getting rid of him."

Haasi looked unconvinced. "Maybe she's in cahoots with him.

You hear *him*? Pretty gruff."

"Yeah. Don't like the sound of that."

Heavy shoes pounded the stair treads along with María's light steps. She didn't stop talking, and it was impossible to understand her rapid-fire Spanish. They stopped, the two lingering in the stairwell, talking over each other. Haasi and Blanche both spoke a little Spanish, but the idiom and the pace were hardly a match for their ability.

Haasi grabbed Blanche. "I don't want to jump out a window, Haas," she said. "Really…"

"Come on. Back here." Haasi headed down the hallway. "Let's go. Must be a way out of here. I've had enough of snakes and earth mothers."

They were almost to the back of the flat when María called after them. "¡*Señoritas*! *Ven acá*. Come. Quickly."

Haasi had seized the doorknob. María stood at the entrance to the living room, the light shining behind her. It also illuminated an enormous figure standing next to her. María was a big woman, but this man towered over her.

"¡*Señoritas*!" The man's greeting sent an icy shiver through Blanche.

Haasi and Blanche tentatively retraced their steps down the hallway. "This better be good," Blanche mumbled.

"Be ready to *get*. I mean it," Haasi whispered.

María said, "*Señoritas* Blanche and Haasi, let me introduce Felix Sono Cardenal, detective for the Mexico City police."

The *señoritas* didn't move. Haasi spoke under her breath. "That's the guy. The one I saw." Blanche bristled.

Señor Cardenal cleared his throat and straightened the string tie that hung from the neck of his impossibly white shirt. His teeth were as brilliant, and his face looked like it had been carved out of rock, dark and angular, well-worn. A don't-mess-with-me face and a chin the size of a melon. He had great brown eyes—

that crinkled in a smile?

He grasped Blanche's hand, then Haasi's. His grip was not something one would want to meet in a fight. "*Bienvenido a DF. Mucho gusto.*" He pronounced it "day-effay."

"DF? Is that where we are?"

He laughed heartily, and for some reason Blanche liked him instantly. "That is what we call Mexico City. You are not *chilanga*. Yet."

"Well, no I'm not *chilanga*." It sounded like something good to eat.

"That is a person belonging to Mexico City. You will soon want to belong here. It is a wonderful place."

Blanche had an urge to get her notebook out and quote him for her stories. *Focus, Blanche.*

"*Mucho gusto, Señor* Detective," Blanche said, hesitantly. "This city is indeed wonderful. I think."

He laughed again. "You must wonder why I am here."

María was already bustling about with more jamaica and the delectable empanadas. She gestured for them all to sit.

"Why were you following us?" Haasi's question was frosty. It dispensed with the last of the conviviality in the detective's expression.

"We don't appreciate being chased down the street," said Blanche, chiming in.

A look of surprise crossed his face. "I did not mean to *chase* you. I do need to speak with you. With both of you. *Por favor.*"

María finished filling their glasses and hurried away to the back of the house. Blanche and Haasi sat on the edge of the blue cushions, and Cardenal perched on a ladder-back.

"I am here because of you," he said.

"What did we do?" What could they have possibly done that would interest the police? *Except for that body in the floor. Shit… Why can't I keep my mouth shut?* She had no desire to sit in a

Mexican police station, but she felt plenty antsy about that body. He had to know. They needed to investigate.

Detective Cardenal was still smiling. Clearly, he was not going to arrest them. Not for a second. Not with such an engaging smile. And Blanche and Haasi hadn't done anything wrong! But this was, after all, another country, and they might as well have landed on another planet. They needed to adjust. Quickly. Everything was happening too fast. It hit Blanche at once. She was almost giddy with fatigue and apprehension, like she was spinning toward a situation out of her control. She needed a break. She wanted another one of those excellent beers and a nap. And the chance to start this whole writing and photographing vacation over again. Without finding a dead person in the floor.

"I think we need to go," she said. "Thank you for everything, but ..."

Haasi jumped to her feet.

The detective did not seem to hear Blanche. "You did something very good. In the Palacio exhibit," he said. Both hands were in the air waving them to be seated, but gently.

"We did?" Blanche's voice squeaked.

"You, and your friend." He bowed his head to Haasi. "You saw something unusual."

Blanche could feel her heart racing. She hoped it didn't give her away, the palpitation, the nervousness. "Yes. The hair clip, or something like that."

Haasi shot her a look.

Detective Cardenal nodded. He leaned in, his eyes like headlights. "What exactly did you see? Please, try to remember."

He could read her thoughts. Blanche closed her eyes and braced herself.

"*Nada.*" Haasi could be as stony as the best of them. "We saw nothing. Just the clip." Cool and calm.

But Blanche couldn't help herself. Now she was drawn to

the mystery of it, and *Señor* Cardenal's smile did not diminish her anxiety and curiosity. He knit his gargantuan fingers into a human boulder of a fist.

"*Señorita* Blanche? Tell me."

She caught Haasi's eye, and that eye said, *Shut the hell up.* But Blanche plowed ahead. "I saw something pink. In the hair. And the skin. It just wasn't *ancient*. It was shriveled dark, like leather, but the texture was not the same as the others. And the hair..."

"You announced to the crowd that the body was *new* dead. No?"

"Yes, No. I mean, I'm not so sure."

"Not sure? Not sure, what?"

"Well, I'm not a forensic specialist. I'm nothing, really. Just a part-time journalist. My cousin, Haasi, and I are on a little vacation. Just to do a bit of sightseeing, writing, eating, that sort of thing."

Señor Cardenal leaned back. He nodded. "That's good. No better place to do that than Mexico. We have the best of everything." His eyes were suddenly merry. He looked like he was about to burst into song. "We should go to Zingo, listen to Maríachi, take a Centenario or two."

Haasi ignored the invite. "*Señor* Cardenal, how did you find us? Before María invited us in?" The steel in her tone made the smile on his face droop.

"You disappeared into that restaurant, and I did not want to interrupt the *comida*. Bad luck to do that. But then I spotted you, and thanks to my friend in the kiosk, here we are," he said, a bit defensively. "I happen to know María. A coincidence. I'm sorry if I disturbed you."

"Yes, you disturbed us," said Haasi. "If you have a problem over there in the exhibit, it is not an affair of ours."

"I don't mean to imply that it is a problem for you," he said. "But it is a very big problem for us."

Blanche leaned in. "Is the mummy really a *corpse*?"

"Well, I might say that of all mummies. But the situation is under wraps now, so to speak."

"Hmmm," said Blanche. "What do you mean, you have a *big* problem? Is there more?"

The detective shifted side to side in the ladder-back. It creaked. He seemed unconcerned that momentarily he might be sitting on a bunch of twigs. "Yes, that is correct. You have fine-tuned our focus, shall we say? This business with the corpse. It may be part of a very bad business."

Blanche began pacing. "Something fishy about the whole situation. What else is going on?" Now she was raising her voice. Haasi put a hand on her arm.

"*Tranquila, tranquila*," said Cardenal. "The body. Yes, it needs investigation. But besides the business of this so-called mummy, many art objects are missing at the cultural center and in other museums in DF. Especially since the turn of the millennium. The black market all over the world seems to have exploded with demand for ancient artifacts. Missing here are travertine and turquoise and greenstone. An obsidian sword from the ninth century. Carved jade beads from tombs, clay figures and masks that are irreplaceable." He stopped and patted the top of his head. Blanche had noticed this tic only minutes before. It was strange, and...endearing? "We can't seem to get traction on this thievery. And now this. These questions concerning the mummy exhibit."

Haasi said, "*Señor*, I really don't see how we can help. We saw very little, after all, and if you have a wider problem, I just don't see how we fit."

Blanche studied the detective, warily. They'd only been at the Palacio a half hour—in the country for five hours. Surely, he didn't want to involve two young Florida tourists. Yet she was pulled in Cardenal's direction. His charm had something to do with it but it hardly matched her curiosity.

"True," said the detective. "It has nothing to do with you." He seemed to be grasping for ways to make sense of it all. "On the surface of things."

Blanche hunched her shoulders. "What do you mean?"

"My emphasis has been to find the thieves and recover the artifacts. Clearly, this is a sophisticated ring. The plan is well-thought-out, and we haven't a clue." He appraised the *señoritas* with a hard look.

Blanche squirmed. "I still don't know what you want with us. Specifically."

"The thefts have picked up. But we're no closer to finding the thieves."

"And?" Blanche pressed him. Haasi folded her arms.

"The body you saw in the floor. You have a good eye, *señorita*, and we need all the help we can get."

"I suggested to *Señor* López, you know, the thin administrator dressed in black, that the mummy with the pink hair clip might be, er, freshly dead. He immediately hustled us out of there. Pronto. No discussion."

"Something strange there. But I ask you now. You may have seen something. Or heard something during your visit to the exhibit. However small." *Señor* Cardenal pulled at a bushy sideburn, his attention riveted on the women. "There may be a connection."

"A connection? Between the mummy and the missing art?" Blanche felt the circle widening. Haasi shifted uneasily in the chair. Blanche began pacing again. An idea never settled quietly with her; it bounced around until it exploded.

He was still tapping his head. "If you can remember anything you overheard from *Señor* López or from anyone in the crowd. Any detail?"

"We'd be glad to help," said Blanche. "You want us to stick around and see what we can find out?"

Haasi's sigh was like a small tornado. "We are not detectives."

"Oh, of course not. You are not even witnesses to a crime, officially," he said. "I do not want to trouble you now. Please, go rest and enjoy. I have taken too much of your time." He jumped up from his seat with surprising grace. "Where will you *señoritas* be staying?"

Haasi remained tight-lipped, but Blanche volunteered. "At the Hotel Rosarita on the Calle Donceles near the Zocalo."

He offered a card, and Blanche took it. "You are part of this strange scenario, and you have certain impressions. No doubt about that. I don't know what that can mean, but something may come of your visit. It is important you think about it," he said with a slight bow. "Your assistance is much appreciated. And, after you rest, and when we have more information, we will find you. Just routine. I hope that will be amenable."

He was warm and official, at once, and almost gallant. Blanche nearly curtsied. Haasi glanced at her, on the verge of an eye-roll. María appeared from the back of the house and pressed another empanada on the detective, but he raised one hand and thanked her before he turned to leave. He glanced at Haasi, then Blanche, and smiled.

"I don't know how we can help, but, please, call on us," Blanche said, a mix of curiosity and dread roiling in her stomach. She went from the roiling to disbelief to determination. *Might as well go with it. What can we lose? Someone has lost her life!*

The detective clambered down the stairs. Blanche's gaze skipped over Haasi and María. "Wow! What do you think?"

"This Detective Cardenal, he is good," said María. "Others I do not trust so much, but he is good. You are safe with him."

"Haas? Should we get involved?"

María cocked her head. "¿*Cómo?*"

Haasi said, quickly, in that level tone of hers: "Blanche, we're already involved. And we've taken enough of María's day, don't you think? We should go." She smiled at María.

Blanche took María's hand. "Thank you. You have been so kind…" Feather balls and snakes, police and mummies jumbled around in her brain. "And, gracias, for the most delicious empanadas!"

"*Muchas gracias, señora*," Haasi said.

"You will return?"

"To say hello, and, at last, goodbye," said Blanche.

"We do not say goodbye. We say: Go with God. *Adiós*."

"Then, that is what it is."

María hugged them both. "Remember Coatlicue."

Blanche leaned into Haasi as they hurried down the stairs. "Let that be a lesson. Watch out for the one wearing snakes."

"Or acting like one."

Chapter Six

THE PILLOW MAN
AND THE ANGELS

"JEEZ, IT'S ONLY OUR SECOND DAY," said Blanche. "That was a creepy start!"

"Yeah, but Mexico City is looking good," said Haasi. "And it smells great!"

They meandered through the vast La Ideal bakery, their senses feasting on all the delicious ways to make a fresh start. With sugar on top. They'd gotten a good night's sleep after their day with the mummy, María, and the detective, and for now Haasi wanted to put it behind them. Blanche wasn't convinced. They needed to go back to the Palacio. A rehash of the whole incident with the mummy was sure to come around, but at the moment, they were hungry. Their mouths watered, their eyes scanned the glass cases and table displays of cakes, cookies, and rolls. Then there were the refrigerated cases of stuffed creamy things and yogurts with fruit and grains on top. The fragrance of the baked treats was overpowering, and they couldn't decide. They selected shiny buns and crunchy pastries sprinkled with sugar, a cone filled with chocolate cream, two fruit tarts, and, for good measure, Blanche reached for a spongy cake-roll with raspberry swirls. They dodged young bakers gliding past with metal trays fresh from the ovens, and Blanche felt her eyes grow bigger than her stomach. They carried their box of goodies to Alameda Park and sat on the grass.

"This is a sin, it's so *delicioso*," said Blanche. She sat cross-legged against a tree, balancing a coffee and an elephant ear.

Haasi carefully picked bits of apricot out of a fruit tart. "I suppose you're ready for a new day of more drama." Haasi's expression said she was less enthusiastic about returning to the scene of the "crime," if indeed there'd been one.

"At least we have the police on our team," said Blanche. She dusted sugar off her fingertips.

"I wouldn't mention that."

"Right. *Señor* López is jumpy enough."

"I'd like to get over there before they think to move that mummy, or corpse, or whatever it is. Do you think that's gonna happen?"

"Cardenal hinted around, so did López. At least that's the impression I got. They said they'd *investigate*. But I don't know, Blanche. Now we've gotten into the mix, and I don't think it's going to be easy to get out. Short of flying out of here—if they'll even let us. What if they decide to keep us in Mexico?"

Blanche eyed the remaining sugared bun and the gooey rim of a tart. "Might not be such a bad thing. These, and the beer. I'm in love."

"Oh, you." Haasi laughed, but she sobered, fast.

Blanche jumped up. "Let's get."

They headed back toward the Palacio and stopped to cross at a crowded intersection. The Mexican sun beat down on them with a heat that was unforgiving. They scooted over to a stop sign out of the glare and waited to cross the busy street. It would be a long wait. Vehicles poured from several streets and merged at the corner. The traffic was dizzying.

The man in front of them stepped off the curb. He carried at least a dozen pillows wrapped in clear plastic bags. Their whiteness bobbed in the blinding sun like earthbound clouds. Sun and clouds all around, disoriented in the heat, Blanche watched him, and waited. She wanted to get going, too. "I guess we can follow this man carrying clouds. Otherwise we're gonna stand here forever."

"Blanche, patience." But it seemed the pedestrians were walking right out into traffic.

She took Haasi's arm. "Let's go. How likely is it they'd kill us?"

The look on Haasi's face was not reassuring. Blanche wiped a hand across her forehead. It was hot, and getting hotter. The air was so dry. Every breath she took felt clogged with dust. The late spring weather was in the 80s, unusual for the city on a plateau, and a drift of smog made the air worse.

Pillow Man hesitated. He was short but solid. He wore sagging jeans and a grimy-white, stiff-straw cowboy hat. He turned then, his face in profile, lined like an old leaf, with straight eyelashes and a proud nose. It was a thing Blanche noticed, and loved here: the faces. They were often not pretty; they were maps of hard work and sun, years of fretting and loving.

"Oh, Jesus!" Haasi prayed. She was a step behind Blanche, a hand on her back. Pillow Man was close in front. Safety in numbers. A bigger target, harder to hit. Blanche checked the oncoming traffic, but Pillow Man did not.

The black motorcycle spun out of nowhere, and the old man went up in the air—the pillows, clouds in the sky. Blanche froze. Someone screamed, or was she the one screaming? Cars and trucks honked. A bicycle sped past them. Blanche saw a straw-hat wheel away like an errant hubcap. Then dead silence. The sun was blinding. The sky had fallen. Clouds covered the street.

The metallic screech of the motorcycle pulled her attention to the right. A black-and-silver blur in a helmet was sliding sideways over the pavement, the sound of metal on concrete.

She squinted at the man on the bike: "Hey!" Blanche yelled.

But he didn't look back. He scudded and hopped off farther down the street, gaining balance and momentum, until he was on the bike and gone.

Pillow Man lay on his side, like he was sleeping. He wasn't sleeping. He was groaning, and his eyes were black pools of fright and disbelief. Blanche stumbled toward him, looking all around her but not taking any of it in. Haasi held her arms out against the traffic, like a human fence. Her straight, strong little body dared anyone to cross.

Blanche didn't think about traffic. She dropped to the man's side. He was breathing, but he didn't move.

"¡Señor!" she said, patting his arm.

She glanced around frantically, loosening the top button on his worn shirt. Long sleeves! She was afraid he'd toast there on the street. The only thing she could remember about accidents was to cover the victim with a blanket to remediate shock. She wouldn't have done it even if someone handed her one. It was hotter than hell out there.

Then he nodded, opened his eyes, watering up as he turned to look at her. She sensed more than heard the creaking of his neck and the effort it took for him to reach for her.

"*Gracias,*" he said. "*Angel.*" He managed a weak smile.

She gently patted his back. His shirt was rough cotton. Someone handed her his hat. Straw and cotton: the earth. His fingers opened and closed, and he didn't take his eyes off her.

The traffic moved in frightening streaks of orange, blue, and yellow, rumbling buses and racing cars. Haasi waved away a small knot of bystanders who were crowding around. He needed air.

Blanche looked around at the mess. He'd lost his pillows,

probably his livelihood, and nearly his life. She felt a thrill of luck that he had probably saved her and Haasi, and how foolish that felt. How foolish they'd been to walk into traffic!

She sighed. "*Gracias a Dios.*"

He lifted his head. "*¿Qué?*"

"*Nada,*" Blanche shook her head.

He shut his eyes, his breathing shallow and irregular. She could hear a siren and hoped it was coming for them.

"Do you see the ambulance, Haas?" She was "organizing" the crowd, thanking a stranger who had called it in. Millions of people probably passed here, or near, at some time or other, and Blanche cursed that they were all here today.

"Why do we have to be the ones?" Blanche looked up at Haasi from where she crouched on the street. "Gotta be a reason…"

Pillow Man touched her arm. "*Angel,*" he said.

"Well, there's your answer," said Haasi. "Though I think that's stretching it." A smile revealed a slight gap in her teeth.

"Remember that. I'm an angel."

His hand crept slowly after Blanche. She grabbed his fingers.

"*No mover,*" Blanche said. The street was a griddle turned up all the way. She adjusted the remnants of a pillow under his head. He closed his eyes; she held on.

"*Estoy aquí,*" she said. She was here, and she'd stay until help arrived. She used the retrieved straw hat to shade him and fan the beads of sweat on his forehead.

"I don't forget you," he said.

Chapter Seven

MEANWHILE, BACK AT THE MUMMIES

BLANCHE WAS HAPPY. A rush of relief put a spring in her step. Pillow Man had rallied. His sister, María Carmen, who was working in a kiosk down the street, arrived, and brother and sister went off to the hospital in the ambulance. He would recover, said the medic. Haasi and Blanche had been involved in the incident for more than an hour, and now they hurried toward the Palacio. They had newspaper articles to work on, photos to gather—if not the mystery of the mummy and the missing artifacts to uncover.

"Wow. Angels. And mummies. It doesn't stop," said Blanche.

"Well, I wish it would," Haasi retorted.

Blanche was practically running, and Haasi tugged at her. "Slow down, B. Too hot to hurry. Let's take it easy, though it probably won't be with this mummy business."

"That detective seemed determined, Haas. He'll be back. With more questions." Her eyebrows scrunched; eyes blazed.

Haasi sighed. "How about a nice cool drink first?"

"I could use a beer."

"It's not even noon."

"So? We be on vacay."

"Some vacay," Haasi mumbled. She pulled Blanche over to the open window of a tiny juice bar. *Agua fresca* (sweetened water), *horchata* (milky rice-based drink), *licuados* (fruit shakes and smoothies). Pineapple, papaya, mango, watermelon, strawberries. Fruit she'd never heard of: Cherimoya? Soursop? A lot of it was cut and piled on the counter, the scent of ripe fruit mingling with street fumes.

"Wow. A Coke seems so boring," said Haasi. She squinted at the list of drinks.

"The drinks capital of the world. I'm in heaven."

They ordered strawberry-papaya smoothies and water. The cold, slushy drink revived them in the dusty heat.

"Here's to Pillow Man," said Blanche. "*Gracias a Dios,* he's all right."

Haasi nodded. "Yeah."

They headed toward the Palacio at a more relaxed pace and soon ambled into the lobby. "Shall we?" Haasi murmured, looking toward a thin crowd in the mummy chamber.

Blanche opened her notebook, a pen stuck out of her topknot. She flipped the book closed. "I guess. We can start there. But I'd like to check out this whole place. All of it."

"Oh, B." Haasi sighed.

"Think I'll head to the restroom first. Meet you in a few minutes." She took off without a look back.

The corridor was empty of visitors and dim as she made her way toward the restroom. She heard a low rumbling. Voices rising and falling. She stopped to listen, ducking into an alcove with a drinking fountain and a dusty plant. She tried not to sneeze, pressing her finger under her nose. Holding still. Then nothing. *Quiet as a tomb around here...*

By the time she came out of the restroom, the voices were back, and louder than before. She crept along in the hallway to the source of the noise. Male. Angry. "It's not real," the one shouted. "What are we supposed to do now?"

"Don't worry 'bout it. We'll have it all worked out before anything happens. Say it came from the Convento, on loan. Not our doing. It's a temporary fix."

Some mumbling. "Fix? You call this a fix? Those women saw something. They created an uproar. The devil is mixed up in this, for sure."

"Don't talk like that, and don't mention anything to anyone, especially the boss. I'm not gonna say it again ..." More mumbling. "...exhibit ..." Then a series of drawers slamming and chairs scraping. A rustling toward the door.

Blanche made a beeline back to Haasi and the mummies.

Haasi was alone except for a couple visitors and those resting in peace in the floor. She stood over the glass case, twisting her long braid. The exhibit of the dusty and drily departed was down by one dead person.

She turned to Blanche. "That's funny. She just up and went? The one with the hair clip?"

"Not so funny. And listen to this. I overheard some men arguing ..." Blanche and Haasi huddled over the macabre figures. The mummy of the pink plastic hair clip was gone, the arrangement of leftover bodies oddly spread out with a few more rocks and dirt filled in. Blanche was about to relate what she'd heard in the hallway, but the black-clad man bustled toward them. He was a fussy sort with his prancy walk and arms flinging about.

"¡*Señoritas, buenas!*"

Haasi and Blanche flinched.

"To what do we owe the pleasure?" It was *Señor* López rubbing his hands in a frenzy.

Blanche took a deep breath. "*Muy buenas,*" she said. "I see Our Lady of the Pink Plastic Hair Clip has got up and gone."

"We have removed her. For now." He chuckled, still wringing his hands. Blanche glanced at his long white fingers. *Like snakes.*

A tall man with blond hair, the top of his head carefully coifed into an Elvis quiff, appeared behind López. His fat, florid cheeks had an orange tinge. He was portly in a cheap blue suit and red tie that hung below his belt. "Ah, the *señoritas*, Blanche and Haasi. Once again," he said, extending a small, square hand. "Please, allow me. Sarloff Blussberg, arts and exhibits director at the Palacio Nacional." His inflection was not Spanish, nor, by any stretch, Mexican. German? Austrian?

Blanche shook his hand. A squishy kind of shake, like wet Play-Doh.

"How do you do?" Blanche was surprised at his effusive welcome. Their voices were familiar—so angry moments before and now seemingly all cheery and hospitable. "And how do you know us?"

"Word travels fast, as you Americans like to say."

"Seems to be some changes here," Haasi said.

"We're sorry to disappoint you, but the exhibit has temporarily been ... altered. What I mean is, it's been reconfigured, but not really. This exhibit is huge and there's a lot to see here and perhaps you would like to proceed into the main room ..." He pointed the way, blathering on. His flat tiny hands opened and closed, back and forth. It was distracting.

Blanche cut in. "Where is she? Did you call the authorities?" She ignored the warning that went off in her head.

Blussberg looked innocuous enough, like someone's fat uncle, but he had shifty eyes. He tilted his blond head and pursed his small mouth. "Why would we do that?"

"Because you should. There was something funny about that body in the floor. I don't think it was a mummy."

He laughed. "Well, I don't know what else you would call it, er, her," Blussberg said.

Blanche was incredulous at his deflection; she checked Haasi, whose expression was flat and cold.

"More visitors will be in here for this exhibit. Many, many come here. We can't stop them. They love it. It's tremendous! I don't know what questions you have, or concerns, but we are happy to have you visit." With that, he carefully attempted to steer Blanche toward the door. "Now, shall we? Unless you'd like to stroll through this excellent selection of some five hundred artifacts. ... Not much time, you see, we're closing early today." Blanche had doorstops on her heels. She didn't budge from her spot next to the glass case even as Blussberg signaled the exit.

Why do I keep getting shuffled out of here?

Haasi poked her in the ribs, hard.

Blanche gave a little start. Haasi had that all-business look about her. They were a team; no "I" there. Blanche gave in with a sigh. She looked up at Blussberg. "*Señor?* Thank you for your time. We will visit. Later."

Blanche, walking away, fast, tried to shelve the unpleasant confrontation for now. She filled Haasi in on the details of her snooping in the corridor as they took off around the Zocalo.

Haasi was listening, but for answer she waved a list of cultural attractions at Blanche as distraction. "Haas, what do you think?"

"Now, Bang, we'll just have to see, won't we? They've taken the mummy out of there, and Cardenal's on it. ... Maybe we should have lunch."

"Don't have much of an appetite after all that."

"Feed the fear and doubt with tacos. Good for the soul."

Chapter Eight

WORK IT

BLANCHE AND HAASI WAITED on word from Detective Cardenal. None came. When he did call, Blanche wanted to share the conversation she'd overheard. It pointed to more trouble.

"He'll come through," said Haasi. "In the meantime, we have work to do." And so, they worked the rest of the day, tearing into the restaurant scene and wearing out sandal leather all over the neighborhoods of Polanco and Zona Rosa.

The next day, after a tour of the warren of streets around the Zocalo, they landed at the sophisticated Bajo del Cielo for dinner, and despite the austere steel and glass décor, the clientele was young and casual, and they seemed to be having a good time. Blanche and Haasi had dressed up in simple stretchy sheaths, Haasi's blue, Blanche in red. Blanche had the feeling the restaurant could be plopped down in Paris or New York and would fit perfectly. Lots of fancy black outfits, long shining hair on the women, and a sharp edge to the men.

Blanche studied the exotic list of selections on the menu. "Who says Mexican food is only beans and tacos? Look at this. They even have moles."

Haasi laughed. "Blanche, that's not mole, as in the little pest that digs holes in your yard. It's pronounced mo-lay! A complex sauce of chiles and chocolate—actually invented by nuns."

"Oh, yeah. But what a weird name for something so delicious. Sounds like 'juice of gopher.' Says here they put mango mole on Cornish hen."

"Or you could have it on armadillo."

Blanche flapped the menu down on the table. She took a large satisfying swig of the cold San Miguel, and sighed. "I don't know. It's all so confusing."

"My stomach is delighted," said Haasi as she bent over the menu. "One thing I'll skip are the *escamoles de hormiga*. For sure."

"What's that?"

Haasi looked up. "The 'caviar of Mexico.' Says it's red-ant roe."

In touch with their island culture, they settled on fish: salmon in maize crust for Haasi and whitefish with pomegranate seeds and bitter orange for Blanche. Their choices were a hit. Five stars all the way.

It was a long walk "home" down the Paseo de la Reforma, but they started out, stuffed and happy. The dead body, the police, and shady characters forgotten. At least for now.

It was Day Four, and Blanche and Haasi had put a dent in their travel assignment. They'd visited the city museum with its impressionist paintings, art studios, and antique maps; the fabulous Casa de los Azulejos, of Baroque architecture, Orozco's mural, and a courtyard where they drank *café de olla*, a cinnamon-and-brown-sugar-flavored coffee. They finished off the day of sightseeing at the immense Baroque cathedral on the Zocalo that was only recently saved from sinking into the city's ancient lakebed.

At every turn, there was more to see, and more to eat. They'd sampled Mexican fare in the *fondas* and in the market and on the street—Blanche had never tasted tacos with pineapple.

They decided to take a break from local cuisine. There was so much to choose from: Japanese, French, Spanish, American, German, International. They chose Italian.

Blanche tore into a loaf of garlic bread at Valpolicella, chewing and thinking. Haasi dug into a plate of meatballs and spaghetti. The wine was a good pinot noir, but Blanche preferred Mexico's excellent beer and every kind of fruit juice imaginable. She swirled the wine and frowned.

"Don't like it?" Haasi sipped at her red.

"I don't like that Cardenal hasn't called."

"Well, let your meatballs settle. You're going to need your strength. When he does call, I'm sure he'll have news."

"Even if he doesn't show right away, I know Blussberg and company think they've gotten rid of us, and I don't like that. At all. They're awfully cagey."

"I'll say," said Haasi. "You can bet Cardenal will turn up. At the Palacio and at our hotel to buy us shots of Centenario. Wasn't he the jolly one."

Blanche sat back hard in the booth, a quizzical look on her face. "Yeah, I gotta say. I like him, and I'm not sorry we met him. I just hope he gets on the case soon."

"Better him than us."

"You know, that argument I overheard at the Palacio. Those voices. Lots of hoarse, low whispering back and forth." Blanche was half-musing, mostly murmuring to herself. "I'm sure it was Blussberg and López. And I'm sure they were talking about our mummy."

"*Our* mummy? She's not a member of the family." Haasi waved a meatball at the end of her fork.

"Well, practically. I should mention that little conversation to Cardenal soon."

"Mention it! He should know."

"You're right."

A disco romp pumped out of the speakers, throngs of mostly young people sat outside at picnic tables and at the booths inside. The 70s were back, and it was *hot* in there.

Haasi's fingers danced on the tabletop.

Blanche laughed. "Disco fever? Wanna go to the club tonight? I'll get you one of those mirror balls for your birthday."

Haasi's expression was intense. "No mirror ball. My crystal ball says let's get our work done and get back to the island."

"You homesick?"

"Not really, Bang. Are you?"

"Always. I miss Santa Maria. But I can't seem to get this bad business out of my head. And we still have work to do for the newspaper."

"How do you want to handle that detective?"

"When I talk to him, I'll be cool. Or try to be. I think I can do that." But her eyes were full of mischief. "What do you want to do now?"

"Order more garlic bread?" First things first. Haasi was on a second round of meatballs. "I don't know, Blanche."

"They took our mummy away, and now they act like the situation is normal."

"Right. Guess we'll see how that plays out."

Blanche raised the last of her wine and clinked with sister-cousin.

The next day Cardenal was still not in touch. Blanche wanted to return to the Palacio. "I'm up for snooping."

"When are you not, Bang?" Haasi sighed. They were finishing a breakfast of coffee and buns on the patio. It was a bright, cool morning with the hum of birds and traffic in the background.

"I'd really like to see if something new has turned up over there," said Blanche.

"What? More mummy woman? Or something else?"

"I love a surprise."

"Blanche, let's give it a rest. We've got ruins to climb, and I'm sure there's stuff I haven't eaten yet."

"I can't imagine what."

They'd get to Cardenal and the Palacio later, but first they headed to the ruins of the Aztec Templo Mayor off the Zocalo, an open-air site of ancient steps and statues of gods and goddesses. It was the seat of the Aztec city center of Tenochtitlan, founded in the fourteenth century. They stood on the edge of the volcanic rock softened from age and erosion. Grass grew in narrow pathways among the stones and steps that ran up to altars. Blanche imagined the thousands who had come here, and the thousands who had died grisly deaths of sacrifice. It was hard to believe they were standing in the middle of one of the largest cities in the world. A bustling, sprawling megalopolis of almost twenty million people spread out over four hundred *colonias,* or neighborhoods.

Blanche glanced in the direction of the Palacio across the plaza at the cathedral and the arcades and shops. Streams of workers and visitors rushed out across the center of the busy modern city and ancient ruins.

They climbed the steps in the Templo among stone snakes and dragons. "They don't look so fierce with a little weather on them," Haasi said. "Wonder if this is where Coatlicue did her deeds."

"Well, I don't know about that," said Blanche. She held the guidebook open. "Says here this was the seat of death where they sacrificed thousands at a time to that bloodthirsty god of war, Huitzilopochtli. Wasn't he the four-hundred-and-first baby?" They looked up at the rows of stone skulls leering at them from the wall of the temple.

Blanche shuddered to think as she walked in the graveyard of one civilization and thought of the mummified corpses at the

Palacio; suspicion swept through her. López and Blussberg hadn't mitigated any of it by trying to shove them out of the exhibit. And the weird chatter she'd overheard outside the restroom pushed her to dig further.

She looked all around at the result of digging. Nobody would have known the extent of these ruins if the Mexicans hadn't started a construction project at the Zocalo in 1978. What they uncovered was a vast network of steps and altars and artifacts that boggled the mind and gave graphic history to a brilliant and intricate puzzle of a civilization that had burst into flame, and then died with the arrival of the Spanish in the sixteenth century.

"I can't wait to write about this place," Blanche said. Haasi snapped a picture of a stone snake-beast undulating across the ruins.

"Can you believe where we're walking?" Haasi's forehead glistened. Blanche rarely saw her so animated. She climbed a step and kneeled with her camera for a low shot of an Aztec deity. With her Florida roots, and Miccosukee heritage, Haasi maintained a level of comfort in the heat and an appreciation and reverence for history. She seemed at home exploring the ruins. Blanche was amazed, but she was an observer and visitor, a pale foreigner from cold, green Ireland. Oddly enough, Blanche's temper boiled up easily while Haasi had a cool head. Yet, as cousins, with the same great-grandmother, they were kin, and they could read each other, bound together in a world of mutual understanding.

Blanche stood on one of the steps at the base of an altar, her head full of images from Rivera's murals. "Hey, Haas, do you hear that?"

"The subway, Blanche." Reality dashed her imagination. They looked down into a hollow of stones and smooth carvings, stretching for most of a city block.

"I guess," said Blanche. The rumbling under the plaza stopped, the traffic screeched and honked. "It must have been magnificent."

"It still is."

They leaned on a wall, staring down into the maze, then pushed off and started out across the square. The people hurried past, others sought shade and rest under the trees near the cathedral. Blanche and Haasi weren't far from the Palacio. They could see the two leaving the building and walking toward a waiting car: López and Blussberg. They were hard to mistake, an unlikely pair, the pretentious blond director and the vampirish staffer. They climbed into the back seat of an enormous black ride. An Escalade? The rims gleamed, the car polished to a black-diamond gloss. A woman sat in the driver's seat. Even from where Blanche stood, she could see glitz, the shining dark hair and huge sunglasses. A gold bracelet rested on the steering wheel and caught the sun.

"What do you suppose they're up to?" Blanche's question was rhetorical. The car and riders stuck out, rolling around the plaza, past the cathedral.

"Probably not any good, whatever it is," said Haasi. "An odd bunch, if you ask me."

"I really have to talk to Cardenal."

Blanche and Haasi sat in the small garden at the hotel, a poinsettia tree sprawling above their heads, a bird chirping happy sounds. Haasi set her Modelo on the wrought iron tabletop. "Maybe this business will get resolved, and we can get on with this little trip in peace."

Blanche's expression said no such thing. "Ha! Sure. There's just one problem: I'm dying to know what Blussberg and López were up to."

"A date with the nice *señorita*?"

"Nothing nice about any of them."

Haasi pursed her lips. "We have to get back to normal, B."

"Right. Normal." Horns blasted in the street outside the walls of the patio, visitors circled in and out of the lobby through the glass doors. Blanche watched them checking in, arriving from every corner of the world. She'd called the detective, but couldn't get through. She was itching to talk to him and get back in the mix. "I'd really like to talk to Cardenal. Now."

"I know, but I wouldn't hurry. We'll see him."

"Yeah, but, when? Remember what he said? There's all that stealing going on. And a corpse thrown on top of it? I want to tell him what I heard in that hallway. And now this. Could be legit, but I don't know. Creeping off like that in the Batmobile seems suspicious."

"I think the Batmobile is a convertible."

"Well, then, Dracula's hearse. Can't be up to any good, that bunch ..."

"You don't know if there's any connection. Whatsoever." Haasi's expression was blasé. She put a bare foot on the chair next to her at the small square table. It was cool in the shade, and the two had the small patio to themselves.

Blanche took a swig that drained the bottle. She was deep in thought.

Neither one noticed the small woman in the hotel lobby, looking around, talking to the receptionist. The woman hurried through the glass doors. Blanche looked up. The visitor wore long loose pants, a bandanna on her head, and atop that a small straw hat. Her eyes were steely and kind. A Mexican stare. True and piercing.

Blanche was on her feet.

"*Señoritas*? You saved my Eddie," the old woman said. "I am here to thank you." She stood there quietly, hands folded loosely at her chest.

Haasi leaned forward. "Eddie?" She looked at Blanche.

"Pillow Man."

Chapter Nine

THE RIDE OUT

BLANCHE MOVED ACROSS THE PATIO. Her eyes met Carmen's, and they drew toward each other in a hug. It was Pillow Man's sister, María Carmen, who'd arrived at the scene of the accident and driven away with Eddie in the ambulance. Blanche was surprised, and glad, to see her; she was eager for news.

"I can't believe it," said Haasi. "How are you and Eddie?"

Carmen smiled. "*Estamos bien, bien.* Thanks to you," she said. "Come with me." She extended a hand from under her purple shawl. "*Por favor.* Come, see Eddie. He is grateful."

"Oh, I don't know," said Haasi. She looked at Blanche and then Carmen, and her expression softened. "Has Eddie recovered?"

"You will see."

Blanche had the gleam in her eye. Adventure Time. "How far, Carmen?"

"It is close. I will bring you back. Detective Cardenal, he knows I come to you."

"Detective Cardenal?"

"Yes, I know the detective; he knows of the accident. That you saved Eddie. Mexico City is big, but the story of the two beautiful *señoritas* from North America who care for a Mexican man in the hot street. The story goes like the wind."

Cardenal knows?

They climbed into the front seat of the white pickup truck. There was no seat belt, and Blanche thought of the possibility of being thrown out and into a dusty cactus. Not only that, but Carmen didn't look big enough to drive a tricycle.

Tentatively, Blanche gestured to Carmen. "Seat belt?"

Carmen sighed and clambered down out of the truck. She groped around on the floor behind the front seat for the safety belt until she brought the buckle up through the hole. Blanche caught the belt and buckled it around herself and Haasi. They looked at each other. Haasi shrugged.

Carmen did not talk much, and for this Blanche was grateful. Carmen's face barely cleared the steering wheel as the semis whizzed past their pickup on Highway 57 out of downtown. They rumbled away, six eyes riveted on the road: the old Mexican and the young "angels" from Florida.

Blanche was amazed at the quick change in the landscape, only a few miles out of the city. They'd hardly been on the road fifteen minutes or so. Through a bug-splattered windshield, the semi-desert stretched across a land dotted with nopal cactus and dusty mesquite—trees that reminded Blanche of thin women with short feathery hair. The stubby growth sprouted here and there among small, chipped houses interspersed with taco stands and neat piles of old tires in every configuration. Blanche imagined people living quietly inside those small houses of cinder block and corrugated roofs, managing year after year, a hundred years at a time with hardly a change; there was something soothing in it. Lasting and solid. Cut off from distraction and noise of the city, from cable and internet, tourists and traffic. And murder.

But who could escape the city? Many of them traveled into the markets, or to work in the kiosks and stalls, to sew, clean, or cook, and then go back to the country. Like Carmen and Eddie. Blanche had scrounged books on Mexico, in the library and bookshops, mostly travel guides and histories, but she and Haasi hadn't planned on getting out into the country. Not until Pillow Man. She relaxed. She welcomed the adventure, especially now, to see him. The mummy and that drama could wait. It was a relief to get some distance from it.

Pillow Man sat under a shiny blue canvas cover propped up with poles. He was peeling the thorns off flat paddles of nopal cactus with a paring knife. When he saw the truck rattle to a stop on the scrabble of a front yard and Blanche emerge first, his eyes lit up. He dropped the knife and rose slowly. He limped toward her, arms outstretched: "*Mi ángel.*"

Blanche smiled. She was hardly an angel. All she did was put a bit of shredded pillow under his head while he lay in the street and hold his hand until the ambulance came, then she didn't let go of his fingers until Carmen arrived and they drove him off to the emergency room. It was a harrowing experience, but he was alive, and he was smiling. For this, Blanche was grateful. It had only been a few days since the accident, but he looked remarkably fit. His face, though lined and weathered, had a healthy glow.

"¡*Mejorando?*" Blanche held him by his thin shoulders. Was he getting better? He straightened up. She could hear his old bones practically rasping against each other. He had to be eighty. He was wearing the same faded shirt he'd worn at the accident, clean and pressed, the collar and sleeves buttoned up even in this heat. His white hair, thick as pillow fluff, was plastered down on his head.

"*Mejorando.* I am better now," he said. His eyes filled, which brought Blanche right back to the day of the accident. He kissed her cheek.

"Come. Leave her." Carmen fussed, holding onto Haasi's

arm as they walked around the truck. Impatiently, she clucked: "*Vamos*. Time to eat."

The cottage was a rough structure of cinder blocks set on a patch of dirt. One window by the door had no glass, only a gauzy white shawl of a curtain waving in and out in welcome. A mannequin dressed in a green shirt was stuck in the dirt near a rutty road, and in the middle of it, a lonely cow stood, lowing and mooing sadly. Beyond the cow, a small pond with scum the color of the mannequin's shirt lay flat and still. Not a sound for miles. Blanche looked out across the country at vast expanses of tan and green, bumps of cactus, the low black hills far in the distance, beckoning, suggesting cooler places. A mysterious beauty that rolled away under a startlingly blue sky tinged pink and orange in the early evening.

It was dim inside the cottage, but her eyes adjusted to the light. Strings of bright cut-paper flags fluttered from wall to wall overhead. Something delicious was simmering in a pot and sending up a meaty aroma. Blanche hoped it was one of her most favorite things, *chamorro*, the slow-cooked, spicy leg of the pig. Blanche and Haasi had discovered it, wandering through the market one day. They'd ordered two tacos of *chamorro* and orange Victorias to drink and sat on stools, watching the cook stir a vat of meat the size of her whole stove back home.

Young women stood over a *comal*, all of them speaking Spanish at once. A girl flipped tortillas into baskets lined with napkins. Candles flickered on the deep-set windowsills next to tangles of red and white geraniums, and a boy in the corner bent over a guitar. The happy sounds and smells carried them into another world after the lonely dusty desert.

Then, an explosion of laughter outside. Several young men banged through the cross-hatched wooden door. They wore T-shirts and jeans. They stopped, shyly, when they saw Blanche and Haasi and the other girls, then they scattered along a far wall, carrying beaten-up guitars, a small drum, and a flute-like reed instrument.

Pillow Man did not look at the newcomers who guffawed and slapped each other on the back. Eddie shuffled in a straight line, nodding once at the young women in the kitchen. He held on to Blanche's arm and walked over to the boy in the corner. The boy stopped tuning the guitar and unfolded himself from the stool. He was tall, compared to everyone else in the room. He was not a boy, but a man. A crooked smile cut his jaw at a sharp angle and the flash of that smile made him even more handsome.

"*Angelita*, meet Emilio Sierra Del Real," said the Pillow Man whose full name, they'd learned from Carmen, was Virgilio Eduardo Fabian Gustavo, or Eddie. Blanche loved the sound of all the long, musical names.

Eddie took their hands and brought them together. Emilio and Blanche smiled, a spark passing between them, the guitars quiet, the room filled with the warm scent of cooking. Blanche would always remember that moment like she wasn't even in it, like it was a painting of a fiesta that hung in her mind.

"So, you are the angel," said the guitar player. His hair was spiky like the feathers of a blackbird, his nose was aquiline like an Aztec chief. He had powerful upper arms that stuck out of the T-shirt tucked halfway into a pair of tight jeans. He wore scuffed boots. His hand wrapped around the neck of the guitar like he was grasping something easy and familiar to him—kindling for burning, a bunch of flowers, a loaf of bread. With the other hand, he reached for Blanche and kissed her on the cheek, and then the other. A light gesture that hit her soundly.

"No angel. I'm Blanche Murninghan," she said. "And this is Haasi …" But Haasi was already busy at a long counter, a *molcajete* in one hand and an avocado in the other. Laughing with the girls in long skirts who twirled into the room as they set bowls on the table.

Blanche didn't move. She stared back at Emilio. "You speak English well." She blurted, without thinking.

"Sometimes. For example, like now." He was still smiling, a crease around the eyes that added years.

She felt the blush move along her neck. She was glad the room was dim and cool. She hoped he couldn't see the pink in her cheeks.

But she wanted to hear him speak again. The sound of his voice was deep and smooth. He didn't seem to be in any rush. She finally asked, "Do you live here?" They were in the middle of nowhere. *Does he feel like that?* She couldn't tell anything about the way he felt, but they were tied together in some odd way.

He said, "I am not always here."

Then where? She didn't have time to ask him. Carmen clapped her hands. "¡A la mesa!" Everyone gathered at the table, but Blanche's eyes followed Emilio as he set his guitar against the wall.

Chapter Ten

FIESTA

THE PARTY REELED, ROUND AND ROUND in a circle of color and music, flags and flowers. Carmen guided Blanche and Haasi to yellow chairs, the backs painted with blue flowers. Carmen set food on a table covered in a well-worn orange-and-turquoise-checkered cloth: bowls of red and green salsas, chopped onions, cut limes, roasted-salted serranos, and jalapeños, and stacks of warm tortillas in small round baskets. They all sat, except for the boys who gathered on stools along the wall, guitars at rest, and waited their turn.

Carmen began passing bowls. Eddie piled the meat and strips of white pigskin into tortillas. The young men helped themselves to the vat on the stove. Blanche stole a look at Emilio, a head taller in the middle of the bunch. He reached for limes and chiles over Carmen's shoulder, and she swatted him with a quick hand. "To the kitchen!" she laughed.

Blanche watched Eddie and added the shiny white strips of pigskin to her taco. The juice ran down her arm. She mopped it up quickly. "Ah, a good sign," Eddie said. "¿*Le gusta?*"

"I love it," said Blanche. She'd never tasted anything so good.

She should try everything, except, perhaps, for the *chapulines*, the Oaxacan grasshoppers. Eddie enticed her with a plateful of the deep-fried insects, all legs and shriveled bodies. Blanche shook her head. He popped one in his mouth and it crackled in his teeth.

"*Qué cosa, Eddie,*" Blanche sat back in the chair. "You'll be up jumping around."

He threw his head back and laughed. "No. No jumping!"

They ate the tortillas and juicy, salty meat and the roasted serrano peppers, hot and biting. Nopal, roasted corn, a variety of chiles—familiar ingredients that never seemed boring. It was virtually the same diet as what the Aztecs ate.

Eddie nodded approval. "More for *Las Angelitas.*"

"*Está bien.*" Blanche didn't want to trouble the girls, but this detail of hospitality—the warm tortillas—seemed important. "*Muchas gracias,*" she murmured.

"*Me alegro,*" he said. "I am very happy."

Emilio pulled up a chair next to Blanche. "They don't eat *chamorro* often. Or grasshoppers." He spoke softly. "But today they are celebrating, and Mexicans do not need much of an excuse. They are thankful you are here, and very thankful for what you and Haasi did for Eddie." He wrapped a tortilla into a cylinder with one hand and ate it in two bites. He had been hanging back with the boys, but she had seen him watching her.

"They? Isn't this your home?"

"No, I'm visiting in Tepequito. I do part of my medical training in the country. We must all do service to complete the study."

"You're a doctor?" She sounded incredulous. Required training? It made perfect sense, but she'd never heard of it.

"Not yet. One day, I hope."

One of the girls held out the bowl of *chamorro* to Blanche. She couldn't resist. She took a small portion with serranos, the green skins blistered black.

Emilio's eyebrow shot up. "A true *mejicana.*"

She smiled. "Not really. But I like the hot stuff."

He laughed. "You like it here?"

"Very much."

His eyes squinted in a smile. He had the whitest teeth and darkest eyes she'd ever seen.

"*Permiso*," he said. "Excuse me." His hand rested briefly on her arm, and then he strolled back toward the corner. He clasped hands with one of the young men and picked up the guitar. They began to play, and the chords and notes filled the room where fifteen people fit nicely. They settled in groups of two or three at the long dining table and at a spare conversational arrangement of carved pine sofa and chairs with red cushions. Sunflowers drooped out of a vase on a small end table in front of Our Lady of Guadalupe.

Blanche had been sitting too long, enjoying herself too much. She stood up to help. Haasi was way ahead of her, piling dishes and jabbering away in Spanish with the girls. Blanche lifted two bowls off the table, but Carmen shook her head and motioned to Haasi. "Sit." A *Tres Leches* cake, soaked in three kinds of sweet milk with peaches, appeared. Carmen put forks and plates on the table and cut the cake.

"*Toma*," Carmen said, handing out the plates. "Enjoy!"

The cake was light and sweet. "They have a way with sugar!" Blanche nudged Haasi whose expression was blissful. She eyed the second piece Carmen put on her plate. "Who'da thought? Cake soaked in milk? Heaven!"

Eddie nibbled at the cake, clearly delighted. Carmen clapped and moved her feet, humming to the music. She'd changed to a red shawl over a white muslin top embroidered with roses, and her long white hair fell in waves about her shoulders. The young men tuned their guitars for the next song, their fingers picking out the chords.

Emilio's gaze found Blanche as he sang: "*Mujeres Divinas*." *Blanche's Spanish couldn't quite keep up, but she understood something about dying in the cantina and always adoring that divine woman.*

Divina mujer. No one had ever called her a "divine woman."

"First you're an angel, and now divine." Haasi laughed.

"I know. And I haven't even died yet."

"Don't say that!" Haasi did not hide her superstition.

"Sorry."

Haasi sighed. She squeezed Blanche's hand.

They sat close together, scooting their chairs nearer to the guitars. Carmen brought out a bottle of mezcal. *Why not?* Haasi and Blanche each tossed back a shot. A sandal tapped the concrete floor, and Blanche reached for more.

The night was magical—and miles and centuries away from her neat cabin on Santa Maria Island. She might as well have landed on the moon. She looked at Eddie, curled up, a shawl over his shoulders, and as snug as a cat, warming to the music. His head was moving, his fingers tapped the arm of the chair. *Oh, Eddie.* He looked up at her and motioned to the mezcal, rocking his thumb. He pointed at the bottle. "*Toma.* Drink. Celebrate."

Blanche tossed back a shot and warmth flooded to her fingertips. Above her, the pink and red flags waved in the breeze.

Eddie raised the glass in a toast. "¡*Salud, pesos, amor, y el tiempo para gastarlos!*" Health, money, love, and the time to enjoy them.

The door of the cottage stood open to the evening. Dozens of candles burned down, the edges of the room glowed, and their voices blended into one song. Blanche wanted to stop time right there, to enjoy the moment, and stop chasing the nightmares of the city. It was a welcome respite.

It's crazy being here.

Crazy is good.

It was a happy accident that brought her and Haasi here, that the pillows had cushioned the blow, that Eddie seemed to have recovered so well. She eyed Emilio strumming away. She grabbed the bottle and poured two shots, one for Eddie and one for her.

They sang about dead lovers, lost children, cactus, springtime and beer, and the time flowed out around them. They sang about the man whose brother died in Guadalajara, and the dear mother who died in Acapulco. They turned to songs of whales and owls, horses and birds, and laughed until they almost fell down. Eddie leapt up, danced in a circle and sat down again, his hand cupping one knee, the feet keeping time with the music.

The moon threw raggedy silver patches onto the floor; the candles burned away the hours. Blanche requested *Cielito Lindo*. They groaned but sang it anyway.

Emilio was at her side, and she felt the room spin. It might have been the drinks, or not. Carmen said, one, maybe two, with an admonishing glance at Eddie. Blanche had had three, maybe four. She was losing count of everything.

It was now past three in the morning.

Haasi was chatting with two guitar players. Blanche looked around: *How the hell are we going to get home? Cardenal knows we're here …*

As if Carmen heard her thoughts, she appeared from the back of the cottage. She still wore her loose-fitting muslin and red shawl. She took Blanche's hand and patted it lightly. "Emilio will take you home," she said.

"Emilio?" Blanche was hesitant.

Emilio rested one arm over the top of the guitar, his legs angled on the stool. He was watching Blanche.

"OK," she said. Blanche wanted to stay. She wanted the night to go on and on. She wanted to know more about him and Mexico. "Sure, we'll go with Emilio."

Haasi broke away and whispered. "It's all set?"

"I think it's quite all right," Blanche said, smiling at Emilio.

The fiesta did not end when they started for the door. The guests, and their hosts, were still twirling and tapping and playing guitars. Blanche hated to miss it, but their late ride would take them through the vast desert.

Eddie got up slowly. His eyes glowed as he held Blanche's fingers. "*Muchas gracias. Angel.*"

"*Muchas gracias, Señor* Eddie. For everything. For this fiesta, for this evening." She glanced at Emilio. It was getting so she couldn't help herself. Then, she hugged Eddie one last time.

Emilio, Haasi, and Blanche crowded into the front seat of Carmen's truck. The trip seemed to take seconds, their conversation and laughter circling around in the cab of that truck like it was their own private universe. They skimmed the dark desert toward the lights of Mexico City with hardly a soul on the road.

At the hotel, Haasi whispered, "Good luck." She ran off to their room, returning in minutes to drop off a couple of Tecates.

Blanche laughed. "As usual, reading my mind."

Emilio and Blanche sat in the hotel lounge off the lobby. The tile floor the color of an old flowerpot. A poster of Diego Rivera's *Niños Pidiendo Posada* hung over the small sofa. A couple of lamps gave off low light, and the windows were crammed with vines and geraniums.

They talked, their heads together, their legs curled under them on the sofa. They were both only children who never knew their fathers. That was where the similarity ended. Emilio was a child of the desert and horses, a hard life of farming surrounded by dogs and chickens and goats. He'd always wanted to be a doctor, since first seeing his grandmother deliver a baby. Blanche had grown up wild on the beach, with her cousin Jack, climbing palm trees and fishing for pompano and snapper. She'd gone to college, majored in journalism, and led an idyllic life under the eye of her doting grandmother, Maeve Murninghan, and her beloved friend Donald Nicholas "Cap" Reid. Her grandmother was gone, but Cap still kept an eye on her.

They were so different, yet Blanche was drawn to him. He was an open door, and here she was, walking through it. They sipped beer, their eyes locked on each other, and in the hush between stories, she opened the window and let in the early morning breeze and the scent of fresh rain.

"We are bad," she said, raising her beer.

He laughed. "Bad is good."

"I feel like I've known you for years," she said.

"Who can tell about time? No edges to it ..." He took the bottle out of her hand and laced his fingers in hers. Then he frowned. "Why did you have to bring up time, *Señorita* Blanche? I've got clinic in two hours." He looked at his watch. "Wish I didn't have to go."

"Something I need to ask you. Before you go. You're a doctor ..."

He straightened up, a look of concern. "You all right?"

The whole strange discovery at the mummy exhibit at the Palacio tumbled out, along with her suspicions. The detective and the thievery of artifacts. He studied her his mouth set in a tight line.

"I've heard rumors, believe it or not, of this strange business with the 'mummy.'"

"You know about the body, and, maybe, how it's possible to make a mummy?"

He laughed then. "There are good ways to make a 'mummy.' And the bad way."

"Very funny," she said. "We're talkin' the bad way here. Very bad."

He was smiling but guarded. "The rumors … That's all it's been. Gruesome rumors." He was quiet for almost a minute. "Blanche, I'd stay far away from this. It is dangerous. Sinister."

"But did you ever hear of such a thing?"

"What? Making mummies?" He seemed to choose his words carefully. "At the medical school, there's talk of La Capa Plata, a rough bunch of gangsters. And a woman, a doctor. La Escandolera."

"You think she did this?"

"I have no idea. It's just some underground talk about the weird business she does for the mob." He took her hand. "How'd you ever get mixed up in it?"

"I'm not really in it. I just happened to be there, at the Palacio, staring at this body in the exhibit that I knew was not *ancient.*"

"Ask the detective to follow up on a woman doctor who has questionable connections with the medical school. I think she has other business for cover, but I'm not sure what it is. She was once associated with some of the classes, and that's where I heard about her. Maybe I can find out something, but for now, Blanche, stay away from those people. Sounds like a mess."

He reached for a pillow and put it under Blanche's elbow. She brushed his arm, smooth and warm, and snuggled next to him. He closed his eyes for a second. They sprung open: "Pillows." He laughed. "If it weren't for Eddie and his mountain of pillows …"

Chapter Eleven

THE UNREAL

EMILIO AND BLANCHE SAT, HOLDING HANDS, and then he kissed her and slipped away. It was dawn. She left the window open, the rain dripped off the leaves of the cherimoya tree onto the patio. She thought of the weight of sound, the light and the dark. She loved the rhythmic sound of water, she loved the sound of his voice, talking or singing. The cool morning wafted into the hotel lounge. She wished the night had lasted longer, that the party didn't have to end. That he was still here.

She was suddenly deflated, a party letdown after the fiesta and music. She was glad Carmen had come to pick them up, and that they had gone off with her. She'd visited the real Mexico, and she wouldn't forget. She sure wouldn't forget Emilio. She hoped she would see him again.

Intriguing. Everything about him, and then this last reveal about La Escandolera …

She climbed the narrow stairs to the room she shared with Haasi, who was curled into a ball under a white cotton blanket. Blanche was careful not to wake her, and soon she too fell into a deep sleep. Her last thought was of Emilio's dark eyes, falling into them.

"Blanche! It's almost noon." Haasi shook her gently. "Shake off that coma. What the heck did he do to you?"

Blanche sat up, her hair a fright of curls and the dream fading. The daylight blasted her in the face. "Whaaaat?"

"Hope he's not operating today." Haasi laughed. She scooched Blanche's legs over and sat on the bed.

"I hope not, too. He was here 'til after five!" Blanche put her hands on her head and fell back on the pillow. "OMG. I feel drunk. With love."

"Well, can you pull yourself together? For just a bit? Earth calling Divine Angel." Haasi gave Blanche a friendly shove and grabbed her toe. "Detective Cardenal's downstairs on the patio."

"Ooooooo. Great."

"He wants to talk to us again."

"Well, good. I want to talk to him, too. See what he knows about La Escandolera! A mysterious gang member slash lady doctor."

"What?"

"Yeah, wait'll you hear." Blanche staggered to the sink and checked herself out in the mirror. "Think I need a few more winks. No more drinks, for now. But, hey, let's go see *el detective*."

Detective Cardenal sat at a wrought iron table on the shady side of the patio under a vine of pink mandevilla. He seemed perfectly at home. Traffic blared outside the hotel, but the patio offered a cool city retreat. He was flipping through a notepad, a paper cup of coffee at the ready.

Blanche stumbled into the sunshine. She lusted after the coffee.

The detective rose when he saw Blanche and Haasi. "¡*Buenos días, señoritas!*" His brilliant smile rivaled the morning, his gleaming black hair slicked back.

"*Buenas* to you, *señor*," said Blanche. "To what do we owe the pleasure?" She was barely awake but rallying. Haasi was bright-eyed.

"*Señorita* Haasi gave me a call. We need to talk."

Haasi turned to Blanche. "I rang him this morning again. He needs to know what you overheard at the Palacio. And we have other loose ends. ..."

"Let me think." It was difficult after her night of fiesta. "They did complain about us stirring up trouble." Everyone in the vicinity seemed aware that Blanche and Haasi had alerted the world to the fake mummy. "I heard bits and pieces, mostly. There were male voices, saying something was not 'real.' It was a rather weird, heated conversation."

"Could have been talking about the price of beans or a designer watch." Cardenal smoothed back his thick coif and tapped his head. He had that perpetual look of amusement in his eyes, and Blanche guessed that he liked his work as detective.

"Well, *no*," Blanche said. "They were definitely talking about an exhibit, or something to do with the exhibit. Not a watch or anything."

"He could have been talking about that mummy," said Haasi. "It's gone now." Each word struck with authority.

He studied her. "Yes, I am aware of that," said Cardenal. "I'd like a better description of events from you both, if you wouldn't mind. For the record."

Blanche obliged, once again, describing the pink hair clip and bronze skin and the whole aspect as best she could remember. "In that conversation I overheard, one of them said not to tell the 'boss'. Now who would that be? Seems pretty important to find out, detective."

"Yes, it does." He cast a glance to the side. Blanche felt he was holding back.

"And this. They also talked about the *loan* of the mummies to the exhibit." She was foggy, and hung over, and nothing else seemed to pop up.

"The *real* mummies," said Haasi. "I scoped out the crowd. In fact, I identified you, Detective Cardenal, as a suspicious character."

He laughed. "I've been called a lot of things. Suspicious is all right. But I've been visiting these different museums and noting the crowds because of the art theft. Believe me, you two stood out as suspicious, too. Couldn't miss the two *gringas*."

"Fair enough. But, listen. There's something else I want to tell you," said Blanche. "I met a young doctor last night ..."

"Congratulations. I'm glad you're getting out and meeting the people of this great city," said Cardenal. Blanche was struck again. *Seems awfully hearty for a policeman.*

"Oh, it was great, all right," said Haasi, 'til the sun came up." She poked Blanche, grinned at Cardenal. "We had a wonderful time at Pillow Man's, I mean, Eddie's, in Tepequito. They mentioned you."

"*Estupendo*. They've been vendors near the plaza for decades. Good people, and generous. What you did for them—we heard. I'm glad you met him again, and María Carmen. And the young doctor?"

Blanche said, "Yes, the doctor. That's what I want to talk about." She shook her head to loosen the cobwebs. "He told me last night about a woman. La Escandolera. A former medical student rumored to work for the mob. La Capa Plata? I guess she's done favors for them. It's a stretch to connect her to what's going on over there with those mummies and the theft, but it's worth a look. She has a reputation."

"We know of her." Cardenal lost his humor. "Oleantha Flórez." His brows knit in concern a fist clenched on the tabletop. "She's suspected of all kinds of mayhem. And she's hard as the devil to track down. The medical school has facilities scattered in different parts of the city, some of the labs near the Palacio. We'll look into it." He started patting the top of his head again. "Interesting."

Blanche suppressed a giggle.

Haasi looked at her. "Are you still drunk?"

Now Blanche was laughing, and Cardenal was lost in thought. The hand rested on top of the head.

Blanche sat up. "No, I am suddenly very sober." She eyed the coffee. The afternoon of the visit to the Templo in the main plaza snapped into memory. "Detective, we saw someone outside the Palacio yesterday, after we visited the ruins in the Zocalo. A woman. A very fancy one, picking up López and that blond guy, the director. Blusterberg?"

"Ah, *Señor* Blussberg. We have been questioning him, and we've come up with *nada*." Cardenal squinted at her. "Do you think you could identify this woman?"

"She was a distance away, but maybe. Swept-back, shiny black hair, huge sunglasses. Gold bling."

"Not so uncommon in the city," said Cardenal. "But La Escandolera. A real scandal, that one. We'll check around for the latest on her. I'll get her photo and ask you to identify her. Perhaps." He stood up and wiggled his phone at them. "I'll call you." He bowed slightly. "Also, may I thank you, *señoritas*? You are most helpful in our investigation. I hope you will be staying on in DF for a while. At least until we can tie up some of these loose ends."

"*Señor*, I do not think that will be possible." said Haasi.

Blanche felt the mezcal fumes clearing from her head. "Detective, sir. Really?" A bubble of elation. Emilio! *Mummies and thievery*!

"*De verdad*," he said. "Truly. We have an eye on the Palacio and some other locations. Artifacts are still going missing. And this mummy business, and new details. ¡*Dios*!"

He mumbled the last and was gone.

Blanche scratched her head. "Well, that sort of does it. We

need to do some digging. Pronto. And, I guess, settle into Mexico City for a while." She shrugged and smiled at Haasi.

Haasi slipped down in her chair. "Here we go."

"Here we go? We're here." said Blanche. "But first things first. I need a nap."

"You just got up."

"I know, but I'm having a poor spell."

"OK, get some sleep. I'm going to talk to the woman at the desk, see if we can get some kind of deal on this room. Then, think I'll head over to the Zocalo for more photos."

Blanche groaned. "Maybe we ought to call Clint at the paper."

"Maybe not. Let's just handle it. For now."

"I better get myself together." She was still wearing the T-shirt and shorts from the night before.

"I'll bring coffee."

"And maybe a bun from La Ideal?"

"This place is beginning to feel like home."

Chapter Twelve

TO THE CASTLE

LATER THAT DAY, BLANCHE AND HAASI WAITED for Cardenal to call with news.

"It's too soon, Bang," said Haasi.

"But it's been … *hours* since we saw Cardenal." Haasi was right. *Chill, Blanche.*

In the meantime, they worked on the travel articles, but Blanche had trouble concentrating. She and Emilio had a date set up for the next day. She had taken a strong liking to him, and it seemed mutual. And on top of it all, he was somewhat unwittingly adding to the drama of the Palacio. Emilio had told her he'd heard rumors, and she was more than all ears.

The afternoon was cool as Emilio and Blanche sped down the Paseo de la Reforma toward the Bosque de Chapultepec on their rented bikes. The drive to the "Central Park" of Mexico City with Emilio was just the thing to clear her head if not give her a thrill to her toes.

The wide Paseo was crowded with other bikers, walkers, strollers, skaters. It was Sunday. On one of the busiest streets in the world, all the way from the Zocalo to the park. Thousands and thousands of happy people milled around, up and down and across the boulevard, Blanche and Emilio among them. It was a block party like she'd never seen, and a far cry from sleepy Santa Maria Island. She'd been reticent to go bike riding, even slightly freaked out at first, but then they took off, and now she was elated at the freedom of speeding along on such a beautiful day. With Emilio!

They stopped to adjust the straps on her helmet. "You'll be fine," he said, calming her nerves.

"If the doctor says so."

"No major traffic. Just us on the Paseo."

"And a million other people!" She laughed. "Hope you know how to set a broken leg."

"No broken anything. Just stay close behind me. You'll love it."

She didn't doubt for a minute she'd love it. Seeing him again thrilled her. The idea to go bike riding, less so, but Blanche was intrepid, if nothing else.

Haasi had gone off to the tourist bureau to chat up the young director, who had promised to get them freebies at local restaurants and material for the articles. Haasi was excited about the photos she'd taken at the Zocalo and the Templo, and she wanted more *color*. "And then it's my turn for a nap. I've been climbing ruins, running around the plaza. There's so much, Blanche! Right here in the middle of the city." Her face was flushed. Blanche had never seen her so happy. "I'll see you later, or tomorrow. We'll catch up," she said, hugging Blanche and scooting out the door, camera swinging from her neck.

Now Blanche and Emilio rode past the Monumento a la Independencia at a roundabout—with "El Angel" atop a column rising more than a hundred feet into the air. The gold statue was dedicated in 1910 for the one-hundred-year commemoration of Mexican independence from Spain, and, in later years, suffered a couple of horrific earthquakes.

"Hey, Angel, here's the other Angel," Emilio yelled back at her. She laughed but kept her eye on his broad back, his legs pumping. She wasn't leery any more about riding this bike in a city of millions. She had the hang of it. All thoughts of mummies and snakes and police whisked away with the breeze, though none of it was ever far from her mind. For now she'd concentrate on the view: Emilio.

They passed under the lavender-blue canopy of jacaranda trees, past a row of vendors selling everything from leather belts and bags to *tlayudas*, an oval tortilla of blue corn topped with nopal and cheese. She could smell the cinnamon of *camotes*, the pressure-cooked sweet potatoes, a typical street food in Mexico City. It made her hungry, but not for food. She threw her arms wide, "Look! No hands!"

Emilio turned. "Blanche!" The front wheel briefly wobbled. "You're going to make me fall."

She smiled. "I wish."

Emilio led her up a steep hill toward the Castle in the park. The manicured lawn and bushes and ancient cypress trees, fountains, vast expanse of dahlias, sunflowers, ruffly hibiscus, holly, and philodendron with platter-size leaves.

"It is amazing," said Emilio. His arm swept the vista. "All of this out of mud." Indeed, the Aztecs built their empire on lakes and canals. "We have a saying here, '*Así es el fango*'—'That's the mud for you,' but sometimes it means good. Like this." Once a sacred spot for the Aztecs, home to a French emperor, and Mexican presidents, the hilltop garden and Castle were now the site of the National Museum of History. They wandered the grounds and looked out at the city below. Blanche took in the most breathtaking view. "I can die now." Her face was red and glistening, black curls escaping the helmet.

"Please. Do not." He put a hand on her cheek, and a line

formed between his thick eyebrows. "You OK? Here, sit. I'll get us some water."

Blanche went over to a patch of grass under a tree, her legs rubbery from the bike ride. She was more of a walker and swimmer. But it felt good to get the exercise.

He came back with two bottles of water, took her wrist, counting beats, as he looked up into the tree branches. He grinned. "Yeah. I think you will live."

She swiveled her wrist into the palm of his hand and took a long swig of water. Nothing ever tasted so good. "I feel quite alive, thank you."

"You sure do." He sat cross-legged on the grass, the V-neck stretched and damp showing off a well-muscled chest. Blanche could only imagine what the rest of him looked like, and, horrors, what she must look like. She'd removed the helmet and with it the topknot tumbled down. Her face was flushed tomato-red from the ride and, especially, from looking at him.

"How old are you?" she asked.

"Where did that come from?" He laughed. "I'm old. Twenty-nine. You?" He clapped a hand over his mouth. "I'm sorry. Not supposed to ask a lady that."

"Almost thirty-three." She didn't give a hoot about age. Her beloved grandmother Maeve was eighty-seven when she died, but to Blanche, she was seven or seventeen or just plain ageless. "It's only a number."

"True. Some people don't seem to age, or at least it does not seem to matter."

"What? Are you reading my thoughts now?"

"Maybe." He leaned over and kissed her on the ear. He'd been aiming for her cheek and missed. She laughed and turned her head, so she was staring right into his eyes. The darkest, warmest eyes she'd ever seen. She kissed him, and she knew she shouldn't, but she did, and she was glad.

What's wrong with me?

He put his hand at the back of her head and pulled her toward him. Then jerked away. "I'm sorry. I couldn't help it."

"I couldn't either."

They sat like that, in the grass, holding hands, on the top of the hill, a place where heroes died, an emperor lived, presidents reigned, and flowers grew. On top of the world. The city below them, its misadventures and murder out of sight and out of mind. For now. There were things she'd wanted to ask, but they seemed to flit away with the ghosts on the hill.

Chapter Thirteen

HIDDEN PLACES

LATER THAT DAY, BLANCHE SAT ON HER BED while Haasi paced back and forth with a toothbrush shoved in her mouth. The hotel manager had agreed— with prodding from Haasi—to give them a deal on the room. They were feeling right at home and bursting with stories about Mexico City.

"Haas, I can't believe Emilio. He's wonderful!" Blanche stretched her arms over her head and almost fell off the bed.

Haasi stopped walking around and pointed the toothbrush at Blanche. "Wow. You're falling for the guy."

"What am I going to do?"

"Have fun? But remember—you can't put him in your suitcase. And by the way, Bang, how did we get so many clothes in those backpacks?" The floor looked like a tornado had struck the lady's clothing department of Macy's.

Blanche continued her dreamy-eyed pondering of the canopy of ficus trees outside their window. "He says, let's enjoy the time we have. What else can we do? Every day, every minute!"

"Oh, boy. And it's only been, like, a day or two. Like hours you've been together, in fact."

"Yeah." Her expression was a world away from mummies, traffic accidents, art thievery, and the police.

Haasi sighed. They weren't dwelling on the fix they'd gotten themselves into at the Palacio. She gave Blanche a poke. "We have those passes to El Jardín for dinner. From Aracelli at the tourist bureau. Remember? Want to go? Could Emilio meet us?"

"Emilio had to go back to Tepequito." Her smile drooped. "We had so much fun on that bike ride. Plus. Get this. We stayed up at the Castle for a while, then went for a beer. He told me some interesting stuff. Including more about La Escandolera. We gotta talk."

"And eat." Haasi opened a drawer and pulled out a silky black sheath about the size of a postage stamp. She eyed Blanche's faded shorts and T-shirt.

"I'm sorry, Haas. You must be starving!"

Blanche leapt off the bed and grabbed a yellow dress with a flouncy skirt. It went over her head, sash tied. She splashed her face from the sink in the corner, still flushed red, eyes shining. The topknot had not been repaired. Black curls fell over her throat and down her back.

"You look great," said Haasi.

"No, you."

"OK. Us. Let's go."

El Jardin overlooked the Paseo from the second floor of a French colonial-style building—left over from Carlota and Maximilian's reign in the mid-nineteenth century. They arrived for dinner at a fashionable ten o'clock. Inside the door to the restaurant, a tall vase of pink lilies the size of balloons and branches of red berries greeted them, the scent a pungent mix with olive oil and garlic and bread. Sleek, dark-haired women and gorgeous men sat at white tables. Candles flickered. And in the wide, arched windows, city lights twinkled.

"Wow, takes your breath away," said Blanche.

"Well, not your appetite, I hope," said Haasi who was already perusing a menu near the entrance.

The host seated them at a table near a window. An elderly waiter appeared noiselessly at their side, with menus, suggestions, and a warm smile. Blanche sat back and looked out over the tops of the trees with purple blossoms. Dreamily. "Jacaranda. Reminds me of Emilio. And our bike ride." She squeezed her eyes shut and stored away the memory.

Haasi smiled. "Oh, Blanche." She opened the menu and her eyes grew rounder. "You do have it bad."

"I don't feel bad. I feel good. And I've got news." Blanche leaned forward. "But you first. Tell me what you did today."

Haasi lowered the menu. "Blanche, seriously, there's so much to do here. To see. It would take forever."

"Wouldn't that be nice?" she said, her fingers laced under her chin.

"Oh, lookee! Couscous in cranberry and *chapulines*. God, I think that's those grasshoppers again. And nopal cactus with pineapple and tangerine," said Haasi.

"I'll pass but make a note of it for the daring travelers out there. Really, we should finish those articles."

"We are. This place is kind of fancy, but they have been so hospitable at the tourist bureau," Haasi's eyes skimmed the menu. "Thank you, Aracelli!"

They ordered a Camus, and slowly sipped the smooth red wine with tones of chocolate and cherry. The skirt steak marinated in lime and chiles arrived blooming with fried pumpkin blossoms.

Blanche hardly touched her steak. She swirled the wine and waited for a break in Haasi's concentration on dinner. She'd devoured half a mango, most of her steak, and an avocado.

Blanche took a sip. "Wow, this is going down like butter."

"Eat your dinner, Blanche." Haasi grinned and forked the

last pumpkin blossom. "From now on, I'm putting lime on everything."

Blanche shoved her plate aside and leaned across the table. "Listen! I've been mulling something over."

"Uh-oh. You did say you have news." Haasi winced and tore a hunk of bread. "Shoot!"

"Emilio and I drove past the Palacio on our bikes. Part of the old medical school is over there, some labs and offices in a rundown building. The school has moved most of the operation out. It looks deserted, but it isn't. When we drove by, there was a light on and a guy coming out the side door."

Haasi could already tell where this conversation was going, but she needed to hear it to believe it. "And?"

"Wanna have a look?" Blanche folded her arms on the table. "I was perfectly honest with Emilio. I told him we should poke around over there."

"*We*? Is that a good idea?"

"Probably not. Cardenal said he was going to check out that woman. La Escandolera. But the wheel needs some grease. Emilio knows some side doors. I promised we'd wait for him."

"Blanche, why would anyone use the medical school lab for their creepy business?"

"Good question." Blanche started smiling, and Haasi could tell she was floating off somewhere into Blancheland. "I got it out of him when we were on our second beer."

"What are you talking about? Earth to Bang."

"Sorry, Haas. It was such a great day." Blanche drifted back to the table. "Emilio seems to think that whoever is up to all that weird stuff at the Palacio has a lot of pull. And a set of keys, or a code to get in there. They can do whatever they want over there."

"Didn't he try to talk you out of poking around?"

"Yep."

It wouldn't do any good to argue. "Does he really know how to get in there?"

"Seems to," said Blanche, taking another sip of red. "We ought to take a stab at it."

"Don't like the sound of *that*."

"Well, Haas, don't you want to check it out? With rumors of that woman and all that's going on. Pretty suspicious, if you ask me."

"Bang, I don't remember anyone asking you. This vacay is getting crazy."

"Vacay. Well, it is taking on new tones …" She held up the wine glass to the light. Clear and lovely.

"The newspaper, Blanche. Ya know? We should be sticking to those articles and not this other stuff."

"Business is business, and this is serious."

Hassi gave her a sideways grin and shook her head. "I don't know why, but I'm in. How can I not be? You certainly have a way of putting things. Why the hell not?"

"Just the deets, ma'am. Just the deets."

They laughed and clinked glasses, maybe a bit too hard. A splash of wine bled onto the white cloth, and Blanche covered it with her napkin.

They finished the bread, a couple of coffees, and a tray of cream puffs. "Thank you, SunStream Travel and the Mexico City Tourist Office!" said Blanche.

"Let's roll."

"Literally."

Chapter Fourteen

GOING IN

"HE SAID TO MEET HIM HERE." Blanche and Haasi stood under the arches near the jewelry store, rows of gold loops and bracelets catching a sunbeam. It was shady and cool in the arcade. They faced the Zocalo and the throngs of Mexicans spilling across the plaza, out of the Metro, zigzagging to restaurants and shops. Blanche searched the faces for Emilio, her heart racing at the thought of him—and their upcoming visit to the lab. The time to snoop was now.

It was late afternoon. Blanche and Haasi had spent the better part of the day on the patio—their favorite spot, under the trees, sorting through material from the tourist office. Blanche planned to use much of it in her writing to back up the reel of images in her brain. She would concentrate on the city center, from the Zocalo to the park at Chapultepec. The museums, walks, and bike rides, the tours and food. There was a ton to sift through. Trouble was, Blanche loved it all. So did Haasi, who had already taken hundreds of photos. They kept getting sidetracked on their walks around the city, and that's what ate up their time. That morning, they'd headed toward an art gallery and wound up in a museum of architecture, the door almost hidden from view on a busy street. They didn't leave until Haasi's stomach finally demanded it, loud and clear.

"Emilio wants to go in after business hours. Close to dark," said Blanche. "He tried to talk me out of it again, but I told him we were *determined* to go exploring."

Haasi gave Blanche a wry smile. "Blanche, we have no idea what we're getting into. You know this could be real trouble, don't you? And what the heck are we going to do if we find something?"

"Call Cardenal?"

Haasi scratched her head. "It may be too late."

"What's that supposed to mean?"

"I don't know. Sometimes things happen and it's too late to do anything about it. We need to be careful on this. Don't you think Cardenal's checked out the lab already?"

"No, I don't, and I think that's an awful lot to think about right now, Haas. We don't have a single answer. *Nada.* Maybe Cardenal is on it. But probably not. Emilio says it's under the radar that the med school even operated over there. They were using the space up until a year or so ago, but now they're not in there. Something about certification, bureaucracy, funding, blah blah blah. The academics supposedly cleared out, but Emilio says talk is our lady friend is hanging around. Doing what? A classmate said he sees her coming and going frequently."

"I'll bet that was her—La Escandolera—leaving with those two goons from the Palacio."

"I'm sorry, but I think she, and her homies, killed an innocent woman and dried her up like a prune. For what?"

"Blanche! Jeez, that's awful." Haasi's expression was a fright. "Do you hear what you're saying? I mean, we kind of talked around it, but this is not good. At all."

"Well?"

Blanche saw him walking across the Zocalo, easy stride, cowboy boots and jeans. Her stomach took a little dip. His long legs closed the distance, and then he was next to her. He kissed her cheek, squeezed Haasi's arm.

"Crazy, beautiful ladies." He gave them a slight bow. He reminded her of a dashing Spanish gentleman of the eighteenth century, except for the getup. "Blanche, let's not make a big deal out of this. Please. In and out. I know of a side door, a maintenance entrance out of the way in the alley. We'll go in, look around, and leave. OK?" He ducked his head and kissed Blanche's ear lobe. "Will you be done with it then?"

She smiled up at the look of concern on his face. "Just like we talked about. If we see something, we'll tell Cardenal. Probably should have told the detective we're going in tonight."

"You're right. But, technically, we're just visiting tourists. I used to have access to all the facilities, so I'm just showing you around. Visitors. You, me, us. A little tour." He looked serious again, the smile lost.

"Got it," said Blanche. "Just visiting. But you understand, we need to do this. We *really* need to do this."

"*Dios mío*, you are something else," he said, and looked at Haasi. "Is she always like this?"

"Like what?" Haasi was implacable, protective as ever, and reticent to give anything away.

"Determined? Curious? Able to drive a person crazy?"

"Yes," Haasi said.

"Against my better judgment," he said, "but I know you'll be poking around there despite what I say. I can see it all over you." His fingers were laced in hers, and he squeezed.

Blanche's adrenalin mixed with romance. It was a heady brew. Her legs were like cooked spaghetti, shivers went down her back. "Let's go then, move it along. If we see something, we speak up. Isn't that the right thing to do?"

"Well, I don't know if that refers to discovering the source of fake mummies, but whatever." Haasi sighed.

Emilio looked across the Zocalo. The Mexicans strolled in all directions, along the sidewalk and across the plaza. The men with hair slicked back, trim beards, and the women smelling of rose and jasmine. Children ran around, laughing, their faces full of delight. Beautiful. Curls and dark eyes. "Crowds. That's good," said Emilio. "Do you see the façade of the Palacio? We're going past and around back to a separate building down an alley, like we saw, Blanche, on our bike ride. No guard at the side entrance. I have a key code. Let's mix with the crowd and look like we know what we're doing."

They walked briskly, Blanche in the lead. Emilio touched Haasi's arm and grinned. "She knows where she's going."

"Pretty much."

It was getting dark, and the side door was obscured in a niche of the old building. The alleyway loomed up around them like a dark cave, nondescript, hollow, and empty. Emilio punched in some numbers. They were inside. "Put your lights on but keep them low," he said. They each had a penlight, and now Blanche clicked hers on. The floor in the entry was concrete, the stairs to the left, worn, crooked stone. It was damp and smelled vaguely of mold and a chemical. Bleach? Disinfectant? Formalin and alcohol. Blanche recognized it from biology class. She'd never forget that smell, that and the frog she'd butchered, mostly with her eyes closed.

Inside the entry were double doors. Emilio tried the handle. No dice. Blanche was already climbing the stairs, with Haasi behind her. Emilio fell in last.

The top of the stair led to a short hallway and another door at the end. A glass pane shined with a dull grey light. Blanche tried the door. It was open.

"Wait!" Emilio slid past her. "I know this area. It's an old lab. Careful. There are beakers and cords and liquids …"

They stood in the dimly lit lab, a cavernous space of white tile, steel, and high, dirty rectangular windows on one wall. The air was close, an even stronger whiff of chemicals hitting Blanche directly in the nose.

"Yeah. Weird. And look at that!" Blanche held up her penlight. The beam illuminated a strange bed of white pipes, tilted. Hoses led away from the contraption to a drain in the floor.

"Oh, wow," said Haasi.

Emilio was silent. He walked around the "bed," his light working from one end to the other. He retraced his steps. At the lower end where a clamp secured the pipes to a frame were hairs. Long, black hairs, just the amount that would get caught in a fast comb out. "Look at this. Cardenal ought to see this."

"I don't think the police have been here," said Blanche. "Looks pretty much like business as usual."

Blanche's throat constricted, she turned to Haasi. "That mummy. The one that isn't really … Didn't she have black hair? That was the other thing, besides the skin texture and the hair clip. The hair on that one just didn't pass the ancient hay test like the others."

"Righto," said Haasi. She took a step back and stumbled over a tangle of hoses. She lifted the penlight. Some of them snaked up to suspended bottles of liquid on a rack where a web of tubes were neatly coiled, next to hanging loops of hoses. "Not exactly set up for watering your garden. What the hell is going on here?"

"Wish I knew. We didn't take this class," said Emilio. The three huddled close together, their lights sweeping over the lab. The tangles of tubes and hoses like snakes. The sterile, oddly contrived space. Blanche had never been in a mortuary, but this place screamed *cold and dead.*

Nothing good happens here.

Blanche shined her penlight on vials of liquid. "This stuff might be the weird smell. None of it is labeled. What do you think it is, Emilio?"

"No idea, but I'd say from the odor, it's some kind of preservative or disinfectant."

They moved carefully around the perimeter of the room. Emilio shined the light against an expanse of tiled walls and onto an elevated metal table. A long steel counter with tools, some of them lethally sharp, others blunt. "Don't touch anything," he said. He tore a paper towel from a roll and sorted through a bin of tools. Lifting one frightening implement, he said, "This is used to break bones. In order to reset them. At least that's the intended use." He put it back with the rest of the assortment.

Blanche shivered. It was hot outside and like a dark, cool grave inside. She shined the light around the lab. A small round table and a wooden armchair were tucked into a corner, and neatly arranged on top were a coffee maker, filters, a large red can. "This looks so cozy. Somebody's been here lately. Didn't you say this place has been closed up?"

"For the most part. Except for special operations, and certainly, recent operations," said Emilio. He lifted the lid on the coffeemaker with the tip of his finger and sniffed. "Yeah, these coffee grounds are newer."

"Newer? As new as our mysterious mummy?" Blanche stood next to him, spotlighting the coffee pot. "And what's this? All the secrets of youth and beauty." A mirror, several lipsticks, hair spray, and tubes of makeup and compacts of face powder were scattered on a small silver tray.

Haasi poked around the shelves in the opposite corner. "Hey, look at this." Blanche and Emilio joined her. Haasi opened the cover on a ledger with the end of her penlight. Inside, in neat legible writing, were names, procedures, "delivery" dates, all in Spanish. Emilio leaned over the page, and Blanche saw the look on his face. Even in the dim room, she could see the change. Anger? Disgust? Horror.

"They've been busy in here. Gunshot wounds. Strangulation.

Notes on desiccation." he said.

"Desiccation!" Blanche grabbed his arm.

"Not exactly a normal medical procedure, but it has been a preservation practice. For thousands of years," said Emilio.

Haasi flipped pages. The three put their heads together, their shallow breathing the only sound in the lab.

Blanche's Spanish was only fair, but she could still make out the meaning of some notes in the ledger. "Look at this! Says here, these monks used honey to mummify bodies, even stuffing themselves with it before death."

"Sweet," whispered Haasi.

In the next minute, a door at the far end of the lab clanged open. A metal object dully hit the wall. The three froze.

Chapter Fifteen

GOING OUT

"WHAT YOU DOING IN HERE?" The disembodied voice came from across the lab.

Blanche thought of bolting out the door they'd entered. She reached for Haasi's hand and leaned into Emilio. Her head jerked toward that entrance.

Emilio put a finger to his lips. He took one step toward the voice. "What are *you* doing here?" Demanding to know right back.

"Yeah. What?" Blanche's voice reverberated through the cold space. *I didn't need to say that. Wow, what is wrong with me?* She immediately regretted opening her mouth. She'd forgotten to turn off her filter.

Haasi yanked at the back of her jacket. "Bang!" She gritted her teeth, her voice barely above a whisper. "Be quiet."

Emilio had his arms out, shielding the women, but it didn't do any good. Blanche had already taken a step toward the voice.

"Do not move. Stay where you are." The voice became a body, a wide one, dressed in black, so Blanche could only make out his face. It was not a pretty sight. A long mustache curled in a scowl under a bulbous nose. He moved closer. A gun in his hand. From where Blanche stood, she could see the pockmarks and the dull

87

evil glint in his eyes. "Over there, against the wall. *Vayan*." He waved the gun in the direction of the corner next to the bed of pipes. Equidistant from either door. Impossible to run for it.

Emilio turned slightly. "Don't talk," he whispered.

He took a couple more steps toward the man. He held the gun up. Emilio stopped. "I'm a medical student. A doctor in training. I am taking these students on a tour of the lab. And the museum, and the Zocalo ..."

"*El museo* is closed, and the Zocalo is out there." He waved the gun around, and Blanche flinched. "Lab is not for tourists and students."

The man was quick. He grabbed the penlight from Emilio and walked over to the shelf with the ledger. It was still open where they'd left off poking around. The man flipped the pages, and turned to the three visitors, the gun still pointing in their direction. "You have very big eyes. Not so good."

"You can say that again." Blanche hissed. They drew closer together. "What are we gonna do now?"

Blanche had the awful feeling that it wasn't up to them.

A door slammed. Blanche ripped the blindfold off her face, a smelly bandanna that reeked of old grease and sweat. "Great! Now I'll probably get typhoid on top of everything else," she muttered. She looked around. She was alone in a small room. Dark wooden walls, ceiling. A small two-seat, high-back sofa. A high, narrow window, crusty with paint and dust and cobwebs. There was one door, and she tried it. Of course, it was locked.

Shit.

She shook her head, hard, and squinched her eyes. Her first thought: Haasi! Emilio! A cold fright squeezed her middle. She slumped to the floor against the wall. The man with the gun had blindfolded her, and Haasi, she supposed. Before the bandanna went over Blanche's eyes, the gunman whipped the pistol across Emilio's face. A rough hand pushed her out of the lab. She stumbled down the stairs. She winced at the memory of the cold look in the gunman's eyes. He'd put the gun in Emilio's back and told him to steer her and Haasi out of the lab; she'd felt his long fingers between her shoulder blades. A slight caressing, a whisper. "Don't worry, it will be all right."

But it wasn't all right. The scuffling, a protest. Now she was in this room. Alone, and worried out of her mind about Emilio and Haasi. How long had she been here? Hours? She couldn't keep track of time.

Emilio called us students. Good move, but what about him?

She sat, she stared off into space. She got up and went around the room, tapping on the walls frantically not thinking for a second if it was doing a bit of good. "Haasi!" She screeched. She didn't give a damn who heard her. "Emilio!" It dawned on her that the nonsensical wailing wasn't helping. She had to *think*.

She fell onto the sofa, her hands covering her face. Shivering in the small hot room at the thought of all that had gone wrong, and all that could go more wrong. She wrapped her arms around her middle and shook in terror.

Blanche was fully awake. It was near dawn. A sliver of light grey lit the grimy window. She didn't move. She heard something. A faint tapping. Faulty plumbing? Couldn't be. She willed it to be a signal, willed it to be true. It got louder, more insistent. Blanche leapt off the sofa and pressed her ear to the wall. Her hands ran over the walls, up and down. Until she reached a small, framed panel. The tapping was loudest here. She banged on the panel, a newer slice of painted wood, a cheap plywood. She waited for a response. She leaned down and, near tears, yelled, "Who's there? Haasi?"

"Blanche. Shut the hell up."

Blanche was never so happy. It was Haasi. Behind the panel. Blanche fell back on the floor. "Where are we?"

"Not far from that lab. I think."

"I have to get this panel off. Wait."

"Just hold tight. Listen. Remember, Blanche? Listen."

It's what saved them, not even a year ago, when Blanche had been kidnapped and taken off in a van. Haasi had told her on more than one occasion *to listen*, but listening to Haasi was not just a thing of ears. It meant gathering reserve, digging for survival, thinking as well as listening. Listening saved Blanche then, gave her context and understanding of where she was, and strength. She took a moment to concentrate on all the senses. She could see, and she could hear, and smell. Touch and think. Now, she needed everything. She listened. She wouldn't have found Haasi if she hadn't.

Blanche looked around the room for resources.

An axe? A gun? Anything to get us out of here?

She listened, hard. It was quiet outside. They had to be near the plaza, but she heard no traffic. They were in some part of the old building where they'd discovered the lab, she was sure of it, and what good did that do? Well, old buildings were like people. They had quirks. *Let's follow the quirks.*

She called Haasi in a hoarse whisper. "Do you have any ideas about how to get out of here?"

"I'm thinking, Blanche. Can't you hear me thinking?"

"Yes."

Blanche searched the room. There was, of course, nothing. No tools, implements of any sort. But there had to be *something*. She went back to the framing around the panel and picked at it with determination. She didn't even have the nails for it. Her fingertips were getting splinters. "Haas! I'm working this panel on the wall."

"I have one, too."

The picking and scratching weren't working, and so she went about looking for a solution when clearly there was none.

Blanche stood on the sofa and ran her hand along the windowsill. No handles or levers. She jumped down. *Nada.* Nothing in the room of any help. Whatsoever.

Now she was getting angry. It usually didn't take long for that to happen, but the knot of fear in her stomach was turning. And bitter. *What the hell. Those shit birds.* She picked up the sofa and tossed it halfway across the room. It was a release she needed. And then she almost smiled. *Well, lookee here.* The supports under the sofa were held together with a series of springs, and the springs were attached to flat metal braces. It was a cheap piece of furniture, and Blanche gathered confidence in that. She yanked at the web of springs and braces, the anger fueling her strength. She pulled and pulled, using her foot for leverage until the screws popped, and the metal braces gave way and threw her into a heap on the dusty floor.

She sat there, flipping the metal braces and springs over and over. The flexible coils dangled from the holes punched in the flat metal.

She heard the tapping again. A muffled sound. "What are you doing over there, Bang?"

Blanche leaned against the panel. "Haasi, I think I've got something here."

"Whatever it is, we don't have much time. That guy said he'd be back. Don't know when, but we need some kind of plan. Now, Blanche."

"I'm going to try to get this panel off."

"Better you than me. Pancho Villa tied my hands."

Blanche took the flat metal brace and worked it around the frame of the panel. It was a tight fit; the wood was swollen. She once again cursed her choice of footwear. A sandal was worthless as a hammer. What she needed was a good solid boot heel.

Finally, the metal fit a sliver of an opening under the frame. She forced it and worked it back and forth until a section of the wood molding popped off. "Haas, hold on. It's working." The rest of the frame came off easily. Blanche lifted off the wooden panel. Facing her was another wooden panel on the other side of a dark hollow space between the walls.

And a rope? It hung from somewhere above straight down past their floor and into nowhere. Blanche peered into the narrow darkness between the walls, but she could see nothing.

"Haas, can you hear me? I got the panel off over here. But this is weird. Hold on."

"I'm holding."

"Stand clear."

Blanche's karate and gymnastics classes surfaced. She lay on her back. She could barely reach the panel on the opposite wall. It was a stretch, but she kicked at it with all her might. Nothing.

"It's coming, Blanche. I think. Hurry." Her voice wavered from behind the wall opposite.

Blanche lay on her side and used her left leg. "AAAAARRRRGH"

"For Chrissakes, Blanche. Will you be quiet?"

Blanche sat up and leaned into the hollow space. "Did anything give?"

"Yeah, it's going. Just do it."

Blanche scraped her left leg on the raw wood opening, so she tried the right. One solid kick, and the panel flew off into the room where Haasi was captive. Blanche leaned in. "Haasi! Let me see you. Good God. Let me see you."

Haasi stuck her head in the opening. "Howdy, pardner." She popped up like she was grinning in a TV commercial. "Boy, am I glad to see you!"

With a rope, or cable, hanging between them. Blanche held it off to the side. "Howdy, yourself. Are you all right?"

"Well, not really. Here we are," Haasi said. "What's with the rope?"

"Dunno. Let me see your hands."

Haasi reached through the opening and Blanche untied her wrists. "Jeez, what an amateur. These aren't even decent knots." Blanche knew a thing or two about knots. Living on the island, right on the water, she and her cousin Jack had learned early how to fish, how to sail, and how to tie knots. "If Jack could see us now, he'd freak."

"Well, I wish he could see us now. I wish he were here … Blanche, we have to hurry!"

"What have you got over there? Anything we can use?"

Haasi drew back into the room. She reappeared, the penlight in one hand. "Bad guy missed this."

"That's hardly much of a weapon."

Haasi shined the penlight into the space, up and down. They both leaned into the dark hollow. The beam of light slid down the dusty cable. Haasi sat back on her heels. "Just as I thought. A dumbwaiter."

"Uh-huh. Great. A waiter? Get your order in. A slice of ham and some candied yams …"

"B! Don't you know what a dumbwaiter is?"

"I've seen some dumbwaiters in my life. I've been one."

"Blanche! A dumbwaiter is a platform, or a box, that's used to send food and dishes and stuff up and down between floors, usually from a kitchen. Got to be a kitchen down there. And maybe a way out."

"OK. What are you thinking?"

"I'm going to take a little ride."

"You're gonna go down there? On that thing?"

"Do you have a better idea?"

"Not at the moment."

Haasi grabbed the cable and tested it. She pulled and a faint screeching filled the hole as the "waiter" began to rise. She stopped and peered at Blanche. "When it comes up, I'm gonna ride that puppy down and you hold the cable steady. It's old and I don't know ..."

"Haasi, this is crazy."

"I'm small and fast. Right? I'll check around. *Got* to be a window or door down there. I don't have a way out from up here. You?"

"No." Blanche deflated, all the excitement of finding Haasi whooshing away. They were trapped, for sure.

They looked down into the shaft, Haasi directing her penlight along the walls. "We hoist the thing up. This cable is the pulley."

"What if it's sealed up down there?"

Haasi's leg shot up in the opening. "Beware a mighty hammer."

Blanche felt a mix of relief and dread. They had to try. There was a slim chance of getting out of there. Before Bad Nose Mustachio Man came back.

"Haas, do you know where Emilio is?"

"B, I was blindfolded, too. That bad guy was ordering him around. Didn't you hear it?"

"I couldn't understand. His Spanish was too fast, *pendejo* this and that. Emilio squeezed my hand and said, '*Cuidado*. It'll be all right.' And that was it." Blanche froze. "Haas, did you hear that?"

A squeak like an old door opening. Then, quiet.

"What? I don't hear anything."

"I don't want to think right now. We just have to get out of here."

Chapter Sixteen

NEXT FLOOR, PLEASE

HAASI AND BLANCHE PULLED ON THE CABLE TOGETHER and the dumbwaiter started to ascend.

"Blanche, we have one little issue. If I can get out down there, you need to follow me. You pull the thing up and get in. I'll guide you down."

"Most definitely." Blanche jangled a handful of springs and metal braces ripped from the underside of the sofa. "And look! I'm working it. Trying to make some brass knuckles. Sort of."

Haasi grinned. "Well, we need all the help we can get."

They resumed grunting and pulling on the cable. The thing was old. It creaked higher until it was level with their floor, accessible from Haasi's room and Blanche's. Blanche held the platform steady while Haasi crawled into the space. Blanche started to lower her down into the shaft. The last thing Blanche saw were those dark almond-shaped eyes that glittered like black jewels as Haasi rolled herself into a tiny ball. "*Adiós, muchacha.* Lower away," she said. Neither one of them weighed more than a hundred pounds, at barely five feet, but they had the strength of baby oxen.

"If it's a no-go, I'll pull you up."

"It better be go." Haasi whispered hoarsely as the box squeaked into the darkness.

Blanche watched Haasi disappear. The beam from her penlight shot up and down the shaft. She called up to Blanche: "We're in luck. The "waiter" stops here. End of the line. That guy must have stuck us on the second floor."

Haasi pushed at the panel. Nothing. "It's not giving, Blanche."

"Keep trying. Use both legs?"

A loud pop, and a dim light flooded up the shaft. "Blanche. I'm in. There's a kitchen here …"

Blanche stiffened with fright. Now she was sure she heard something. A door banged shut somewhere in the building. She heard the thud of heavy footsteps. She pulled herself out of the opening. Someone was out there on the other side of the door. The steps pounded on the landing. She remembered making that turn in the stairwell. Now the boots made a dull staccato up the stairwell. Whoever was there was yelling into a cellphone, and he wasn't happy. He stopped, yapping away in Spanish so fast Blanche couldn't understand a word. But none of it could be good. She looked around like a wild woman.

She called down to Haasi. "Holy shit, Haas! Hang on. Be quiet down there. Someone's out in the hall."

Blanche dragged the sofa toward the wall. Tears of happiness for the high padded back. She moved it over the panel opening, just about covering it. Barely. She sat down and prayed.

The door blasted open.

"*Buenas, señorita.*" It wasn't Bad Nose Mustachio but another man equally ugly, his face sharp angles and menacing. He looked like a walking, ragged-edged rock. "Are the accommodations adequate?"

"Quite," said Blanche. "Not."

To her horror, he threw his head back and laughed, stood there arms akimbo, head tilted at her.

"I want to leave now," she said. *No, I don't. Not without Haasi. And where's Emilio?*

"*¿Qué pasa?*" He looked around the room. "Why is the sofa over there?"

Oh, Blanche, think fast, you idiot. She coughed. A lot. "Sorry. Must be the dust."

He shot one boot forward. Blanche's stomach twisted.

"The sofa. Why you move it?"

"It was drafty over by the window, so I shoved it over here."

"*¿Qué es eso?* Drafty? It is twenty-eight *grados* out there. You *gringas* are very sensitive, no?"

"Sensitive. Yes." She smiled, and it was difficult. He stood so close. She could smell him, a musty mix of citrus and odd pungency, like an old fried cigar. She cringed, her hands clenched on her knees clamped together. Desperate to get him to leave, she was on the verge of passing out. How to get him to leave so they could get on with their escape? He did not look ready to leave.

He leered, blackened teeth showing in a lopsided grin. "I'll be back. Maybe I bring you tortillas. I'm a nice man."

Sure.

"How long will that be, *señor*?" She kept her voice level. Even pleasant. "How long are you keeping me here?"

"Do not know. We have business," he said, shaking his head. "*Qué pesadita.*"

Pesadita? The word from *pesado*, meaning weighty. It also meant troublesome, annoying, tedious, boring, all in one. It was a Spanish word that had no direct translation. She and Haasi were not *pesado*. He should let them go, but how to convince him?

She decided to keep her mouth shut, for the moment. Hopeful she could think of something, or he would leave. They needed time. She didn't move.

"Now I go see chica next door. I pay her a visit." He had the most evil, leering look on his face Blanche had ever seen. The fear she had for herself was half the fear she felt for Haasi.

Think, Blanche.

"*Señor*, would you mind, could I 'trouble you for that tortilla? Now? You see, I have a condition, a blood sugar condition, that requires I eat small meals. I'll start to shake something awful, and I don't want to cause trouble and I know you said you would ..."

"¡*Silencio*!" He had his hand on the door handle.

"There is that little bitty taco stand near the corner of the plaza. That nice cart. If you wouldn't mind. I would be so grateful." Blanche couldn't believe the words that were coming out of her lying mouth, but she wanted him gone. Distracted. Away. At least until Haasi searched that room below and found a way out.

"I'll think on it. Taco cart is not there now," he glanced toward the dirty window, now with a dull grey dawn light. "But I'll get something, a bun or tortilla. I'll get them so you shut up now." He sighed. "Maybe."

He was gone.

Blanche waited until the boots pounded away, and for her heart to stop thudding with fear. Just a beat or two. She slid the sofa away from the panel and leaned into the shaft. "Haasi!" Her throat was a constricted whisper. Frantic. She held her breath.

"I'm here, Blanche. Pull the thing up and get in."

Blanche scrunched into the box and rode it down, thanking God she and Haasi were blessed with small bones and short stature. She jumped out of the "waiter" and into a dim old kitchen nearly as big as the lab. Pocked porcelain sinks, high, dirty windows, empty shelves except for a torn box, a stack of old newspapers, and a can.

"Come on. We don't have time for a cooking class." Haasi was standing on a counter, her fingers curled around the bottom of a window frame. "I found a big metal spoon."

She wedged the bottom of the window open. "Afraid to break

the damn thing. We have to get through it. Without bleeding to death."

Blanche looked back at the hole in the wall from which she'd emerged, praying the devil didn't jump out at them. The day had turned into pure hell, and there seemed to be no end to it. She leapt up on the counter next to Haasi and helped push the window out as far as it would go. The thing hadn't been opened in a hundred years. Now they were disturbing the homestead of generations of roaches and spiders. Blanche shook the silky web off her fingers as she followed Haasi through the window.

They stood in a small courtyard, overgrown with tangled vines and scattered with a few pieces of rusty old furniture.

"Jeez, we've gotten this far. Must be a door out of this place," said Blanche. She turned round and round, staring up at the vacant windows of the building they'd just escaped. "How do you think Emilio got out of here?"

"He's a big boy. I have a feeling we were just in the way. Bet they have other designs for the guy."

"I don't like the sound of that." It was unsettling, a thread of doubt and worry that Blanche did not want to deal with now. But it did not stop the worrying. "Do you think he'll be all right?"

"Bang! Look for a way out of here."

Haasi wielded the spoon, whacking at the thick growth on the walls. "Gotta be a door somewhere in the secret garden."

Blanche thrust her hands into the growth. "Ever read that book?"

"No time for a book report, B." Haasi was all legs and arms, working away at a patch of vines. "Wall over here, lots of plain old brick." She pulled at clumps.

Blanche could hear the low thrum of traffic. They were near the Zocalo, a place where they could run. Get lost in the crowd. Blend with the masses and escape their captors. She renewed her efforts.

"Over here!" Blanche yelled. A black metal gate with no handle. The rust and paint crinkled and flaked. One hinge was missing. They pulled on the gate. It gave way into an alley. They checked up and down the long empty stretch, and they ran. They were covered in sweat and dust and leaves. Blanche had a length of ivy in her hair. Haasi's braid bounced off her back as Blanche sprinted behind her.

Throngs were spewing out of the subway stop on the Zocalo.

"Let's get lost," Blanche yelled. She gripped Haasi's arm.

"I'll say."

They took off toward the crowd. It was a perfect cover.

Blanche didn't see the woman until she came out from behind the taco stand. She almost knocked her down. "Sorry," she said, and turned to keep pace with Haasi.

The woman disappeared. She fell back out of sight and kept looking up in the direction of the dark windows of the lab. She was crying.

Chapter Seventeen

STUFF IT REAL GOOD

"THEY GOT AWAY," said Antonio "El Jefe" Sánchez.

"How, and why?" Oleantha Flórez de Losada stood with her hands on her hips, feet apart but ably planted in the five-inch, taupe patent leather heels. "And why do they call you El Jefe? You couldn't push a fruit cart with any success."

His expression visibly drooped. He hated it when she talked to him like that.

"They're small? They got into that dumbwaiter between the rooms and ran out through the kitchen. I don't know where they came from, but I know they're not coming back."

"And the *pendejo*, El Doctor Emilio?"

El Jefe grunted. "Not my problem. The boss has him. I think."

"You think," she huffed. "Nothing but problems. And those women will go to the police and make trouble. Just our luck."

"They were kids. Students on a tour with the *médico*. You will not see them again. Believe me."

"You better be right," she said. "We have to move the goods."

"Sí, Ole."

"And don't call me that. It's Doctor Flórez to you."

El Jefe (and Oleantha Flórez, for that matter) worked for La Capa Plata, a bunch of Mexican mobsters who specialized in smuggling and drugs. He'd been ordered to keep an eye on the lab, and when he found the intruders, he'd dealt with them. Admirably, he thought. But he could never please these people. So what that they got away. Good riddance. They were scared out of their minds, and it was a strong bet they'd disappear and never show up again. But the young doctor, the "tour" leader, that was another matter. He had been delivered …

The boss, El Patrón, was one remote old bastion of evil. Had to be up there near eighty. "Knowledge is power," he was fond of saying, "and I'll keep it for myself." He shared little about his plans and schemes, and he made certain that he kept his minions separated as well as uninformed until the last. It seemed better that way. For him, at least. He was best known for ordering the killing of dozens, blackmailing mayors and political leaders, and stealing goods right out of the safes of rival cartels. El Jefe feared El Patrón, but he feared Doctor Oleantha Flórez in equal measure; she could skin his *cojones* with a look. He still had to give her grudging props. She was pretty good at putting the thugs back together when they caught a gunshot or knife wound. Sometimes she seemed more inclined to finish the job on her patients, but apparently she had not succumbed to that practice. The population of La Capa Plata was fairly healthy under her watchful eye and expertise.

They called her La Escandolera, and she was a scandal in high heels.

Oleantha moved over to a closet and unlocked it. It was hidden in the wall. No one would have known it was there unless he, or she, had a damn map of the place. She gingerly rolled out a long, dry hunk of ancient human being. "You had your eye on the lab, and even though you screwed that up, it's done. I don't want to deal with it again." She shot him a nasty look. "Right now I have to pack this baby. Blussberg gave me the goods."

El Jefe cringed. He didn't like the criticism; it could mean his head. But at least he didn't have to look at the newly dead one. Instead, the bundle Oleantha now fussed with was a pile of tightly wrapped old rags, the real mummy stolen from the original exhibit on loan to the Palacio. Not the "new" mummy—the poor young woman who Oleantha had drained and dried and baked to leather only recently and installed with the other three in the floor. He'd had a hand in that whole grisly switch. Out with the old and in with the new. He'd delivered Lalia Solis Iglesia to the doctor. He felt a new wave of disgust for himself, and more than a twinge of guilt, especially when he recalled her fright as he came after her. He'd burn in hell, for sure. But he didn't want to think about that now.

He sighed and awaited the doctor's orders. He was unsuited for the job, but he'd be damned before he showed himself weak to Oleantha, or El Patrón. The woman had more iron than any ten men. He'd just go along with what she demanded and then get the hell out of there and back to his stucco hovel on the outskirts of Mexico City. The screaming feral cats and wild dogs that roamed his tire-littered yard were better tempered than the doctor.

She opened a black satchel on the counter and lifted out a dozen small objects, each wrapped in white flannel. She carefully lined them up, opened each packet, and wrote down the contents in a ledger. Travertine beads. Gold necklaces. Bejeweled obsidian daggers. A statuette of Moctezuma. She handled each piece lovingly, a lust for the goods gleaming in her eyes. He knew she'd restrain herself. The price of the stuff dissuaded all of them from pocketing any of it. The black market was a cesspool of wealth; it bubbled up from hell and kept bubbling.

El Jefe mumbled under his breath. *Por dios, o, el diablo.*

She rewrapped the bundles with packing tape. "Hand me that shopping bag by the door. And hurry up." El Jefe jumped and deposited it on the long counter.

"Well, open it all up, and lay it out," she demanded.

He did, dropping each item like it was hot from the oven. Glue gun, sponges, alcohol wipes.

"Scissors." Her voice cut like a blade.

He found them in the bottom of the bag. He felt unsuited for this operating theater, but the sooner they got it done, the sooner he was out of there and downing tequila and sucking on limes.

She stood back, her gold-tipped fingers entwined, the diamond bracelet picking up a feeble ray of sun through the dirty window. El Jefe waited. He knew she was not a hasty one. Always meticulous down to the last damn detail. She seemed to take pride in her job to get things right, even when what she was doing could not be more wrong. It made him all the more regretful that he'd bungled the "detainment" of the little chicas. The doctor would surely find a way to make his life all the more miserable.

Now Oleantha had donned a white lab coat, sparkling with starch and sunshine for the next awful job she was about to do. From a tray she withdrew a scalpel and dove into the long-dead body. El Jefe looked away but kept one eye on the procedure, fascination and horror mixing in his blood—with a healthy shot of adrenalin.

"Are your hands clean? Get over there and wash them anyway," said the doctor.

El Jefe swaggered to the sink and returned to the counter. Oleantha was carefully pulling apart the flaky remains and creating a cavity in the body, which was an unrecognizable mix of old flesh and rags. "Well, *gracias a Dios*. The organs were removed."

El Jefe wasn't sure if he should cheer or turn and run out the door. El Patrón would kill him if he left her hanging; he'd stick it out and beg to be let go of duties related to the doctor in the future.

She eyed the items on the counter, ignoring her "assistant" for the moment.

He was just glad the thing had been dead for hundreds of years and the gushy stuff was long gone. For a gangster, he had a remarkably weak stomach for the business of torture and killing.

"This *mierda* has to fit," she mumbled. "Now. You are going to hand me each item as I call for it."

He peered at the wrapped bundles on the counter. Each was numbered.

"One," she said, a slender hand upturned, the fingers curled like a golden claw.

He placed the object in her hand. She inserted it into the cavity, shoving it up into the thorax. "Next."

And so it went, until all the bundles of art were placed inside the body. Oleantha drew the folds and flakes and patches of leather-like skin and crumbling fabric together, using the sharp fingernails like pincers, and with the precision of a surgeon (for that was her original intention if she hadn't run afoul of the examiners and licensing boards) she carefully glued the creature back together. She had to make do. Only recently, she'd taken some of the wrappings from this ancient mummy to camouflage the newer mummy when they did the switcheroo in the exhibit. Now, the procedure to hide the goods was tricky at best, tugging gently here, patting and molding in place there. "Sorry, I had to take some of the shirt off your back," she mumbled. But she had enough to work with, and she was up to the task. The smell of hot-glued, desiccated flesh and old, dried-up linen filled the air. It stuck in El Jefe's nose with an acrid stench that almost made him gag.

She flipped the glue gun into a bag and ran her hands down her slim hips. Not a hair of her sleek, black shoulder-length helmet was out of place. Her face wore an implacable smile, partly drawn into place with a thick application of a glistening, slightly gooey red lipstick.

"Ready for travel. It should go first class, if you ask me," she said. "Be careful with the cargo when the time comes."

El Jefe went to the closet and drew out a pile of sheets, a role of bubble wrap, and a long, large wooden case. He knew the drill, though they had never sent the stolen items off in a mummy. He swaddled the body in the sheets and put it in the case. Next, several layers and wads of bubble wrap. Oleantha watched him pack. "Pretty good. You should get your own show."

"No. Gracias. No."

Sarloff Blussberg licked his lips. The lovely Oleantha stood before him, filling the air with orange blossom and spice, but the look on her face was pure venom. He wished the woman were as sweet as the fragrant package she was wrapped in, but, alas, he knew too well, she was poison.

"Great job, Ole," said Blussberg. His small hands flew apart and back together like he was swatting flies. He wore the same blue suit and long red tie. A sunlamp and make-up created his orange aspect. The hair was another matter—a distinctly blond version of an Elvis Presley do meant to cover thinning tresses and a bald spot. None of this mattered; Sarloff Blussberg was the Palacio director, but he fancied himself a kind of lord about town. He'd made the deal with El Patrón to get the priceless artifacts out of the country, and Oleantha had been a splendid help.

"I'd like to go over that inventory, Sar," she said, taking a seat in a leather armchair and crossing her legs.

Blussberg couldn't resist glancing at the long silken gams, and, as ever, her tiny narrow feet tucked into stiletto heels. He had dreams of her walking all over his body and his face, but that would never happen. El Patrón had her tied up in jewels and cars, and Blussberg could not compete. He would check his lust at the door and continue to dream.

He cleared his throat and produced a small journal. "Let's see. A fortune here. I must thank El Patrón again for putting me in touch with you (how he wished). I'm delighted to have this little project all sewn up."

"Glued up," said Oleantha. "Never mind. The inventory?" Oleantha produced her own ledger and a gold pen. She was poised and ready.

He eyed her. "As I said, a fortune. Two obsidian daggers with carved stones on the hilt; six large travertine beads, polished and inscribed with Aztec lettering; a gold hair ornament, extracted from a queen's tomb; two necklaces of beaten gold encrusted with turquoise. Some other items listed here, most of them dating from the Aztecs, pre-Hispanic, fourteenth to fifteenth centuries."

"That is what I have," she said, diddling the pen back and forth. "Priceless. I'll let El Patrón know the shipment is packed. He's working on the other end for you."

"Oh, that's great. I plan to fly to Frankfurt next Thursday, Lufthansa. I hope to make the connection at the airport. I don't want to be traveling around Germany with the goods. We need to set this up in the next few days."

Chapter Eighteen

THE MISSING

BLANCHE AND HAASI HADN'T SPRUNG THEMSELVES an hour when Cardenal called Blanche. Their phone calls practically crossed. She was on the case to find Emilio, and the detective needed Blanche to come by the station. He didn't say why.

Blanche was eager to oblige. She was frantic. Emilio was missing, and she needed help.

"Calm down, Blanche. We'll talk when you get here," the detective said.

Blanche stormed into Cardenal's office, and she immediately stopped short.

"*Señora, le presento a Señorita* Blanche Murninghan." Detective Cardenal was on his feet behind the desk as he introduced Blanche to the mother of Lalia Solis Iglesia. "*Señorita* Blanche, Amparo Solis." The two women locked eyes, worlds of sadness and fear passing between them.

Blanche had seen this woman before, and she couldn't for the life of her remember where. *Mexico City is a big place, and I've seen a lot of faces. But this one …*

The detective was still on his feet, concern etching his normally happy features. "It is conclusive. We have identified the person you alerted us about in the exhibit, *Señorita* Blanche. The person in the floor under the glass." Here, he cleared his throat. "It is the señora's daughter, *Señorita* Lalia." The detective spoke softly, bowed his head slightly, and held one arm out to the older woman huddled in the chair at the front of his desk. Her eyes seemed vacant, her shoulders slumped. She had lovely long black hair, like her daughter, but streaked with silver.

Blanche stood frozen to the spot, but her heart was melting. She reached for Lalia's mother, took her hand. "*Lo siento.* I am so sorry," she said. Blanche sank into the chair opposite the señora and didn't let go of her hand.

"Amparo. Please call me Amparo," she said. "It means protection, safety. It means nothing now." Tears welled in her dark eyes. Blanche was having trouble keeping it in. The detective didn't move except to clasp his hands together. She was on the verge of asking Amparo if they had met before, her face was so familiar, and then she thought better of it. The air was thick with grief. Blanche left it alone, for the mother's sake.

"I thought you two should meet, since you were the one, Blanche ..."

"This is terrible. How did you find out?"

The detective and the mother stared at each other. Amparo dabbed at the tears. "I filed a missing person's report, fearing the worst. Lalia had gone to that club on the outskirts of Zona Rosa. I'd warned her. It was late, and there's a bad crowd there. She knew better." She seemed to be working her way into the anger phase of mourning as the detective and Blanche looked on.

"No," Blanche said. "She should be able to go out with friends and not have this happen." Now Blanche was getting angry. The detective fell back in his chair and pushed away from his desk.

"With friends like these, I don't know. They were not good people," said Amparo. "Not like my Lalia." She dissolved back again into that drowning sea with no bottom and no shore.

Blanche turned to Cardenal. "What are you going to do about

it? You said you were going to check …" She stood up. "We have to talk."

Amparo was already headed toward the door. Blanche looked down at the distraught mother's hands. She was clutching a pink plastic hair clip. Blanche wondered if it was *the* hair clip. Had Cardenal shown a bit of empathy and handed it over from the evidence locker? No telling. Amparo clutched the last vestige of her daughter's presence and set her lips in a grim, sad line. Blanche reached for Amparo, but it was a feeble gesture. She saw something in Amparo's eyes that would haunt her every time she thought of her and the terrible loss she suffered.

Amparo was gone. Blanche leaned on the detective's desk, both arms taut, her eyes blazing. "You found her? Lalia? A missing person?"

"*Sí*," He hunched his shoulders. "*Suerte pura*. The mother was over here, fearful, pressing us. We ran some tests and other ID on that 'new' mummy, and it turned out a match for Lalia. Poor girl."

"We need more luck. We need to find Emilio." The detective didn't know the details of the "detainment" in the lab, so she filled him in.

Blanche started pacing the small office. The windows looked out on a park, children chasing each other, pairs sitting on the benches. It looked so peaceful out there in the shade. She wanted to go back to the beginning of their vacation and capture some of that wide-eyed excitement, but that would not be possible. It had been one crazy mishap after another.

Cardenal rubbed his enormous chin and studied Blanche. "Well, you're back safe. That's what matters now. I wouldn't worry about Emilio. Did you check with Carmen and Eddie?"

"I don't have a number for them. Do they even have a phone? Besides, I don't want to upset them."

"I'll check around, get over to that lab and look for clues. Seems strange that if he got away, he didn't alert us about your detainment."

"That's why I'm here. I don't think he got away."

He leaned back in the chair, crossed his fingers over his large middle. "How well do you know him? The Mexican man, the *machote* ..."

"I know what that means. He's not some tough guy. He's sweet and thoughtful."

"Ah. But the hombre ... In general. You might say, sometimes he disappears. On purpose." Cardenal smiled, slyly. A man in on the secrets of all men. Their desires, their play, their irresponsibility.

"No," said Blanche. "That is not the case. You need to look for him." Blanche told him more details of their lab adventure and the findings—the clump of black hair, the strange bed of ceramic pipes, a description of the goon who had "detained" them in rooms upstairs. And Emilio! Where was Emilio?

"You shouldn't have gone in there in the first place. Trespassing. It was dangerous," said Cardenal.

"*No.*" Now she was getting hot, her temperature rising despite the window unit that rattled like rocks in a blender. "No, that's not it at all. Emilio was a med student in that lab. He had a code to get in." She flopped in a chair. "He was taking us on a little tour."

"Some tour. *Bienvenido a DF,*" he mumbled, obviously ruminating on the situation.

"La Escandolera," she said. "Have you looked into her background?"

"Blanche. Not much in that department. It was a miracle we found Lalia, that the mother didn't let up." He stood up and jabbed a finger at the pile of folders on the long cabinet behind his desk. "Do you have any idea the workload over here? Poking around in a lab when thousands out there are disappearing? Killing each other over drugs. And territory?" Blanche glanced at the folders and papers, stacked haphazardly, teetering against the wall. She wondered how many names were noted, how many were in there lost forever. In front of the stacks, a small photo of a little girl and a little boy grinned widely, innocent and oblivious.

"This is big, detective. You need to get over there. We got in, and out, fortunately."

"Where's your cousin, Haasi?"

"She's waiting for me back at the hotel, hoping Emilio will call."

"Good idea. You are full of good ideas."

"And here's another one," said Blanche. "*That woman*. La Escandolera. Emilio talked about her. She might be set up in that lab. You can't let this go."

The detective looked weary. He ran fingers through his hair and shook his head. "That woman. No end of trouble there. She thinks she's a doctor, even acts like one. She's patching up those gang members of La Capa Plata."

"Well, I think she also has a talent for making mummies. Lalia Solis Iglesia, for one. You've got to see the odd stuff in that lab. And remember when you said those ancient artifacts have gone missing? Don't you think it's kind of strange, the thievery, and the mummy business are happening altogether?"

"Maybe. We haven't gotten anywhere with those thefts at the Palacio, and now other sites are reporting losses."

"Just seems super strange to me."

"We'll look into it. *Pronto*." He came around the desk, tilted his head at Blanche. "Hasn't been much of a vacation for you chicas. How about you and Haasi come over to our house for some pozole? You need a proper welcome to Mexico, and my Sylvia makes the soup of the gods. With all the trimmings."

"That would be great!" Blanche jumped up, eager not only for soup but a lockdown on getting the detective's help. He needed work.

"I'll call you," he said. "Enough of this mummy business for you two. For now. I'm glad you're safe. Just relax. I'm the detective here."

"You won't forget about Emilio? Call out to Tepequito, check around? Right away?"

"Blanche, it's only been *hours*. But, yes, I will. Let's hope he turns up."

Chapter Nineteen

POZOLE

DETECTIVE CARDENAL DIDN'T WASTE TIME extending the invitation for dinner. He called Blanche that afternoon and asked if she and Haasi would be free that evening. Haasi was delighted, while she was constantly calming Blanche's fears about Emilio: "If *we* got away, bet he could, too."

Blanche was glad for the invite but had less interest in eating and more interest in what Cardenal was doing to locate Emilio. It all seemed tied to the bad business at the Palacio.

They took a nap to sleep off the travails of their adventure in the lab and then set out for the detective's home around eight o'clock.

The Cardenal family lived on the outskirts of San Angel, a neighborhood, or *colonia*, of Mexico City. The neighborhood was sleepier than the Zocalo, and happily residential. After the taxi swung off the Paseo de la Reforma, the colonia soon greeted Blanche and Haasi with cobblestone streets, pastel houses, and bougainvillea blooming over arches and walls. Detective Cardenal had told them to make arrangements for a cab through the hotel's concierge desk. At times, the local *sitios,* or taxis sitting randomly on street corners took tourists for a ride, literally, but the hotel cabs were generally trustworthy.

Blanche wore a short skirt and a stretchy top that read "Santa Maria Island" on the front and "In Your Dreams" on the back. Haasi had slipped into a plain gold sheath. She looked like an Aztec princess.

The taxi pulled up to a residence typical of the *colonia*, one of many attached houses tucked on a narrow street where all the front entrances had wrought iron gates and an abundance of flowers and greenery. It was still light out. Blanche picked up the aroma of cooking, a lovely mix of onions and garlic, rice, chiles, and beans, and though this wasn't home, it felt like it. It seemed all of Mexico stopped when it was time to eat. In the middle of the day, if workers and residents couldn't get home for *la comida*, they were seen swinging the white boxes in plastic bags, headed for the park, a restaurant, or office lounge to eat, rest, and visit.

The detective came bursting through the carved front door and headed for the gate. "*¡Bienvenidas, bienvenidas a nuestra casa, señoritas!*" As always, Blanche was amazed that a policeman could be so jolly. She clutched the spray of mums and lemon leaves for *Señora* Cardenal and smiled. Haasi held a box of chocolates in two hands, ready to thrust it at their hosts. Before she ate them. Blanche had seen the look on her face in La Chocolatera when she selected the caramels and bonbons. Haasi loved all food and treats. She said she'd even give in and try the bugs and grasshoppers—should the opportunity hop onto her plate.

The entrance of the Cardenal home was dark and cool, terracotta tile and white stucco walls. A candle flickered with a scent of pine on a heavy wooden table. "*Ven, ven,*" he said. They followed him to the back of the house where the sun lit the bright, long room, a kitchen to one side and a comfortable salon to the other. Sofas lined the walls and an enormous coffee table in the center was loaded with *antojitos*, which Blanche learned meant "yummy bites." Here were platters of red, green, and yellow peppers, olives, cheeses, breads, slices of cucumber and jicama, radish roses, and curly fried pigskin. The detective directed them to sit and brought them beers. Haasi helped herself to a napkin full of olives, peppers, and cheese. Blanche gazed out at the patio garden where a bird was splashing in a tiny birdbath.

Sylvia came bustling out of the kitchen, arms extended. "¡*Mucho gusto!*" She was a striking woman with black wisps around her face and startling dark eyes that crinkled with welcome. "*Señoritas. ¿Como están?*"

"We are very well now," said Haasi, balancing her olives and extending a hand. "¡*Gracias!*"

"You will be much better once you eat the cooking *de La Reina*," said the detective. "She is truly a queen of the kitchen." He helped himself to a fistful of pigskin and jicama.

In the dining room, a table was set with an embroidered cloth and bowls of sliced avocado, chopped green onions, shredded cabbage, radishes, bits of fried tortillas, strips of pigskin, oregano, and chopped cilantro. *Señora* Sylvia emerged from the kitchen with a steaming tureen of the pozole, a soup of hominy and pork shoulder, and placed it before the detective, who did the honors.

"How do you say it?" He held the ladle like a baton. "Dig in."

The detective took a bite and stared at the ceiling. "*Divino, mi amor.*" He smiled at the señora. Blanche topped her soup with a little of everything. It was delicious, a regular adventure in flavors. Haasi seemed to be off in another dimension of enjoyment.

Their host lifted his Tecate. "You know," he said, "originally, pozole was a celebration among the Aztecs after human sacrifice. In fact, he, or she, became the next meal."

"Really?" Blanche held the spoon halfway to her lips.

"They believed eating the human flesh after tearing the heart out gave them strength and pleased the gods."

"¡*Felix, por favor!*" *La Reina* was incensed. She straightened in her chair. "I assure you, this is pork!"

He threw his head back and laughed, nearly tipping over in his chair. "Just a small history lesson, *mi amor.*"

Haasi and Blanche looked at each other. And although Haasi's appetite did not seem dimmed by the news of the ancients, Blanche considered the chunks of pork floating in the soup. She took a hearty slug of the Tecate.

Haasi and Blanche sat on the detective's patio at the back of the house. Blanche was somewhat relaxed after the soup and beer. Cacti, jade plants, and other succulents, potted marigolds and lantana, flowering vines of every sort flourished in the patio paradise. Small, compact, and citified. A high wall shut off the outside world, and despite its location not many miles from the Zocalo, it was remarkably quiet. The patio stones were white and worn, the furniture also worn but comfortably outfitted with bright orange cushions. The detective brought out a tray with shot glasses, a pitcher of tomato juice, salt, limes, and a bottle of tequila. The festivity reminded Blanche of the night she met Emilio. "What have you found out, detective? About Emilio," said Blanche.

He sighed. "No news. Yet. Carmen is checking at the clinic in Tepequito. He was supposed to be there today."

Blanche sat on the edge of the cushion. She had the awful deep-down feeling Emilio would have contacted her—had he been able to—and somehow he had *not* been able. "I don't feel good about this business." Now Blanche was on her feet. Haasi was on the edge of her seat, and Cardenal's eyebrows shot up. "We should have heard something by now. Did you go over to the lab and look around?"

"Yes, I sent someone over there, but the place was clean. Now, Blanche ..."

"Clean? No chemicals? Weird bed of ceramic pipes? Diaries?"

"Nothing like that. Nearly empty."

How had they cleared out the lab so fast? Blanche wondered, but they'd had a good day to do it after discovering them snooping around.

Cardenal filled three shot glasses with the tequila and three with the tomato juice, or "sangre." He sat down and motioned for her to do the same. He spoke quietly. "We're looking into this. Trust me."

He offered her the bowl of limes. She took a wedge without looking at them. She studied the detective. "Are you putting me off?"

Haasi visibly stiffened. She reached for her cousin's arm, and Blanche relaxed. Slightly.

"I don't want any more trouble." He smiled. "You helped identify the problem at the Palacio. Invaluable. And this morning you were particularly warm and consoling to Amparo about her daughter's terrible death. I appreciate it, and I know she did, too. Terrible business." He grabbed the tequila bottle by the neck. "But, officially, you are not a witness to the crime, and there's nothing you can do at the moment to find your friend. You need to step back from this and let us handle it. We may be slow, but we will arrive." He lifted the shot glass and downed another.

"Please. You need to stay on this. I know they did something with him."

He shook his head wearily. "Blanche, we have little to work with." He leveled a hard look at her, and she returned it. "I'll see what I can do. I promise." He still held the bottle like a truncheon. He poured the shots of tequila and tomato juice and threw back one of each, took a pinch of salt, and sucked the lime. They followed his lead. "*Ah, bueno.* To mark your visit to Mexico." He clapped the shot glass on the table. "*Sin problemas.* Or, at least, without more problems."

Blanche felt sad. *Where is he?* She clutched her glass. She wanted to have a couple more of these excellent tequilas, but she figured that would not be advisable. Especially with Haasi sitting there staring a hole through her. She needed focus. She finished off the tequila, but she wasn't finished with the detective.

"There must have been *something* in that lab." The tequila warmed her and sparked questions. "Did you find out anything more about that woman doctor? Did you contact Emilio's academic advisors?"

Haasi sat with her legs crossed, seemingly entranced by a cactus on the other side of the patio. One foot went up and down. She sighed and gave Blanche a rueful smile that read Blanche would not let this go. And if Blanche wouldn't, Haasi wouldn't either.

"In answer to your questions, yes, we are working all angles. On all the cases." The detective downed another shot of tequila, not bothering with the tomato juice. Blanche's wheels went round and round. She just hoped the room didn't start spinning. She kept an eye on Cardenal.

Ah, yes, Señor Detective, get nice and toasty and loose-lipped. Please. She had the feeling he knew more than what he was letting on. He tried to derail them with smiles and tequila and placating. She wasn't having it. She could feel the words forming, about to shoot from her mouth.

Sylvia appeared with a tray of coffees and a plate of delectable-looking, spongy rolled cakes. Haasi immediately lost interest in the cactus. Blanche moved over on the sofa so that Sylvia could join them. "What mischief are you stirring up, Felix?" She had a merry look in her eyes as she poured very dark coffee into demitasse cups and passed them around.

"I'd say the mischief is sitting right here. Direct from Florida, USA," he said.

Blanche's knee was bouncing. She leaned forward her hands clasped into a knot. "Detective, sir, please remember that I brought the whole thing up when I discovered that body in the floor."

Cardenal downed a shot. Sylvia frowned. Her eyes opened wide, and she looked from her husband to Blanche. "¡Qué cosa!"

Haasi hunched her shoulders and sat back. She didn't seem inclined to enter the discussion—after two tequilas, a slice of cake, and a cookie. She balanced the demitasse on one polished knee.

"¡Pobrecitas!" Sylvia straightened up. Her husband visibly shrank under her reproachful look. "Felix, you must help them. What is going on here?"

"Mi amor. It's complicated. The señoritas are involved, to be sure. Involved in this murder, but peripheral-al-ly." The word came out with an extra syllable. "Señorita Blanche also overheard some talking, some argument. She thinks, quizás, there is a connection between the death of this poor girl in the mummy exhibit and the thefts of art from the exhibit. And now her friend is missing."

"Bueno. Felix, you must help." She pointed to her eye. "Ojo. Sharp talent you have here." She patted Blanche's arm.

He threw his hands up. "I can never argue with this woman. She is always right."

Hope flickered and caught. Cardenal was nicely lubricated, and thanks to Sylvia, primed, so Blanche pounced. "Do you know anything else about this team at the Palacio? The director, that woman? Anyone else? There are others involved, you know. They didn't take us out of that lab and lock us up for nothing."

"¡Por Dios!" Sylvia clutched the gold crucifix on her necklace. "Felix, this is horrible. What welcome is that to Mexico? How can you help the señoritas?"

He rolled his eyes. "There's a whole cast over there at the Palacio. And beyond. We're running them down."

Blanche sensed more was coming. He was poised to go on,

and she read the hesitation on his face like she was looking at a map she intended to follow.

"What else, *Señor* Cardenal?" Blanche asked, quietly. Haasi hadn't moved, except for that sideways look, as penetrating as an arrow.

"There is more. Someone else is in the picture. Someone called El Patrón. We know now that he is head of the operation—a major plan to steal art objects all over Mexico City. What's happened so far is just the top of *El Popo*, you might say." He shook his head. "Smoking and ready to explode."

With a straight face, Blanche nodded. It was the confirmation she was hoping for: El Patrón. The "boss." She was already planning what she was going to do with this bit of information.

Chapter Twenty

WRITE A WRONG

"BLANCHE, DON'T BE RIDICULOUS," said Haasi. The day after dinner at Detective Cardenal's, the two were sitting in the Alegría Hoy coffee shop near the Zocalo. Despite the name of the place, she didn't feel much "Happiness Today." The whoosh of the espresso machine and the aroma of fresh ground beans filled the air. Blanche was stabbing a piece of raspberry cake. The place was definitely a hipster destination; skinny dudes in tight jeans, girls with faces studded in silver buds and loops, hair that defied description, and that seemed to be the point. Haasi's eyes lazed around the small cozy shop. A delectable, sugared confection hovered close to her lips. She turned her attention to the donut, rather than dwell on Blanche's suggestion.

"Well, why not? I can't hold it in any longer, Haas. I think it's a brilliant idea." Blanche pushed the cake aside and cradled her latte, a bit of foam on her cheek.

"Blanche, you're foaming at the mouth." Haasi finished the donut and got up to buy another. Blanche watched her walk toward the counter. It was a miracle of genes and humanity that she weighed so little and managed to be the healthiest person Blanche had ever met.

Blanche turned to the mirrored wall and checked herself.

Wiped the foam off her face. She sipped the hot coffee, and winced.

Haasi plopped down with more goodies.

"If you don't want to go, I will understand." Blanche sounded just a bit petulant.

Haasi laughed. "You know damn well you're not going out there by yourself." She bit into the donut and red jelly oozed onto her fingers. "Ah, *sangre*. Blood seems to be everywhere you look."

Detective Cardenal was standing at the vending machine. Kicking it.

"Now, I'm going to have to arrest you for that. No beating up the vending machine. Punishable by a fine of a thousand pesos." Blanche stood back, out of his kicking range, hands on hips.

He turned. "¡*Señorita* Blanche! ¿*Qué pasa*?

"Still no word from Emilio. Did you hear anything?"

He resumed perusal of the candy bars and chips as if the display behind the glass was a prized exhibit. "No, not yet."

"Not yet?" Blanche had a temperature that could go from normal to boil in about one second, and she was perilously close to the boiling point. She followed him back to his office. "Can we talk?"

His glance cut to her. "How did you get up here?"

"Well, I had to surrender ID at the desk and promise to donate my kidney, but they let me past. The señora down there is a real sweetie."

"Don't bet on it." Cardenal ripped open the candy bar and bit off half. Blanche thought of a Rottweiler, though a benign one.

She made herself comfortable in the padded metal armchair and determined to sit there until she got what she came for. The detective acted like she wasn't there. He shuffled a couple folders on his desk, checked a pile of yellow message slips, and then after a barely audible "¡*Carajo!*" or two, he sat down. The rest of the candy bar was rolling around in his head and his glazed expression was directed past Blanche and out the window.

"That was a lovely dinner," Blanche said. "Thank you so much for having us. Haasi loved it, too." She would play the game.

"It was our pleasure. And *gracias* for the flowers and candy. Very nice gesture," he said. "Where is *la Señorita Haasi*?" The detective's voice was pleasant, even soothing.

"She's taking pictures at Chapultepec park for the stories we're supposed to be working on. That project seems to get shoved further aside every day. It *is* the reason we are here, though."

He leaned back. The corners of his eyes crinkled in what Blanche determined was not really a smile but a thoughtful gaze. "Blanche, you better get to the business you came for. The situation at the Palacio is moving slowly. And we don't have anything on Emilio. But I'll let you know when we do. He'll turn up. I am sure."

"I'm not so sure, and I can't wait around for something to happen." Blanche jumped out of the chair and started pacing the office.

The detective's hands raked through the documents on his desk. All of a sudden, he was busy. "We are doing what we can. And now, I have work to do, a meeting at noon. Maybe I'll have some news this afternoon. If you please …"

"Are you trying to get rid of me? Or are you being nice?"

"Both."

Blanche ignored the flurry of activity at his desk. She'd give him a minute. She was not about to leave, just yet. She turned toward the window and looked down at the vendors on the curb, a young man pushing a baby carriage, people hurrying, people resting. Life was going on down there with an easy rhythm, and up here her heart and head were out of tune.

She went back to his desk and positioned herself next to him, not across from him. "Detective, I have an idea."

"*Dios mío.*"

"No, it's perfect. It's a great idea." She raised both hands as if to stop the objections she knew were coming. "You know I'm a journalist. Again, that's why we're here, to write stories of Mexico City. I want to use that business. I want to use my press card."

"To do what?"

"To interview El Patrón." It was all she could do to keep a straight face, something Blanche was totally incapable of.

The detective hardly looked up. "*Loca loca loca.*" He took a swig of something in the Thermos and slammed his chair against the wall. "Blanche that is *imposible.* Do not even entertain the idea. Besides, you don't know who he is or where he is."

"Oh, I've got pretty good interviewing skills. I was over to see our friend at the tourist bureau, and I asked her to get involved here. We did a little digging. She's going to set up the interview."

"Blanche, this is a terrible idea. Read a couple of books or magazine articles, if you want, to get, what do they call it, *flavor.* You can interview me about life on the hacienda ..."

Blanche looked around his office. One sad dieffenbachia, nineteen thousand manila folders, and a bunch of yellowing citations on the wall. "*Olé.*"

Now the detective was on his feet. The room was small, but he managed to fill it with his pacing and his fretting. He looked at her ferociously. "Don't you think El Patrón knows about your little 'detainment,' as you call it? He probably ordered it."

"He doesn't know who I am, or Haasi. Emilio told our abductor we were kids, young students on a supposed tour. El Patrón never clapped eyes on me, and he certainly doesn't know his thug locked up a travel writer."

"The abductor will be out there. On the ranch. He might identify you ..."

"That's the chance I have to take. It was dark. I was blindfolded.

I'm going to wear a blonde wig when I pay my visit. And glasses."
She didn't want to mention the addition of a particularly thuggish
one who looked like a jagged rock, the one who paid her a visit in
the lock-up and promised tortillas. She'd worry about him later.

"Blanche! Let me handle this." Cardenal was bent over his
desk, fingers tented on piles of papers, blood pressure spiking.
He sat down, hard. "What did the tourist bureau tell you?" Now
softly, disbelieving, he eyed her.

"Background. El Patrón's name is out there, especially for his
involvement with the Palacio and the arts. My contact told me
how to get in touch for the interview. First Amendment and
such," she said. The words tumbled out fast, and the detective was
having difficulty stepping around them.

"Now, wait one moment, Blanche. We don't have a First
Amendment here in Mexico comparable to what you're thinking.
Not like what you have in North America. You have twenty-seven
amendments to your constitution? Ours has been amended five
hundred times!" He raked the top of his head. He reminded
Blanche of a lion with all that hair, and he was roaring. "Blanche,
we have brave journalists, and a lot of them have been *killed* for
their reporting. Don't you read the newspapers?"

"This is not an exposé on the cartels. I'm hardly here to do that.
I want to go in as a travel writer. I think Aracelli at the tourist
bureau can get us in." She was firm, arms crossed. She hadn't
budged from her place next to the detective. Every word pushed
her further into her plan, and she couldn't help it. She didn't want
to help it.

"This is ridiculous!" He sat and studied her. Calmed down
just a bit. "What in the world are you thinking?" It was pin-drop
quiet.

*He wants to know what I'm thinking? He actually asked me
that?*

Blanche sat down. Now she had control of the conversation.

This was her territory. The business of writing. She smiled. "He's a longtime patron on the hacienda, a businessman of central Mexico. Don't you see? I want to get in there, get him to talk. Under the guise of getting *color*, as we say in the trade." She held back.

"Color. The only color I see is red. *Rojo*. The color of blood."

"Do you want to go with me?"

"How would that look? The detective and the travel writer. I'm sure the information you are looking for would flow ..."

Blanche cleared her throat and clasped her hands. Set her lips in a tight line, and then she leaned on his desk, just inches from his nose. "I am not looking for information about tourist attractions around Mexico City. I'm looking for who's behind all this stuff at the Palacio. I'm looking for Emilio."

Chapter Twenty-One

OUT ON THE HACIENDA

Rodrigo Ortiz "El Patrón" de Avila lived on a hacienda north of Mexico City in the foothills near Hidalgo. The locals knew the exact location of his multi-acre spread. His family had lived in the area since the Spanish Crown gave the Avilas a land grant in the sixteenth century. It was said that they were nobility from Toledo on the outskirts of Madrid, but El Patrón did not tout the royal connection. Instead, he let it linger in conversation and local history. He believed in aura. Fostering a bit of the unknown and keeping those he dealt with off balance and uninformed. The Avila *escudo* hung on his enormous carved front door as a reminder for all who entered, and it was emblazoned above the grand fireplace in the great room at the center of his house. For all his rapacious dealings with the land and the local people, El Patrón exuded *royalty*. He had power. He also had wealth, and where it came from was questionable. He had vineyards, fields of corn and alfalfa, and cattle; his hacienda was nestled in a particularly fertile area of the country. But the enormous amounts of money he threw around did not come from the fruits of the land; the pesos (and American dollars) mostly came from evil transactions. Some people knew this, and El Patrón paid them handsomely to work for him and keep their mouths shut.

He kept his staff lean, and himself lean. He was even known as a kind of an ascetic, posturing as an El Greco figure with his gaunt face and pointy beard.

Blanche had done a bit of research on El Patrón so she would know what she was walking into.

I have no idea what I'm walking into.

Aracelli had been prompt about getting a time for the interview—the next day, after Blanche's meeting with Detective Cardenal. He was so adamant that she *not* go out to the hacienda that she left his office with her plan hanging in the air. Promising to get back to him.

Soon. After I make a visit to the "boss."

The detective didn't need to know the timetable. She'd be so quick about it, out and back. Why, what could go wrong?

At the tourist bureau, Blanche had been casual, leaning on the shiny counter and fiddling with a pamphlet, while her insides were pinging around just south of her throat. She wanted "a taste of old Mexico," including a feature about a longtime *hacendado* with ties to old Spain, and his view of living on Mexico's lush plateau farmland in comparative luxury. She'd really worked on that list of areas to cover in the articles. Aracelli had reached out to the old rancher on the spot, and it clicked. He had been reticent, but then he agreed to meet with Blanche. If the interview went well, they would get photos later. Or maybe they would use stock photos for the stories. Blanche did not relish the thought of making more than one trip to El Patrón's hacienda.

Blanche sat in the middle of the bus. Her blonde wig was itchy, but she would endure it. She'd spent a pretty penny on it, but it still itched. She took some Benadryl and sat on her hands so she wouldn't keep scratching her head, which was not a good look. She'd practiced wearing it, being suave and smooth with not too much sexy thrown in. A lot of breathing exercises were involved, and some yoga stretches. El Patrón was not known to be a womanizer, but he did have a reputation for charming the ladies. Blanche had even succumbed to make-up! Haasi had lined her eyes, blushed out those cheeks with some sparkly Pink Rose, and applied a bit of glistening Peel-a-Grape lip gloss. Blanche wanted to throw the wig out the window and wash her face. She concentrated on doing neither; she focused on getting her head wrapped around interviewing one of Mexico's notorious lords of corruption.

Haasi was driving. She was somewhere out there, probably north of Mexico City by now, or maybe already parked near the hacienda. Waiting. She'd rented a car and planned to meet Blanche after the interview. Blanche stared out the window of the bus at the fields of brilliant yellow sunflowers that blazed for miles. They'd gone back and forth about how to travel to the hacienda and decided the best way was to go semi-incognito. They were not to appear together on this mission. But they were very much together—Haasi as back-up to Blanche's scheme to get into El Patrón's ranch, interview him (check around for any clue of Emilio's whereabouts), and get the hell out of there. Haasi and Blanche were good at escaping. They were a team. Blanche's stomach tightened at the thought that this might be one of their trickiest capers of all.

They were close now to Blanche's stop near Huehuetoca. She gazed out the window of the bus.

I'm on official newspaper business, and I must act like it. She recited the mantra about ten times. It helped, but she was still nervous as hell.

She pulled at the tight black pants and shot the sleeves on her high-necked, cream-colored top—with a mesh panel below the throat. She'd picked it up in a resale shop near the hotel. She was going for a 50s Hollywood look. The wig had cost ten times the top and pants.

Back at the hotel, Haasi had taken one look at Blanche in the get-up and asked: "Why?"

"Dunno. Just seems to fit the times and the challenge. Don't ask me why."

"And that wig! Pretty cool."

"I want to look real."

"Oh, you look real. *Fur-ril*," said Haasi. "Ready for central casting."

"That's it."

Blanche wasn't very good at acting, and she had no filter. Now she was having second thoughts about the get-up, but it was too late. She had to try. She focused on the fields and small houses and signs whipping past the window of the bus, and it calmed her. Blanche fumbled in her bag for the cellphone. She longed to call Haasi, but she resisted. She was glad to have the cheap burners to communicate, just in case, and to finally check in and leave together. Haasi would pick her up, posing as a hired driver. It should work. It had to work.

If Detective Cardenal knew she was minutes away from meeting El Patrón, he'd probably kill her. If someone else didn't get to it first. She'd left the detective nearly in mid-sentence and gotten out of his office before he could argue further.

She shivered at the thought she was pretty much on her own, but she couldn't sit still and let all this happen around her.

Blanche withdrew the notebook from her bag and flipped through her notes. *The W's. Who, what, where, when, why, and how.* She would cover all that in the interview and hope there would be a shot of tequila involved during which time her interviewee would relax and open up. Maybe he'd even let her roam the ranch a bit. That was going to be the tough part. If Emilio was out there, or El Patrón knew where he was, Blanche was going to have to follow that trail.

Be flexible, Bang. And don't shoot yourself in the foot.

Staring out at the vista of scrubland and cactus, the mesquite and oaks, the farmer pushing a plow by hand, she felt a burst of love for Mexico, mostly centered on Emilio who seemed to care so much for the people around him. It saddened Blanche that she was dealing with a seedy underside, but it was as Maria Obregon had said: the history of Mexico is complicated, one of generosity and kindness, and snakes. The bus rumbled past acres of sunflowers, a thing of beauty used for food and dye. They revered flowers here. She'd seen pictures of the altars and carpets of marigolds and dahlias during the Day of the Dead. She imagined the Aztecs growing them and blessing them for food and worship. Tradition lived long, and hard. It was something she appreciated. It was different for Blanche, an island girl who was used to waves and shifting sand on a bit of land that changed shape regularly and depended on tourism and fish.

Blanche gathered her things and stood up in the aisle of the bus. She was the only one traveling from Mexico City who got off at the dusty terminal. It had been so dry. She'd read there was little rain now in late spring, but soon in the next half of the year, the rain would start and come down in torrents, with little warning. Everything—the colorful outdoor display of fruit, the Pacifica beer sign on the small corner grocer, a narrow café open to the interior with a table and dog out front—all of it seemed to be coated in a fine, hazy film, the sun beaming through it like in a dream. She could hear the faint mechanical creak of the local *tortilladora* turning out tortillas, the music of many Mexican streets. This street was eerily deserted, except for a dog.

Blanche sighed and hefted her purse. She was getting used to the wig and the glasses, and even getting psyched for the meeting. She'd made it this far. It was show time.

A couple of taxis waited next to the portico outside the bus station. She ducked her head at the first, and he waved her in. "*Buenas.*"

"*Buenas, Señor. A la casa de Señor Rodrigo Ortiz de Avila, por favor.*"

The cab driver's thick eyebrows shot up, a mix of surprise and curiosity. For more than a beat, he said nothing. "*¡Vámonos!*" And the cab lurched away from the bus terminal.

Blanche was taken aback by the cabbie's reaction. She thought to ask him about it, then decided the better part of valor was to shut up.

Put on your game face, Blanche.

She caught sight of herself in the mirror of the taxi, the dark eyebrows and green eyes. The cat-eye glasses with green rims. *And that hair.* She wanted to think she looked stunning, like Haasi said, but shocking was more the word. They drove out into the farmland, and once again Blanche was struck by how quickly the landscape could change, from gleaming buildings to donkeys in the field. She saw the occasional tractor, but mostly it was a stretch of sleepy beauty, the struggle in green and brown under the harsh sun. The cab passed over a bumpy dirt road under an arch of laurel trees. A small stucco house lay deserted in the shade, tires in the yard holding down a blue tarp. A single chair sat next to an incongruous, beautifully carved door, and vines of flowers looped around a gate.

Blanche looked for Haasi's car but didn't see it anywhere. It gave her a sinking feeling, but Blanche knew she could depend on sister-cousin. Haasi was good at hiding. Blanche settled on this and felt better.

The cool length of trees ended at a sunny vista of flatland, and the road turned to fine gravel. Off in the distance, a startlingly white *hacienda* rambled on and on like a mirage in the dust. Its whiteness, its humps of separate additions with small windows, shown against the stark landscape. Blanche sat back on the seat her hands braced on the frayed upholstery. She caught the taxi driver's eyes in the mirror, watching her, gauging her. She leaned forward more resolute than ever. She paid the driver and leapt out. The taxi zipped in a circle and was gone in a flash.

A dog as big as a cow ran out of the front door across a landscape scattered with various types of cacti—one more than a story high, another with a fountain of shoots, a few with paddles of prickly pear and red buds of "tuna," a cluster of tiny round ones like a herd of baby hedgehogs. And behind the dog, a tall figure in black, loose-limbed and casually strolling toward Blanche. He held a cane, but he didn't lean on it. He waved it at the dog. "Bella!" he shouted. The dog collapsed in a puddle of fur, almost blending with the sandy earth of a flowerbed.

They walked toward each other. Blanche felt her knees wobble, and her insides were worse. "Ah, the writer," he said.

"El Patr...," she started. Then she caught herself. "*Señor* de Avila. *Encantada.*"

"*Bienvenido a mi casa.*" His eyes were black and unreadable, but his voice was so soft she had to lean in. He had a frightening pallor and slicked back hair.

"*Gracias, señor. Me allegro.*"

She offered her hand and he bowed slightly. She wanted to yank her fingers out of his grasp. She looked around for Haasi, more of a reflex than anything else. She did not expect to see her close by, but she had to believe she was out there.

"*Por favor, ven,*" he said, and stepped aside so that Blanche had no choice but to walk up the paving stones to the grand front door that stood ajar. It was deadly quiet, except for the chirping … of birds? Frogs? Edible grasshoppers? The sounds of the hacienda, of the sun on slithering things and shimmering growth.

El Patrón followed Blanche, and the dog loped behind.

Blanche stepped into a vast entryway, the terra-cotta tiles polished a deep red. A center table blazed with a crystal vase of lilies, allium, and gold branches shot through with sunlight from a far window. Carved benches layered with exquisite blankets lined the whitewashed walls under two enormous oil paintings of Spanish royalty, maybe a duke on the left, the duchess on the right? Blanche glanced at both, their dark gaze, the white ruffs on the duchess's neck above a tight bodice. As for the duke, Blanche could see the resemblance to El Patrón. The narrow nose, patrician brow, and a piercing look that could surely kill. Blanche took a deep breath. Her host walked ahead. Slowly. He seemed to have a limp. She held her bag tightly.

The house was built around an enormous courtyard of red roses and purple bougainvillea; the flowers grew wild and full but obviously had been tamed with shears into attractive cascades around arches and an altar to Our Lady of Guadalupe. It was jaw-dropping. So beautiful—and Catholic? *He prays to Our Lady?*

A colonnade with a walkway surrounded the courtyard on the ground level. It created a continuous balcony with stone balustrade on the second level. Blanche felt like she'd been removed about five hundred years. She had to focus on *now.* More doors led to darker corners of the rambling house. *So many doors, so little time. Where is Emilio? Could he be here, or through there?* Blanche glanced at all the ins and outs and archways that led off in different directions.

She guessed she was in the heart of the house. She listened for the least clue, but all she heard was a lullaby of luxury. A fountain trilled, a bird in a white wicker cage added to the music. Faint symphony music in the background. It was truly an oasis in the desert. Blanche felt an odd isolation, cut off from the real world. And cut off from help, should she need it. She drew on her inner reserve. It was there, like a warm stone holding her in place. Anchoring her. Haasi was out there. And Emilio was *somewhere.*

"*Tranquila, señorita.*" El Patrón was making his way around the patio, while Bella sniffed along behind him. Her host gestured to the seating area. "*Por favor,* take a seat. What better place to relax than here?"

She could think of a number of better places. The white beach in front of her cabin on Santa Maria Island, that little patio back at their hotel. Even the middle of the teeming Zocalo. All of a sudden, she wanted to be anywhere but here.

"It is very beautiful. Are you a gardener?"

He chuckled, a peculiar growling sound. "No, no green thumb. A thumb of poison. I kill everything I touch, or rather, *plant,* I should say." The grin fell away, and his brows knit in a serious look. "I employ people who do things for me."

Blanche felt the knot twist. She wanted this thing *done.*

They sat at a U-shaped seating arrangement of couches with crisscrossed straps of leather on the bases and splashes of flowers on the wide cushions. It was much too comfortable, and distracting.

"Please. Enjoy." El Patrón took a seat on a chair with the sweep of a peacock carved into the high back of gleaming wood. "We will take *café.*" He shook a small bell on the glass-topped table.

Blanche sat up straight on the edge of the sofa. She took out her notebook, eyeing an elaborate altar off to the side of the patio. "Our Lady of Guadalupe?"

He turned slowly to the statue framed in a niche in the wall with sprays of cabbage roses in silver vases and candles in tall glass holders set on the paving.

"The Church has a long history in Mexico. You must know that."

"Yes, a conservative history, siding with military leaders and the rich ..."

Oh, jeez, shut up Blanche.

He smiled at her, and he didn't have to say it: She was an indulgent child. Maybe delusional. She desperately wanted to find that neutral, professional track, and stay on it. If she could only control her mouth.

"Well, yes, that is true, but the Church has done many things for the poor in this country. You know, *Nuestra Señora* appeared to a poor peasant in the north of Mexico City. You should visit the shrine. It is ... I think the word you norteamericanos use, often, is 'awesome.'"

"Yes, so I have heard. We will try to do that." She tilted her head.

"We? Who is *we*?"

Already she'd lost it, giving away her position. It happened like that, word by word. She had to be more careful. She needed to keep her distance, but not allow him to do that. She did not want to be the subject of an inquisition. He stroked his pointy beard.

"Uh, an acquaintance, a traveling companion. Busy taking photos in the Zocalo." She crossed her legs. Pen poised. She smiled. She breathed slowly. What was it her gran told her? *Breathe diaphragmatically*. She scribbled in her notebook about the Church and the shrine. It gave her a second to compose herself. The writing always did.

A round, little woman wearing a starched white uniform and a black apron appeared in a dark archway. She carried a silver tray laden with china and tiny glasses, a crystal decanter of amber liquid, and coffee service. She put the tray down and offered Blanche a crisp linen napkin embroidered with a rosebud. She hoped that lovely golden liquid was booze; the knot in her stomach started to unwind. Just a bit.

He lifted the decanter. "Sherry? From Jerez de la Frontera."

She held the small stem glass and watched him take a tiny sip, his eyes closed. She brought the amber liquid up to her nose. The aroma of golden grapes, with a hint of honey. She sipped. Blanche knew a thing or two about sherry, and this was extraordinary.

"*Maravilloso*," she said. It was like a stream of sunlight had gone from her lips to her toes.

"Age is more impressive than quantity, don't you think? Time is the greatest of vintners." He seemed lost on the southern Spanish coast, five miles from the sea, where the sun kissed the grapes and the cathedral-like wine cellars aged the priceless wine.

Blanche let herself be carried away. For a brief moment.

Time. What had Emilio said? It has no edges to it. All her thoughts went back to him.

She snapped back. She took another sip and eyed her host. He put the sherry down with a slight tap. "Now, what are we about? Where should we begin?"

"At the beginning? In Mexico?"

"Oh, that is quite a long time ago. About four hundred years."

Blanche nearly drained her glass. *Well, maybe I'll just skip ahead a few hundred years. And have another glass of this marvelous stuff.* "What about this beautiful farmland, *señor*? What is your business here? Crops and such."

"Ah, I love my grapes. I want to grow this one." He lifted his glass. "But it is only in Andalusia. It doesn't travel well to Mexico." He swirled the sherry in the glittering crystal and studied it. He leaned toward Blanche. "I don't believe you want to talk about grapes."

She contained herself, and the sherry helped. "I write travel articles for a small newspaper in Florida." She held the pen over the notebook. "I would like to capture a bit of your lifestyle for readers."

"Why me? I am just an old ranchero, living out the days at home." He waved an arm, taking in the surroundings.

"Some home." She relaxed, smiling. "It is gorgeous. Did you build all this?"

"This is the original courtyard, built by my great-grandfather. Many greats back. The generations have built on from here. Would you like a tour?"

Would I?

"Yes, I would."

She stood up and followed. Like stepping off a diving board, she would jump in feet first. She imagined Emilio was locked up somewhere, but she wanted to be realistic. He might not be here at all. She had to keep an open mind and not be charmed away from her mission to look for clues.

One archway led to a salon with every shade of blue. At one end of the room, blue and white tiles surrounded a huge fireplace, hearth to mantel. Blanche whistled softly. "The Moorish influence, from Spain," he said. Blue linen-covered loveseats were positioned in the center of the room. Blue-and-white-striped side chairs with carved arms and legs. A thick cream rug with blue swirls. Blue, blue, blue. A table was blooming over with orchids of every color. The wide window looked out on a vast green stretch of cactus and low shrubs against a vast, bright blue sky. "Stunning," she said.

"Yes, my ex-wife Carlina decorated this room. She liked to match the inside to the outdoors. I didn't understand what she was talking about, but it works. Don't you think?"

"It works." The flow of blue from inside out to the sky, a bench covered in light animal skin that echoed the tan earth. The flowers. "Oh, definitely, it works. It's just lovely."

And ex-wife. Make a note of that, Blanche.

He was almost charming. She floated from room to room. Luxury had a way of doing that, a lovely distraction carrying her from one cloud to the next. There didn't seem to be anyone around but the two of them.

"I imagine you love living here." A little on the gushy side. She checked herself.

"Yes. But it can be lonely. And too quiet."

She didn't feel the least bit sorry. He'd certainly made his bed, about a hundred of them from what she could figure. *Where the hell is Emilio?*

They continued the tour, on and on, through the house, to a masculine great room with an inlaid chessboard game table, another fireplace, and huge, tan leather sofas. Stone and stucco and leather. And splashes of deep red. They entered a long, narrow dining room with carved straight-back chairs lined up down the length of a table for thirty, easily. Oil paintings of more Avilas looked down from the walls. Subdued light filtered over the elaborate sideboards with silver service and a wall-to-wall silky Oriental rug. All the luxury money could buy.

At the far end of the dining room, a door stood ajar. The sun shined on great clay urns potted with topiary under a portico that led to a separate building. She could see a door beyond. She started to move forward, and El Patrón put his hand on her arm. She stopped like she'd been burned.

"*Señor.*" The housekeeper with the lovely calm face was back.

"*¿Ana, qué pasa?*"

"*Teléfono.*" She inclined her head slightly and turned to leave.

"I'm sorry. I must take this call. Will you have a seat for a moment? Perhaps in the blue sala, or on the patio?"

Blanche smiled. "Yes, of course. I might look for the ladies' room while you're busy on the phone."

"Of course." He bowed his head slightly. "Ana will show you."

Shit-ski to that-ski.

Ana was gone. Blanche waited until El Patrón disappeared down the hallway toward the other end of the house. Her feet seemed rooted to the thick red rug as she watched him go, but now the sherry mixed nicely with her usual curiosity, and she thought quickly to retrace her steps. He'd shown her the salons, the suites, the game room, and the dining room. But he'd steered her away from the kitchen. *Why not the kitchen? And where are the storage sheds, the closets, the hiding places?*

Blanche hurried through the dining room toward the kitchen. The portico separating the two areas was a blast of brightness after the dim interior, the cool stucco walls, the dukes looking down from their gold frames. She crossed the tile. The door to the kitchen was unlocked. Once inside, she gaped, struck by the modern convenience of hanging copper pots, herbs growing on glass shelves in the windows, an expanse of marble counter space. The ovens nearly covered one wall.

Where is the staff for all this stuff?

She was struck, but not surprised. Why did she feel like he was hiding something? That this gorgeous house, a marvel straight out of *Architectural Digest,* was just a cover? It was odd; he was odd. She started flipping open doors. Drawers. Slamming them shut. She was making noise, and it felt good. She'd been tiptoeing around the hacienda like in a dream, and now she'd had enough.

She didn't think about who might be listening.

The more she lurched around the kitchen, the angrier and more frustrated she got. *Well, Emilio's not here, and I'm not getting anywhere ... At some point, I have to get out of here.*

She had an urge to check in with Haasi and leave now. But she couldn't do that. El Patrón was expecting her back on the patio.

She unhooked a copper pot from the rack above an island counter and nervously, absently tapped it on the butcher top. She looked around, waiting for inspiration. It was last-ditch. She didn't have much time. She dropped the pot and went to the pantry. It was empty of food, except for some bags of flour and a couple of *cucarachas.* A few cans. Blanche shut the door, hard. She ran her finger over a marble countertop. Dust. *He doesn't use the kitchen.*

The dog appeared from behind the island counter and cocked her head at Blanche. She was a beauty with fluffs of fur around her sweet face. Reddish brown. A setter and lab mix? She sat, eyes fixed on Blanche, and sniffed. Blanche reached down and scratched the dog's neck, and Bella stretched one way and then another for more. Blanche laughed. "You old cutie."

Bella seemed to have enough of the scratching and petting. She got up and started toward the door at the far end of the kitchen. She sniffed some more. Whined a bit and flopped in front of the closed door. It was a Dutch door, the top half open, and Blanche could see beyond the kitchen to a shed. Bella let out a soft, "Gruff."

"What is it, girl?" Blanche crept up behind the dog.

She didn't hear the footsteps.

"*Señorita*? Do you need something?"

Blanche jumped. It was the housekeeper, and the expression had turned from sweet to salty. Her hands were clenched in a knot. She didn't move.

"*Sí.* I am looking for *el baño*."

The woman's face softened, slightly. "Not in kitchen. And not out there." She turned aside and pointed through the portico and back toward the main house. "*Por allá.* Bella, *ven.*"

The dog seemed reluctant to move away from the door, and Blanche, but she slowly turned and followed the housekeeper out of the kitchen, Blanche right behind. She wondered at the furry one's actions, plopping down like that at that kitchen door and then "speaking." Blanche thumped the dog gently on the head, and Bella arched her neck, begging for more. *Do you know something I don't know?* Blanche watched the dog and the housekeeper retreat toward the patio. She had an urge to return to that kitchen door, but her host would surely come looking for her. She decided to find the ladies' room. The farther she walked away from the kitchen, the more unsettled she became with each step.

A kitchen that's not a kitchen? A prop? It's not like he runs out to McDonald's every day ... And Bella. That gentle whine. Was she trying to tell me something?

Chapter Twenty-Two
THE DOCTOR IS IN

EL PATRÓN MET BLANCHE BACK ON THE PATIO after his phone call. She was seated on the edge of the sofa, bending over her notebook. She looked up at the sound of his steps. Hardly any sound at all. He crept along on those long, slithery legs, wearing that gaunt smile. *Creep-ola.* "*Señor,* I was just looking over my notes. A couple of things I wanted to ask you ..."

"I am sorry, *señorita.* I have pressing business. Perhaps we can continue another time. How long are you here?"

"In Mexico City? I'm not sure." She'd been wondering about that herself. Cardenal said he wanted them to stick around. As unofficial witnesses to theft and murder?

"Perhaps we talk one day soon. Tomorrow? Day after? I have contacts in *El Centro* and must go there from time to time, though, I must say, the traffic and the inconvenience are deplorable."

She stood up, a bit too quick to her feet, so obvious that she wanted out of there pronto. "You are so kind. Of course. May I call a driver?"

"Certainly."

"I will call you later and we will talk."

He was so courteous; she was so courteous. She wanted to scream with frustration more than anger. She hadn't found

Emilio. And she'd be damned if she'd tell him where she was staying. She would, indeed, check in with him later.

The driver pulled around on the gravel drive. A woman was at the wheel, her hat pulled low over her eyes. She was very small, hunched down in the front seat.

Blanche didn't hesitate. "¡*Adiós!*" She jumped into the back seat. She couldn't even breathe until the car drove out from under the laurel trees. She grabbed Haasi's shoulder and squeezed. Their eyes locked in the rearview mirror.

"You all right?" Haasi focused on the road, and then looked back at Blanche.

"Could be better. Boy, am I glad to see you. Just knowing you were out there. Somewhere …"

Haasi smiled. "Have to say, I was getting a little nervous. A car drove by and surely whoever it was saw me sitting off in the weeds. I had to move. How'd it go in there? You find anything?"

"A whole lot of nothing. And a very bad vibe, except for the fact he must have had the team from *1,001 Decorating Ideas* in there."

"Really? Nice, huh?"

"*Grandísimo.*" Blanche whipped off the blonde wig, spun it around, and looked at it. "Not done with you yet."

"You talkin' to me? You talkin' to me?"

"Very funny, Robert DeNiro. No, I'm talkin' to the damn wig."

"Now what?"

"I don't know. I want to get back in there, but I'm not sure how we're gonna do that."

"Look, Bang, we need to get this car back, and then somehow get back to normal." Haasi's eyebrows furrowed. She puffed out her cheeks. Blanche's eyes were on the fields and hills and sky. Haasi gave it a full minute. "No, Blanche. Come on. No more fake identities and shady characters and snooping around in dangerous places."

"I'm just thinking. Something about that dog …" She stared off into the cornfield as Haasi sped along the road.

"Dog? He's got a dog? What does that have to do with anything?"

"It's just the way she acted." Blanche smiled and caught Haasi in the mirror. "Cutest dog in the world, so sweet. Don't know what she sees in him."

Haasi drove, steady and fast. "I love dogs."

"Oh, you'd love her." Blanche grinned. She leaned forward. "Haas, just one more look-see? Maybe that'll do it."

"How?"

"Don't know."

"No," said Haasi, her hands at ten and two. Eyes on the road.

"Why not?"

"Bang." They were flying down Highway 57. Haasi shook her head. She was smiling. "Oh, well, you know already what I'm gonna say …"

It was hot. And dark. Except for slivers of light that shined through the cracks in the walls. He guessed he was in a storage shed of some sort. It smelled of pigs. And grease, like that used in mowers and leaf blowers. And chain saws. Even as hot as he was, he shivered.

He'd been here for days, or hours. He didn't know. He'd been drugged. No question about that. They were short men who had grabbed him on either side, and he was strong. He remembered at the time he couldn't resist. He'd tried to reach out to Blanche and Haasi, but he couldn't do it. It was almost as if he collapsed. He couldn't give in. That wasn't him. Emilio Sierra Del Real.

The door creaked open. A man stood against the backdrop of light. A dark shape, skinny legs, and shrunken frame in a long jacket. Emilio saw a stranger but knew this man was after him;

that made him less of a stranger. He wanted something from Emilio, and Emilio had not a clue what that could be.

"Qué *tal*." It wasn't a question. It was a demand, and the stranger came closer to Emilio, his boots scuffing the dirt floor of the shed.

"What do you want." Emilio was not asking either. He wanted answers. To know why he was stuck in this filthy shed that smelled like pigs. It was inconceivable he'd been kidnapped for his little side trip to the lab with the women, but maybe not. Now he was being held against his will. For days? And for what? But who was he kidding? This was Mexico. Shit happened. He was surprised he wasn't dead. His pulse started racing; his mind was running to keep up. *If I'm not dead, then why not?*

This realization hit him with a jolt. He should be dead, and the fact that he wasn't was a certain clue to this whole business. They wanted something from him, but what could they possibly want? He was a poor medical student with no real means. His family had not been wealthy. Indeed, his parents were both dead, his relatives scattered all over Mexico. He knew very little about the cartels and their seedy network. He liked to keep his distance and do the work of a doctor. *The work.* The medical training. That was all he had, the sum total of his worth. Was there a connection between the work and this bunch of goons?

He was just a doctor. He'd play along for now; he had no other choice.

The man drew closer, reached for a string above Emilio's head, and turned on a light bulb hanging from a rafter. Emilio's eyes, long accustomed to the dark, slowly adjusted, and he raised his head to look into the gaunt face of his captor. He pulled on his goatee. Emilio had never seen him before.

"*Lo siento, doctor.*"

"Sorry for what?" Emilio could barely hold his head up.

"For the accommodation." The old man pulled a stool from

the corner and sat on the edge. He crossed his arms. "You should be coming to by now. After all it was such a small dose. ..."

"Dose of what?" His head swung back and forth. It was difficult to focus.

"A cocktail? *La rocha*, perhaps?"

"¡*Hijo de puta!*" Emilio tried to stand. "Son of a bitch!" he repeated. He wanted to grab the scrawny neck, throw him down, and stomp on him. But that was not going to happen. Besides, he could hardly move, and what sense would that make? He'd be dead in a second. He fell back. He felt a wave of nausea and disorientation.

"*Tranquilo.* It should be wearing off about now. You won't remember a thing."

"What things?"

"Such things." The man resumed stroking his pitiable beard. "We need to talk."

Emilio had a hard time imagining how he was going to talk. He was sinking after some brief moments of lucidity. He couldn't hold his head up, much less stand. He stumbled to a bucket in the corner and back to the dirty cot pushed against a wall. "Let me rest."

That was the last he remembered.

The man turned to the door and snapped his fingers. Another figure appeared. "I think our doctor needs another shot, but lightly. He's in no mood to talk just yet, but I need him to. Soon."

Emilio woke up with a start. Disoriented. The awful smell, the scratchy cot disgusted him. He threw the raggedy blanket onto the dirt. He'd heard banging. Or was it some kind of nightmare? But, no, he was sure someone had been slamming doors, or drawers. Punctuating his unconscious, pounding on his brain. There'd been another, and another. He tried to rise up on his

147

elbows. He tried to find his voice, but it was somewhere down a deep dark hole. He couldn't reach it. He lifted his arms and they were as useless as dead branches. He lay down again on the cot, and he was gone.

Chapter Twenty-Three

BRING ME
THE HEAD OF A GOAT

OLEANTHA FLÓREZ DE LOSADA WAS IN THE MIDDLE of putting in a few hours at her alternative medicine clinic, *La Hierba del Cielo*. She opened a crate of vials and lifted them out, one by one, and checked them off in her inventory. The purples, the pinks, the yellows. She opened a purple one and took a whiff. "*Ah, lavanda.*" She closed her eyes. The lovely smell of lavender brought her back instantly to her grandmother's bedroom, to the pressed and tatted white linens, the little dog seated on an embroidered cushion. The view of the orchard from the window, cherimoya and apricot, plum and fig trees. It was paradise there, playing at her dressing table with her beautiful silver combs and mirrors and brushes.

The hacienda in Hidalgo was gone. The cartels had taken it long ago. Her grandmother was dead.

But the memories are not gone. She peered into the mirror behind a wall of glass shelves. She was happy with what she saw. The sheen of her black hair. The striking blue eyes—the gift of a Viking forebear who had landed on the Spanish coast. She was a special *mestiza,* and she liked that. She liked being different, set apart. She'd worked hard at it.

She went to the desk, a Louis XV marble-topped work of art with beech marquetry and gilded shell, doves, and dolphins, supposedly left over from the ill-fated French occupation of the mid-nineteenth century. She felt like a queen seated at that desk. The armchair fit nicely under the secret pull-out drawer where she'd found that dagger, such a priceless jewel. It was pure beaten silver, inlaid with mother-of-pearl on the hilt, not bigger than her palm. She often wondered who had used it, who had hidden it in the folds of her voluminous silk gown, who had stuck the thing in some *idiota* who had tried to take advantage of her. Oleantha fingered the dagger now, always close at hand, and felt like she channeled that spirit, wherever she was—in heaven or hell. It was all the same to Oleantha; there was just one place for her, and that was here.

She took the ledger out of the drawer. This one had records of the legitimate herbs and oils, vitamins and healing lotions that Oleantha sold in her clinic. The herbs and grasses and teas were moneymakers, not that she gave a hoot how much she made from *chicura, cholla,* or *palo bobo,* and *batamote,* whose various leaves and barks and seeds treated everything from asthma and diarrhea to madness, foot odor, and scorpion bite. She had the Aztecs to thank for their catalogue of thousands of plants and trees that provided relief in times of disease and discomfort. The ancients were noted for their impressive codices, and so was she. Irrepressible. She flipped through the pages, satisfied with her work.

If any government bureau or department demanded to snoop around in her business, for tax reasons, or, God forbid, worse, Oleantha had it all right here. Her other ledgers, well, that was another matter. She didn't want the police getting to any of those. All of the books were under lock and key. She clicked the pen madly on the desktop. *Except for that one ledger she left out in the lab* ... El Jefe had graciously reminded her of that slip-up when he caught those snoops. Well, one little slip-up.

Here she was, doing a tremendous service, dispensing herbs and alternative medicines. Practicing medicine in all its many, er, ramifications. She was carrying on her country's valuable tradition and doing a booming business. She had it all, and she was prepared. She never knew what they'd ask for. Bullet extractions? Cauterizing amputations? In the herb clinic, relief for labor pains? Gonorrhea? Boils? Every once in a while, she prescribed *mata ratón* for killing rats; it was also used for fever and stomach conditions, but she often wondered if her clients followed all the directions and only killed rats. She didn't want to know. Some of these medicinal ingredients had side effects.

She sighed. She couldn't control *everything.* Several herbs with lovely yellow flowers bloomed in pots in the front window, along with a miniature hibiscus, widely used for cholesterol control and digestion. Her patients and clients believed in her and the prescriptions and advice, and, after all, she was a doctor.

She had the world in her talons. She loved the work. The herb clinic was perfect, and it complemented her other business. Working for the mob, assisting in art theft, and making mummies.

She balled up her fist and pounded the open ledger. These bursts of anger flared up suddenly, but they passed, especially when she thought of her "projects." They needed to go off without a hitch, and she was most proud—and worried—about the outcomes of her latest for El Patrón. Just thinking about it began to calm her. In fact, she reveled in thinking about it.

She'd dressed for the occasion. She always did, whether she was retrieving bullets from a gang member's torso or making a mummy. She wore her gold leather, four-inch heels with wide

T-straps. Always the straps. They gave her footing should she slip. The floor tended to get slick where she worked.

The Day of the Mummy, she'd shrugged into a starched white lab coat over a pink tweed Chanel skirt and pink silk blouse. She'd removed the Tiffany bracelet, but she rarely took the peanut-size diamonds out of her earlobes. She felt better when she looked like a million dollars. Literally. She checked her reflection in the small mirror hanging on the lab wall over the sink, and she was happy with what she saw.

For this project, Oleantha bustled about putting tools in order: scalpel and suctions, scrapers and jars and tape and tweezers and sponges. She had it covered although this was a new recipe, as far as she knew, and she feared she'd have to wing it at some point. She'd studied up on the procedure and come up with her own method. She hoped it worked—there was a new condo riding on it.

She was about to get after it when that *idiota* had appeared in the doorway:

"You can come in, you know, for a minute or so," she'd said. "Our girl won't bite."

"Muy graciosa." He had his hands in his pockets and disgust on his face. "That her?"

"Who else would it be? Once again, meet Lalia Solis Iglesia." Lalia, very dead, rested on a bed of ceramic cylinders, her lips blue, her dark hair cascading from this makeshift platform, feet slightly elevated.

He grimaced. "You got it?"

"Sí." Oleantha wanted him gone. She preferred not to have visitors while she worked.

"¿Cuándo?"

"When I say."

He hunched his shoulders. "El Patrón says, the sooner the better. But you're the boss lady. La Jefa." He smiled at his little joke.

Nervously. "I'll be back soon."

She'd had no idea how soon she'd be able to cook this mummy. How hard could it be? She knew the human body. Fiddling with it was nothing more than acting as a glorified mechanic, although the comparison gave her sensibilities pause. She had graduated from medical school, but she hadn't quite made it over the hump. The licensure required a stint of social service in the pueblos, and she demurred. She was a city girl. Born and bred, mostly, in Mexico City. The dust and poverty and endless slap of tortillas on the *comal* out in the countryside were not to her liking. She'd also failed to go all the way to licensure because she didn't have the patience for testing and the pesky board requirements, though she'd taken a run at it. She had to admit, she'd run afoul of it, after offering the board a bribe and getting a reprimand in return from a particularly chaste number of uptight officials. She intended to practice medicine (if that's what one would call it) her own way.

El Jefe had brought her the body of this woman. Maybe in her thirties. Maybe strangled. She had a thin red line around her neck. She hadn't been dead more than eight hours. Oleantha had insisted on a more or less fresh corpse for the procedure. She felt a twinge of guilt, but not much. What they were paying her to conduct this little experiment would put her in Rolexes for every day of the week and buy her a condo overlooking the Paseo near the Four Seasons. It was the practice of medicine. Sort of. It was a dead body. *She* didn't kill the woman; she'd only *ordered* the body. Besides, mummification was seen as "a miracle, a direct intervention from the gods," she'd read in one of the manuals on ancient history that she consulted. She was performing a miracle. Even if she did have to move the process along a bit to suit the bottom line.

Still, she had that twinge of guilt. It was fleeting; Oleantha didn't have time to dwell on it. She had work to do. Her recipe: "A mixture of arsenic, alcohol, and conifer resin. Formalin and salicylic acid to kill bacteria and fungi and preserve tissue." Some of the ingredients she stole from a five-thousand-year-old practice. Back many years, they used honey for its antibacterial properties; she dispensed with that and went to chemicals.

The thugs had placed the body on a contraption of Oleantha's design—a bed of ceramic tubes that alleviated pressure on the underside of the body so the blood would flow. (Ceramics wiped nice and clean, she figured.) The "bed" was elevated slightly in the leg region to encourage action.

She'd washed down the body in white vinegar—the perfect ingredient to start. It had so many uses, for getting rid of soap residue in her hair, and the maid used it in the laundry and on the kitchen floor. She hesitated over the removal of the internal organs, but that was done as part of the "miracle," so she would conform. She grabbed a scalpel and went to work. She used a hook to extract brain tissue through the nose. She pondered whether or not to leave the eyes and then decided she'd let them be. For now. They were the windows to the soul, and if one were still in there, Oleantha damn well didn't want to disturb it any further.

She attached the tubing at the carotid artery and in the legs and started the pump. So far, so good. Most of the bodily fluids drained away, the chemicals were doing the job and leaving the skin like fresh leather. It took most of the day. The body had had a creamy brown hue, but now it grew paler.

She fixed that. Gave her a nice tan. Overhead, a sunlamp with equator-like strength began shining down on the remains. In no time she was shriveled beyond recognition, taken back a thousand years to her forebears. At least in appearance.

Oleantha was still dreaming at her desk, off in mummy land, when she looked up to see a young blonde woman standing outside, staring into the clinic. Her face was alive with interest and animation as she peered through the window at a wall of flowering plants on a tall wrought iron rack. She was definitely a foreigner. Generally speaking, these visitors annoyed Oleantha; they always had so many questions. As if Mexico invented herbs and how to use them and Oleantha knew everything about them. Even so, she loved their dollars.

The door swung open. The blonde walked into the clinic. A wig, no doubt, but an expensive one. And her clothes were understated, even tasteful. A *norteamericana*, maybe a celebrity. They did have a way of thinking they were disguised, but Oleantha could spot bling and glitz and *je ne sais quoi* a mile away. Oleantha straightened up.

"*Buenas,*" the blonde said, and stopped at the *cojón de toro*, an intricate plant whose fruit looked like castanets but was named for the testicles of a bull.

The blonde turned and came toward the desk. "*Hola, soy Blanche.*" She smiled and stuck out her hand.

Oleantha extended limp fingers and nodded, "*Buenas, Oleantha Flórez.*" She waved at the interior of the clinic. "*Por favor.*"

Blanche meandered past the shelves with a look of amazement. Oleantha had to admit the array of tubers, roots, seeds, and leaves, the watercolors of plantain, larrea, and allium, the painting of an Aztec marketplace made up a spectacular display. It gave the place a modern boutique feeling with old-world appeal. She folded her hands under her chin and waited while Blanche, the *yanqui*, made the rounds.

Definitely an American. Oleantha came around the desk. "What can I do for you, *señorita*?" She prided herself on her command of English, courtesy of a pre-med scholarship to a Texas university, plus the fact she'd studied the language since primary, some of it in London. She'd finished the undergrad and couldn't wait to get out of there and back to civilization in Mexico City. It gave her a shiver of regret that her grade point hadn't been quite up to par, which was the real reason she was back in "civilization." Yet, she fondly told anyone who would listen that her work was here. El Patrón had listened. He needed her.

Oleantha smiled, a frigid ear-to-ear that revealed large white teeth.

"I just love your shop!" Her gaze spun from one end to the other. "Could you tell me a bit about all these herbs and things?" Her smile was radiant, the green eyes earnest.

Oleantha fiddled with a pamphlet. *Caramba. I'm not going to give the inventory of three thousand herbs.* "Certainly."

"These are so beautiful." Blanche picked up a packet of magnolia leaves and another of sunflower leaves with glossy pictures of the flowers.

"Most people don't know all the uses of our many flowers. The sunflower—besides its value for dye, flour, and feed— also has properties for headache, anxiety, and scabs!"

Blanche tilted her head. "Really! All those fields and fields of sunflowers! Gorgeous."

Oleantha couldn't help melting a little. She really had little social contact, except with grumpy wounded gangsters. Dead people didn't count. Now she felt herself warming to the small friendly chica. She was busy going from shelf to shelf, reading labels, sniffing packets of leaves and seeds, and oohing and ahhing.

She turned to Oleantha and held up the echinacea, winter cherry, and voodoo lily.

"Interesting," said Oleantha. "Those are snake bite cures. You weren't planning on taking a walk in the Sonoran Desert, were you?"

"Well, no." Blanche held the packets tentatively, put them down, and picked them up again. She seemed drawn to that shelf, probably due to a fascination with snakes. "You have a lot of snakes in Mexico?"

"Oh, yes, the usual rattler and fer-de-lance. Then the corals and various pit vipers. I don't think you'll find them in the city."

"Snakes are everywhere," Blanche said. She drew out a wad of pesos and bought all the snake bite cures. "For souvenirs. Or insurance?"

"*Señorita*, you are safe here. Just keep your eyes open."

The comment was sobering. Blanche studied the doctor, for more than a couple of heartbeats.

"Souvenirs? I think I'd select a hand-woven basket, or some nice embroidery," said Oleantha. "The Nahua make lovely linens."

"I'll have to do that," said Blanche. She pocketed the change and stuck the herbs in her bag. Oleantha turned back to her ledgers, trying to signal how busy she was. But the girl didn't move.

"Tell me, how long have you been here?" Blanche was smiling, her sandals planted near Oleantha's desk, and she didn't appear to be ready to leave. She was winsome. Engaging.

Despite all, Oleantha couldn't resist. She loved to talk about herself and her many talents. She sat down at her desk and gestured to a small bench. Blanche sat. "I'm really a doctor," she said. She glanced at a certificate with florid gold writing hanging on the wall. Blanche squinted at it, but it was long, involved, and in Spanish.

"What kind of doctor? Alternative medicine?"

"I guess you could say that. Yes, alternative." Oleantha nodded, and Blanche waited while the doctor filled in. "I do some surgery, some private practice. But my love is this clinic. This ancient art."

"Wow." Blanche's expression was enrapt. Maybe just a bit too much. "Where did you study? Your English is so fine, and I'm so glad because my Spanish is so bad."

"We study English here from a very young age. I also studied in the United States. And London."

"Hmmm. Do you know any doctors here? From medical school? Do you work with other doctors?" Her question was super casual, but there was an intensity about her. She sniffed the packet of voodoo lily. A basket of dried leaves and berries on Oleantha's desk emitted a spicy fragrance. She closed her eyes. ¡*Mierda*! *Always with the questions.* The doctor flinched, but then she laughed nervously. "Many questions. Why are you interested in medical schools? And the doctors here? Are you thinking of studying in Mexico?"

Oleantha's thoughts raced like a rat in a cage to El Patrón's plans for Doctor Emilio. She wasn't exactly sure what those plans were, and El Patrón made sure of that. No one was ever really in his tangled loop. It made her nervous. She hated the least bit of loss of control. She had some vague idea that El Patrón wanted to use the young doctor for some nefarious scheme. For what, she could only guess. There seemed to be no end to the scrapes and wounds and amputations that El Patrón's band of crazies came up with. She'd have to sit on this situation and see how things played out. El Patrón was a wily one.

How strange all of this talk was now, but there were very few coincidences in the world. Things happened for a reason.

She stood up, straightened her tight knit skirt and silk blouse with the bell sleeves. Caught a glimpse of herself in the wall of mirrors behind the glass shelves. *Fabulosa.*

Enough already with the chitchat. It was time to get rid of the girl. She was about to speak when Blanche of the green eyes behind the cat-eye glasses smiled and leaned forward, all ears.

"I'm not interested in medical studies," she said. "But I am interested in your amazing practice."

"Here it is." Oleantha was uncomfortable, and she couldn't exactly put her finger on why. The girl was intense, yes, and nosy. Oleantha loved the attention, but she decided to turn the table.

"Tell me about your visit here. How do you like *El Distrito*? What have you been doing here?"

Blanche slapped her knees. "What haven't we been doing! Eating. Walking. Admiring the amazing wealth of art. I wish we could stay. On and on."

"What is your favorite?"

"The murals, and the wonderful paintings. Rivera and Tamayo and Siguerios and Kahlo. So beautiful ... And the food! Well, my cousin is the real eater between the two of us."

Oleantha's thoughts jumped ahead, caught up in the enthusiasm of the moment. "Have you tasted *barbacoa*?"

"You mean, barbecue? Like steaks and hot dogs on the grill?"

Now Oleantha laughed. "Ah, no. Not exactly. In Mexico, the *barbacoa* is a ceremony."

"Well, for us we get the lighter fluid and charcoal going and slap those doggies down."

Oleantha's eyebrows shot up. She laughed. "The doggies down? Hmmm."

"Yeah, we love hot dogs, hamburgers, that sort of thing."

Oleantha was more amused than she wanted to admit. And now she was about to open her mouth and put her five-inch Louboutin into it. "You must come to the *barbacoa*," she blurted. "We will do the head of a goat. Or two. It's *delicioso*!"

Chapter Twenty-Four

IN THE PIT

"How in the hell did you manage that—you and La Escandolera chatting it up?" Haasi was incredulous. She and Blanche sat in a bistro off the Paseo. Blanche had just left Oleantha's clinic in the fashionable La Condesa area of the city and met up with Haasi. She'd been sorting photos on her camera while Blanche finished snooping. Now she was devouring a *torta*, a glorious Mexican sandwich piled with meats, tomato, lettuce, jalapeños, avocado, and dripping with refried beans and melted cheese. The bread had been dipped in hot sauce and the whole thing served warm.

Blanche was glad Haasi was enjoying the sandwich, but she wasn't hungry. She was too excited. "I can't believe how lucky we are."

"Or unlucky?"

"Haas, you know I was digging. You just know she's involved. Somehow. And now this!"

"Now what?"

"We actually have an invitation to El Patrón's. For a *barbacoa!*"

"What's that? Sounds like barbecue. I'm in."

"It is, a Mexican barbecue, not exactly hamburgers and hot dogs, I'm figuring. I'm just dying to get out there."

"Wish you wouldn't say that." Haas picked up an errant jalapeño and stuck it in her mouth. "It does seem unbelievable. When is this happening?"

"Tomorrow around noon? This is perfect. Maybe we can get a clue about Emilio's whereabouts. If they have him… She said she'd send a car around to pick us up. If we wanted."

"Nuh-uh. We get our own wheels. I don't trust her, or that whole bunch, and I don't want them coming around our hotel. I'll pick up a rental again."

"I'm glad I kept the wig. I'm sort of getting used to it."

Haasi shoved the plate aside and put her chin in her hands. "I don't know, Blanche. You look like Scarlett Johansson on the verge of an explosion in that thing. I want my Blanche back."

"I'm here."

They left the café and zigzagged back to the hotel, passing Alameda Park, the French neo-Gothic Iglesia de San Francisco (on the site of Mexico's first convent in 1524), and the stunning House of Tiles with its dazzling iron grillwork. They stopped at the Torre Latinoamericana, a sort of "Empire State Building," rising modern and shining with glass and steel in the middle of a historic street corner. Blanche was madly taking notes, catching up on the travel writing. Haasi put a dollar in the tip jar of a silver-painted Michael Jackson mime. "I need a cream puff," she said.

After a stop at a pastelería for the cream puff—and a sugary bun and an almond-filled crescent—they ended up back on the hotel patio. To plan. Blanche sipped a Modelo; Haasi was blissfully nibbling at the crescent. The travel articles sat on the back burner while they brainstormed their invitation to the *barbacoa*.

"Let's be flexible," said Haasi. "And careful. We can't be running off into different parts of the hacienda."

"Stick together," Blanche said. It was the only rule that Gran had insisted upon during those long wild years growing up on the island. Lord knows, she and Jack, and later, Haasi, would have been in a world of hurt if they hadn't.

They talked long into the evening, strategizing, to figure out how to handle the visit to El Patrón's. The empty Modelo bottles seemed to sprout from the patio stones.

"I have no idea what we're going to do when we get in there," said Blanche. Her legs were tucked under her, and the curls were a fright.

"Well, that's a start. A clean slate. Of sorts," said Haasi. "But I'm sure we'll figure it out."

Blanche and Haasi knew the location of the *barbacoa*—El Patrón's hacienda. The occasion was a long-planned fiesta to honor several art *aficionados* of Mexico City. Indeed, Oleantha told Blanche it was "an opportunity to celebrate Mexican art." It all seemed so aboveboard. Blanche was wondering if the fiesta was also a thank-you celebration for the treasures the doctor and her *compadres* had lifted from the museums and cultural centers. She had no way of knowing. But she was going to give it a good once-over and hoped she lived to tell about it. She still hadn't heard from Cardenal with an update on Emilio or the Palacio. She was more worried by the day. She needed to do *something*. Cardenal had gone silent again.

Oleantha wore a long skirt with crocheted tiers and an enormous rose in her hair. Blanche stole a look at her feet. Sensible gold espadrilles. Just the outfit to wear on a sunny afternoon to a barbecue with art thieves and murderers. Blanche was wearing her blonde wig, the cat-eye glasses, and a new thrift-store find, a tight 40s chambray dress with tucks on the bodice and a flared skirt sprinkled with tiny daisies. She looked like she'd escaped from a Bette Davis movie. Haasi had redone her long black braids, tucked it into a pageboy of sorts, with a red-ribbon headband. She wore dark glasses, and black leggings with a belted shirt.

Oleantha air-kissed them both—on both cheeks—and led them through the patio and out a set of French double doors. "¡Ven, señoritas! I will send you drinks. ¿Cervezas, tequila?" She was tripping along, snapping her fingers at a young woman carrying a silver tray, waving to a man in a large white cowboy hat.

Haasi and Blanche followed. "¿Cervezas? Ah, gracias," said Blanche. She'd never met a beer she didn't like. Oleantha flitted off, and Haasi and Blanche stood alone, suspended in a sort of dreamscape.

The scene was a blast to the eye after all the dust and scrubland they'd driven through. A white tent strung with lights and greenery opened to a buffet table loaded with silver service and a long bar where the bartender sailed back and forth clinking glasses and bottles; linen-covered tables and upholstered chairs dotted a wide, elevated plank deck, polished to a honey-hued gloss. Six-foot tapered rose bushes in a riot of colors straight out of *Alice in Wonderland* were arranged on the deck, around the tent, and on the white gravel path from the house. Off to the right a cluster of men, mostly in Western shirts and boots, stood around a pit. They were stocky and wore knives on their belts. A wisp of smoke rose from the ground.

Haasi was right behind Blanche, holding the back of her arm. "Let's do this."

"Do you see those kidnapping goons anywhere?"

"No, but that doesn't mean they're not here. Somewhere. Keep your face turned away."

Easier said than done. Blanche realized her blonde wig was a beacon. All of the men stared at the arrival of the two *señoritas*. *Well, too late for the low profile.*

A waiter arrived with two ice-cold bottles of Bohemia Especial and linen napkins. El Patrón broke away from the group and approached Blanche. "Ah, delighted to see you, *Señorita* Blanche!"

"My cousin, Haasi Hakla." They all shook hands in a round of spasmodic good will. Haasi's face was warm stone. Blanche could feel her brain cells clacking as if she stood inside her head.

"I am sorry we have not resumed our interview. Pressing business," said El Patrón. "Perhaps this week some time? I will be back in *El Distrito*." A Mariachi band of horns and strings rose above the laughter and the shouting.

The fiesta was heating up. Blanche wished she were in the mood for some drinking and dancing. She tried to look calm and relaxed. "Oh, of course. I'll contact you," she said, quickly. "It was so kind of Doctor Oleantha to invite us. Who would have thought? The coincidence and such."

"*Sí*. The coincidence." His fingers went to the pointy goatee. The dark eyes, bottomless. "Now that you have arrived, please, come, see the *barbacoa*!"

The men broke apart, and Haasi and Blanche, their faces turned down, followed their host to the pit. The aroma of roasted meat was overwhelming, and Blanche thought she'd never smelled anything so good. Haasi's eyes were shining behind the glasses. Waitstaff lifted the head of a goat out of the pit. It didn't look happy to be part of the feast. The rest of it followed, wrapped in maguey leaves. "You see below, we have the *maronga*. With chiles. So *delicioso*. The blood drips into the pan to make this dish. You must try it."

Blanche didn't move, except for her stomach that was doing a somersault. She tried not to look at the goat. "How delightful," she said. "A sort of blood pudding. Like the Germans do, in their sausage and such…" *The Nazis. Oh, wow, I need to get a grip. Before I throw up.*

"*Señor*, truly, it smells divine." Haasi's voice was low and even. Her eye went to a shovel stuck in a small hill of dirt off to the side of the pit. As if he read her mind, El Patrón said, "Yes, we bury the goat wrapped in the leaves for many hours over the low fire. The meat becomes tender. Here, you must try these other dishes."

He led them to the buffet table. Blanche hardly recognized any of it, but the platters and bowls were labeled with florid writing on cards stuck in silver holders: *nopal en su penca*—paddles of cactus cooked with chiles, onions, garlic, shrimp, and chorizo; *frijoles charros*, a broth with beans, pork, and vegetables; Oaxaca cheese on burnt tortillas. "Good for digestion," said El Patrón. "And this. From the ancients. *Insectos* in dough, wrapped in corn husks and cooked in lime water."

Blanche looked around for a sandwich or a piece of cheese. "*Fantástico.*" She whispered.

"Tradition. I have a distant grandmother, you know, from Oaxaca. We serve our Mexican foods, and then, of course, the addition of the modern." He touched the silver eagle clasp on his string tie. Just then waiters arrived with splendid fruit trays, most of which Blanche could not identify. There were tiny kebabs of skewered meat, mushrooms, peppers, and grape-size tomatoes, pinwheels of tortillas with fillings, jicama, radishes, and carrots curled like flowers, fried blossoms, and pastry cups filled with creamed seafood.

And there, in the middle of the buffet table, for all to see and greet, and gag over, was the guest of honor. The head of a goat nestled in leaves on a silver tray. Its eyes glazed over, the mouth suitably clamped shut in dismay.

Blanche took a step back.

El Patrón smiled benignly. "She—and other family members—

gave their lives for a good cause. Don't you think?"

"Try to remember why we're here," Haasi whispered.

Guests were starting to line up and fill their plates. It was a fine time to get lost in the crowd.

Blanche and Haasi had purposely arrived fashionably late, after the fiesta got into full swing. It was good cover for the real reason they'd come to the party.

Chapter Twenty-Five

THE SHED

BLANCHE GRABBED A PLATE, helped herself to some nopal, and promptly scooted it aside. She remembered its gluey consistency now—sort of like the okra that Gran cooked in jambalaya, and Blanche had only managed to tolerate growing up. She selected some fruit and a skewer of roasted veggies. She smiled and chewed. She avoided El Patrón and Oleantha and pretended to be enjoying the fiesta even though she didn't know a soul in the crowd that milled in and out of the tent, and she could barely contain her anxiety. But she smiled and nodded, kept to herself. On the lookout for Haasi, who was gone on a mission. She was first up to do a recon of the house and grounds as best she could. It was to be a circular route, and then she was going to report back to Blanche, who would take a turn.

Step One: Should anyone ask, they were looking for the ladies' room. Blanche noticed that staff was scattered in every corner. The first phase of reconnaissance might prove difficult. Too many eyes on them.

"Your turn." Blanche jumped and a strawberry rolled off her plate. Haasi was back already.

"That was fast."

"Just preliminary. I couldn't get upstairs. Too many staffers hanging around, but I didn't see anything out of the ordinary. Maybe you ought to see about that kitchen again. You had your suspicions. Remember? And the dog? I don't see the dog anywhere."

"I'll be right back. Here." She thrust the plate at Haasi who stuffed a piece of melon into her mouth.

Blanche slid away toward the French doors, determined to have a good look around. There were so many rooms spread throughout the house, and she wanted to choose carefully. She remembered a flight of stairs off the patio, and found it, and climbed it to the balcony around the courtyard. She tried the doors. Four-poster beds, vases of lilies and roses, silks and satins and pillows like she'd never seen. Rugs that must have cost a fortune. No way Emilio would be stored away up here, she decided. Nor Oleantha's mummies and stolen art. Blanche was deflated.

She raced back down the stairs and retraced her steps toward the kitchen. The rooms on the ground floor were open to guests with views of the festivities, and it wouldn't do to waste time poking around there. Clutches of guests stood around with drinks, wandering drunkenly, swaying to the blast of horns. She slipped past them. She pushed the door open at the end of a long hallway into a near empty dining room, and there lying in a circular heap of reddish fur was Bella. She stood up and wagged her tail in greeting. Her sad eyes seemed to light up at Blanche's touch. "Oh, girl, where you been? We're having a party without you!"

"Gruff!" It was as if she understood. A soft acknowledgment, girl to girl. She stretched her neck for an extra pat. Blanche regained her sense of urgency. She stooped down next to Bella.

"Remember when I was here before?"

Bella cocked her head, nuzzled her snout under Blanche's hand.

"Tell me, Bella. Come on, let's take a walk."

At the word "walk," Bella did a little paw dance, and the wagging became more frantic. She took the lead, and Blanche followed her through the dining room, out to the portico, and into the kitchen. Oddly, the place was empty. Again. For a party of a hundred? Odd, indeed. Blanche ran her finger over the marble counter. Still dusty. The kitchen was a good distance from the fiesta, yet why would it be off limits?

"Let's go, girl."

Bella padded toward the back door of the kitchen. It was open. A shed stood off to the side, some forty feet away, in a small clearing of mesquite and cactus. It looked like an old maintenance shed, in fair condition. Painted wood slats, no windows, a large lock on the door. Blanche took a tentative step outside. Bella zipped past her, straight to the shed. She stood at attention, and whined.

Blanche's heart was beating so fast and hard she thought she'd faint. She knew what she'd find even before she found it.

She lifted the lock on the shed door. No way she'd get in here. She hoped for a window. She crept around the shed, Bella still on guard at the door making soft doggie sounds. The walls were sealed up tight, except for the rear wall. Weathering had opened cracks between the planks. The paint peeled, the wood splintered. Blanche pulled at one of the old boards and it broke away, opening a small window into the interior. She peered inside. A thin streak of sunlight beamed in. It was dark, but it appeared to be empty of equipment. No mowers, tools, mechanics of any kind. Blanche craned her neck. Only a stool and a shelf. In the corner was a cot, and on the cot a shape. A mound, a dirty blanket, some movement.

Bella had been at Blanche's side. Now she ran around to the front of the shed and started to bark. A major personality change in the dog. She went from sweet to sassy to downright, well, angry. Then Blanche heard it. Someone was working the lock on the door. "¡Callate!" A male voice snarled. "¡Carajo!" Bella growled. Blanche crouched down below the broken plank and waited.

The door creaked open. Blanche peered between the cracks. A wide man stood against the sunlight, a black shadow. Blanche could feel the blast of meanness from where she hid. He went over to the cot, put a boot up against the side, and shoved it against the wall. "Coño."

The shape on the cot moved, in slow waves, the face, streaked with dirt and reddened with misery, raised above the blanket. Emilio! Blanche gasped, then caught herself. She flattened on the ground. Bella was still barking. Thank God for that. No one had heard Blanche, choking on fury and curled at the base of the wall.

"Acá. Toma." The wide man threw a plate on the ground next to the cot. Beans and tortillas. He set a jar of liquid (water?) on the stool.

Blanche heard the man lock the door and go tramping off outside the kitchen. Bella kept up the barking. At one point, she squealed. Blanche clutched in anger at the prospect the man had kicked the dog, and she was so furious that Emilio was locked in the shed. She couldn't see straight. *But I have to see straight. I have to do the right thing here.*

She peeked around the side of the shed. The man lingered there at the back door of the kitchen, drinking from a flask. He looked like the one who'd surprised them in the lab, but she couldn't be sure. She needed to steer clear. And she had to figure a way to get Emilio out of the shed. At the moment, she was caught in the dilemma; an escape seemed impossible.

She waited, crouched on the ground. She had to get away. And find Haasi. And tell Cardenal. And get back here. She was sweating. The party food and beer churned away, and she thought she'd vomit.

Bella was still yapping. Boots pounded into the brush. She was still terrified he'd find her. Instead, he seemed to be walking away. Blanche could hear the zipper, the man relieving himself. He was a distance from the shed. Bella backed off and stopped barking. Blanche whistled gently, and the dog immediately turned and ran to Blanche's side. She lay down. Blanche ran her fingers over the fur on Bella's neck and down her flank. Bella whined softly. Blanche's anger spiked at the sign of obvious bruising on the dog's back, but Bella snuggled up with a sigh of comfort. She didn't stay. The man was moving again. Bella shot off after him. Barking.

Chapter Twenty-Six

WAKE-UP CALL

HAASI WAS INFLICTING HER SPANISH on an elderly lady with high-teased hair and a ton of jangling bracelets. Blanche had rarely seen her cousin so animated. The woman was laughing. "¡*Claro, claro!*" She held a goblet of foamy liquid that sloshed every time she threw her head back. Fortunately, they stood on the edge of the crowd. The host and hostess were nowhere to be seen.

Blanche sidled up to the edge of the group, smiled at the laughing woman, and pulled on Haasi's shirt. The woman threw out one more titter and drifted away.

"Criminy. What happened to you? Where have you been?" Haasi still smiled, trying to mask her alarm.

Blanche was red and sweaty, her dress flecked with burrs and dirt. "That's a lot of questions. I'll tell you later. We have to get out of here. *NOW.*"

"What the hell, Blanche?"

"No goodbyes, we gotta talk. Plan something!"

Haasi kept the smile plastered on her face and drew Blanche further off to the side. She knew, like she always did, when to stop and look both ways. "Blanche. Wait. I'm guessing you found something. Major. Now how's that going to look if we disappear?

We have to do this right." She was nearly hissing under her breath. "Go to the ladies and pull yourself together and meet me near the double doors."

"Seriously, Haas, we need to go."

"Yeah, but we can't draw suspicion. You have news written all over your face, and it can hold for ten minutes."

Blanche headed to the powder room. The young attendant jumped when Blanche burst in the door, but she resumed her calm and handed Blanche a linen towel. "¿*Señorita, está bien*?"

"Oh, sí, sí." Blanche looked in the mirror, the wig askew, and the glasses coated with dust. "Oh, I'm real *bien*."

Haasi was standing next to Oleantha. "Please, our gracias to the *Señor*, and to you. A lovely party."

Blanche appeared at her side. "Oh, yes, lovely. Thank you so much." She could barely contain herself, and, fortunately, Oleantha was likewise distracted. And half in the bag. She held a small crystal glass, nearly full, with a wedge of lime perched on the rim, and her eyes were a glazed deep blue, darkened with the fervor of too much liquor and fiesta. Blanche was fairly giddy they could make their goodbyes quickly.

Haasi looped arms with Blanche, and spoke softly. "Smile."

They made it out the front door, past the valet, and headed at a walk-run straight down the path of laurel trees. The car was parked off to the side of the road in a secluded spot.

"Tell," said Haasi.

"Emilio," she said. Out of breath. They were almost to the car. She reached for the door handle. "I found Emilio."

"You *what*?" Haasi's hands were on the wheel, but her eyes were huge with shock.

"Yes. *What*." Blanche's head bounced off the head rest. "What the hell are we going to do? We have to get him out of there."

"Where is he?"

"In a maintenance shed of some sort. Behind the kitchen."

"You couldn't let him out?"

"He wasn't exactly dressed for a fiesta. Locked up, lying on a cot in the dark, filthy. He appeared to be nearly out of his mind. Oh my God!" Blanche buried her face in her hands. "The dog started barking. One of those goons showed up with a plate of beans and then hung around. I was lucky he didn't see me."

"One of our kidnapper amigos?"

"Couldn't tell. Except he was very wide and very ugly and not in a good mood."

They sat in the car, in a patch of mesquite and scrub, and stared out the windshield.

"We have to get to Cardenal. Now. Do you have his number?"

"No, and my phone's out," said Haasi.

Blanche was near tears, and Blanche was not the crying type; she was a rager when she got upset. Haasi squeezed her arm. In unison, they both took a deep breath.

"What have they done to him? But the bigger question is, why haven't they killed him? That's good, and not so good," said Blanche.

"You're right. They haven't killed him. That's very good, B."

"We're right back to *what* and *why*?"

"You have any ideas?"

"You bet I do."

"I mean, that don't involve guns, knives, poison, and explosives."

Blanche looked over at Haasi. "Got any?"

"Not on me."

"Come on, Haas. We have to go back. The bad guy should be gone by now, and I can handle the doggy." Now Blanche's teeth were grinding with anger. And revenge. "We just can't leave him there."

"Psssst. Emilio!" Blanche's face was framed in the opening of broken boards at the rear of the shed. She made a concerted effort to be calm and comforting and keep from losing her mind. She could hear the faint strains of the mariachi band in the distance. At least she had the cover of fiesta on her side. For now. "*Emilio!*"

The blanket on the cot moved, an arm appeared. Then nothing.

She tried again, now desperate to get his attention. Haasi crouched fifteen feet away behind a barrel, keeping watch. She signaled to Blanche, thumbs up. So far, so good.

"Emilio, can you hear me? *Please.*"

Now his face appeared above the blanket, his eyes were shot red with fright and surprise. "Blanche!"

"Oh, Emilio. What have they done to you?"

He sat up, with great effort, and scratched his head. He had several day's growth on his face, and along with the streaks of dirt, he was almost unrecognizable. But then he smiled. "Blanche? A blonde Blanche?"

Blanche melted at the smile, that he was alive. She was so relieved she thought she'd fall down. "A little disguise. I've been snooping around, looking for you. Come on, you have to get up and get out of there!"

"Blanche, no. They gave me drugs. They'll be back. You have to leave. Now. They cannot find you here. And I know Haasi's out there. In the weeds, in the bushes. Please, leave now, when you can." He rolled off the cot and tried to stand, but his legs wouldn't hold him. He wore boxer shorts and a ripped T-shirt and nothing on his feet. It was all Blanche could do to keep from pouring herself through the hole in the wall to hold him. Wash his face, dress him. He sank down next to the cot, his arm resting on the edge. He looked like he'd lost twenty pounds. In only a few days?

"Emilio. Get up! Come on."

"No, Blanche. I can't stand up."

She ripped and pulled at the boards, her arms straining. Her palms were full of splinters. "I'll help you!"

"Listen, Blanche. Stop. I have to find out what they want. I can't believe I'm awake and I'm not dead."

She stopped grunting and yanking at the boards. "What?"

"They haven't... killed me. Maybe they won't. They want something. I need to find out what it is." He managed a smile. "Blanche, it is good to see you. I don't know. I like the hair...*un poquito*."

"Emilio, listen to me. What do you think they want?" She was leaning half into the shed, yearning to reach him.

"I don't know. Yet. *Por Dios*, Blanche, you have to get out of here. I mean it. Where's Haas?"

"She's keeping watch. They're having some art fiesta at the main house. They'll probably leave you alone for now."

"Art fiesta? With all the art that is missing..." He drifted off, his head hit the cot. He lifted it again and smiled. "I have to find out. Now, go. And be safe."

"I can't leave you here."

"I'll be all right. For now. They didn't kill me. I need to find out..."

"We're going to call Cardenal."

But he didn't move. He'd passed out, half on the cot, half on the floor.

Blanche slumped, pulled back, and ripped a large hole in the dress. It wasn't fair. She looked like she'd been partying hard, but she'd not had any fun at all. She wanted to strangle the host.

Blanche and Haasi scooted around the edge of property, Blanche thanking God and all the angels that the house wasn't fenced in with barbed wire and Rottweilers. The only barrier was a four-foot stucco wall that ran across most of the front. They ran off to the edge of the property and skirted it easily. By the time they arrived back at the car, they were covered in grass, dirt, and tiny seedpods. Blanche's legs were scratched and bleeding from holly bushes and cactus.

They sat in the front seat, panting and out of breath. "You know we're just gonna have to go back there again. Probably tomorrow," said Haasi.

"Yes, but I'm not going to wear my party dress. At least not this one." She tugged at a sweaty, ripped sleeve. "And I'm gonna bring reinforcement."

Chapter Twenty-Seven

THE PROPOSITION

EMILIO HAD NO IDEA WHAT TIME IT WAS. Only that it was pitch black, and he couldn't hear a sound, except for the occasional slithering wild life and cicadas and the low howl of a four-legged creature. He sat bolt upright on the cot. He was surprisingly clear-headed after days of what? Knockout drugs? Bug-infested beans? A cot with so many lumps he would have been better off sleeping on the ground?

His mind was going in circles. He was sure he'd seen Blanche. But a blonde Blanche? Why hadn't she opened the door? All he remembered were the green eyes and she was angry and she said she'd be back. He could hardly remember anything. His brain was so foggy. *I hope she brings the key, or a crowbar. And a bottle of water.* But, no, he didn't want her here. It was too dangerous. He had to figure a way to get out of here, especially before she came back and got herself into this mess.

His eyes adjusted to the light. At the rear wall, a rectangle shined blue-black against the night. He swung his legs off the cot and started across the dirt floor, only to lose his balance and wobble to the ground. He stumbled to his feet and threw himself against the wall. An opening. He felt along the boards. They were thin and weak. Old and weathered. He pulled at the edge of the opening and a board came loose.

Then it struck him. He couldn't have been dreaming. Blanche had been here. He'd seen her face framed in the wall. He smiled at the thought. He couldn't imagine her without the riot of black curls. But there she was. A blonde Blanche.

They had talked. *I have to find out what they want.*

He looked around frantically at the cot and the dirt floor, and he panicked. He had to get out of there. He didn't want to wait around to find out what they wanted, but he had to do that. Isn't that what he and Blanche talked about? He was conflicted, and confused, and half out of his mind. If they find me on the road like this, in my boxers, looking like an escaped loco, it's going to be hard to talk my way back home.

He wanted her safe, and he wanted out of there before they came back and shot him up again with more of those drugs. Made him paralytic, wiped out his mind again. He needed his mind, and he wanted to get back to medicine and helping people, but he was wondering about even doing that with all the crazies running around out there. He raked his hair, rubbed the filthy growth on his face.

He groped at the bedding, on the ground, looking for his boots and pants and shirt. He found them rolled in a ball under the cot. He quickly got dressed. Now he felt strength seeping into his bones, a will to survive. He stood up and stretched. He took deep breaths, bent over, and exhaled. He went back to the door. Locked. Then back to the boards at the back wall. He pulled. Snap! A board came away and almost knocked him over. He pulled at another, rocking it back and forth until it popped loose. He could just about climb through the hole.

He heard a dull sound behind him. A metallic sound of chain and lock and key. Someone had lifted the lock and was fumbling with it. A visitor.

"Going somewhere?"

Emilio held the jagged board. It had old rusty nails in it. He was just about to greet his visitor with it when he saw the gun. The door hung open and it was dark in the interior of the shed, but not so much that he didn't see the flash of grey metal. He dropped the board. Anger spiked in his chest, in his brain, and he struggled to contain it. He wanted to live. He needed to get out of there. Intact. "Enough," he said, taking one step toward the visitor. "What the hell is going on?"

"*Dios mío.* We are impatient. Sit down. *Calla.*" The visitor yanked on a cord and the light bulb flashed on. The old craggy face, the glittery dark eyes were familiar, but he couldn't attach a name to his captor. His aspect was truly something out of a horror movie, and Emilio wanted to end it. The visitor waved the gun toward the cot and leaned against a stool next to the door. Emilio fell back on the cot.

"How do you feel?"

"Great. How would you feel?" Emilio clasped his hands between his knees and stared at his host. "Who are you?"

"I am Rodrigo Ortiz de Avila, and you are Emilio Sierra Del Real. Sometimes I am called El Patrón."

The introduction was chilling, as if the preliminaries had made the horror of the experience official.

El Patrón laughed. "I'm sorry we had to resort to these… arrangements. But you need to know we mean business."

"What business? This is no way to do business."

"Ah, you will be interested in what we do. And if you're not, well, we have means to convince you."

"Are you threatening me?" Emilio didn't raise his voice, but he was sick of the game, and he had nothing left to lose. If they were going to kill him, they'd have done it. He meant to force the situation. Yes, he was impatient, and he was getting angry again. He folded his arms and sat up straight.

"Oh, no, no. I do not threaten my employees. Especially ones who have valuable prospects." He studied Emilio. The compliment hung in the air, seemingly to soften the harsh edges in the tone of his voice.

Emilio didn't budge. He eyed his captor with a stony look.

"Let me tell you what I have in mind, and maybe you'll come around," said El Patrón. "I have a *business*. One might say it's a dangerous business. People get hurt. They need medical attention. We can't go to the medical authorities with our problems." He pushed off the stool slowly and paced the length of the shed. "And so, I need my own medical staff, if you will." He waved the gun carelessly, at times pointing it at Emilio who was becoming increasingly uncomfortable. On the discomfort meter, he was already about to explode.

They want me to be the gangster doc.

The idea of it hit him hard. They were serious. He'd been afraid, for an instant, that something like this was coming, and now he couldn't believe it when it was dumped in his lap. He wanted no part of their *business*. Emilio had not gone to medical school for this type of work. Let them go to the emergency room like everyone else—and get arrested. He needed to extricate himself from El Patrón's design.

But first, he needed to find out more. It was a fine line he walked, but he meant to make the information useful. He took a deep breath to steady himself. "Your recruitment methods are very bad."

"I do what is necessary."

"And if I decide to take you up on the offer?"

"Things will be very good for you. Nice apartment in DF, maybe a *casita* in Puerto Vallarta. Many benefits. We provide a full insurance policy too… the comforts."

Emilio felt a cool breeze, a window of opportunity opening. He had no interest in an apartment or beach house. But he did want to know about the *business,* and he didn't care how shaky was the ground he walked. "I understand you have a doctor. One Doctor Oleantha Flórez?" He stopped and waited to see what would come of that revelation.

"How would you know that?"

It was an impossible guess, a rumor, but Emilio took it. Knowledge was power. Maybe. "There is talk, at the medical school, about a woman doctor who helps the, er, cartel."

"Pfffft! Cartel! Scum. As I said, we are a business, and we need medical assistance." El Patrón's eye, even in the dim light, had an evil gleam. "Yes, the esteemed Doctor Flórez. We have used her... Employed her services." He took a step toward Emilio with the gun. "What more do you know of her?"

"Her name is around. She uses old lab facilities near the Palacio, and I hear she is involved in the arts." He almost choked on the last word.

"Sí." His face became a mask of displeasure. "But she is a woman who talks too much. Like many women. She is demanding, and, I'd say, costly in many ways. I have called upon her many times, but I find she is difficult to work with."

"What type of work?"

"You have just touched on it. The lab, arts." He cleared his throat, clearly brushing over the subject. "And she has assisted with wounds and other medical procedures, but the men are not happy. A beautiful woman poking around in their vitals. They like it to a point and then not so much. Even when dying of infection..." He shook his head with disgust. "Even if it means saving their lives. It does seem strange that someone bleeding on the ground would care if a woman doctor or a male doctor comes to help, but such is the case."

El Patrón resumed his pacing. Emilio couldn't move yet; he still had to take this one step at a time. He could practically see the balancing act going on inside El Patrón's head, wondering if he should reveal details of this *business* plan. Or not. "We have much work," he said. "You will see. We have a large project now. But aside from that, we need someone to attend to these, ahem, occasional knife wounds, broken limbs, gunshots…"

"A project?"

"*Sí*. An art project, if you will. But that is not your concern. Oleantha…" He stopped then. "We're moving forward. I believe you are suited for much of the work."

"*Señor*, I am from the country, a medical student. I don't have experience with the procedures you are talking about. These require emergency room equipment and staff, many different supplies and medications, access to long-term care…"

He cut him off. "We have all that. You will see, and you will learn. One reason I've selected you is that you are young, intelligent, and trainable. And you have few close relations and connections. We've checked on you. You can take it or leave it. I suggest you take it."

He hasn't mentioned Blanche…and Haasi. Thank God for that.

"But surely you can find a doctor who is eager to do your work. There are many…"

"I do not care to spend more time on this. I have influence, and I have found you. This is no accident. You should consider taking the offer. No, you *will* take the offer."

Emilio didn't look up. It was as if cold water had been thrown on him. But he was drained. He sat on the cot slumped over his knees, hands clenched. He had to ask: "How did you find me in that lab?"

"Ah, yes. The lab. We had been watching you, and when you took the young students on the tour, it was a perfect opportunity. Apparently, I am told they ran away. So be it. But we have you."

The young students! He thinks I was on a college tour! Emilio felt better already. Blanche and Haasi seemed to be in the clear. He almost smiled.

El Patrón took this as agreement. He stood next to the door

and folded his hands, his expression relaxed. "*Vamos a la casa,*" he said. "A nice meal, a shower? You don't look like a doctor now."

Emilio didn't look up.

Chapter Twenty-Eight

STAND-OFF

EMILIO BRACED HIMSELF AGAINST THE TILE WALL and let the hot water beat down. He didn't care how long he stood in that shower. Until his brain was fried, his skin was boiled. He couldn't think right now, and he didn't want to. Except he worried that Blanche was on the way, and he was afraid of what she might run into when she arrived. He prayed she'd called the police instead. Let that be the end of it. He didn't want her hurt, or involved any more. He had to handle this, and he had to get away from El Patrón.

For now, he had to play the game. He and Blanche were on the same track there.

He put on the white terry cloth robe and went into the bedroom. His host had not spared any expense on the decorating. Emilio's toes sank into a fur rug—whatever poor animal wore this, it had been well dressed. The four-poster was covered in a navy-blue damask silk bedspread with a dozen pillows in white, cream, and navy. The draperies opened to reveal a splash of purple bougainvillea climbing a white stucco wall behind a fountain. A jet of water shot from a shell in the hands of a naked goddess.

There was a soft knock on the door.

"*Señor. Buenas.*" A small round woman leaned over a side table

185

in the hallway and picked up a silver tray of fruit, coffee, and rolls and bread. She carried it in to the bedside table. "*Por favor, con permiso.*" She turned. "The clothing, *señor*. I will wash it."

"*Gracias.*" He looked down at the robe, then to her hand on the door, and she was gone. The bread was warm, the yeasty fragrance rushing to his head along with the scent of orange and papaya. The breeze lifted the sheer curtains under the heavy draperies and floated them into the room. He was only half awake. He fell back on the pillows and slept.

"Detective Cardenal!" Blanche's fists pounded his front door. She was furious.

She stepped back her arms taut at her sides. Footsteps stomped across the front hall inside the house, and the door burst open.

Cardenal stood there dressed in a red velvet robe, his normally sleek hair looked like he'd taken an eggbeater to it. "What in the name of God! What is happening?"

"We found him, all right. You've got to get out there, to El Patrón's. They're holding Emilio in a shed on the property. I found him during a fiesta. Today!"

"Slow down, Blanche. You what? What fiesta? You were out at El Patrón's? I thought we were going to discuss…"

Haasi sat in the car at the curb, her head craned toward the window, watching Blanche, and scanning the street. They'd made it out of the hacienda grounds and driven straight to the detective's house. It was near eleven o'clock at night.

"We wanted to spring him. But there are men walking around with guns. And there's a padlock on the shed. It's right outside the kitchen door," said Blanche. "Oh, thank you to that lovely Bella."

Cardenal scratched his head and gave it a good pat or two. "*Dios y todos los santos*, Blanche. Do not think of going back there. I will sort this out," he said. "And who is this Bella? Blanche, *tranquila, por favor!"*

"The dog. She led me back there. To the shed."

"You actually *saw* Emilio in a *shed*?"

"Yes, and an awful man and the plate of diseased beans, and Emilio was on a cot all filthy and bleary. He could hardly stand. Oh, I wish I hadn't left him there."

"I'll get the locals on it now. We can't wait on this one. You two get back to the hotel and stay there."

Emilio awoke to a ruckus of banging and shouting. *"Policía, policía!"*

He sat up on the bed, alarmed to find himself in this room. It was beautiful, luxurious, quite a change from the hog shed. He had no idea how he got here, then he remembered. Blanche! Fright shocked him awake, and thoughts of the awful threats of his host, the guy with the goatee. Now he could hear that voice, like old rubber twisting, faraway, talking in a steady hum.

It was late, the longest day he'd ever lived through, but he was still alive, and he wondered at that. He got off the bed, stiff and sluggish, and went to the door. El Patrón was droning on in a low, somewhat agitated, voice. "…of course, but I don't understand. We were having a fiesta and there were many people about the grounds."

"The report is from DF. About the detainment on these premises."

"But I have not detained anyone. I am sure everyone has left the property."

"The only details we have involve a man. Under lock and key. Here on this property." The voice was staccato, demanding and piercing.

"That is absurd. No such man is here."

The cold tile under Emilio's feet revived him. He slipped down the hallway and stood at the top of a gleaming oak stairway. A blazing chandelier in the entry shed broken bits of light on the exchange between the two policemen and El Patrón.

Emilio decided right then what card to play.

"*Buenas, señores. ¿Qué pasa?*" Emilio took a few steps down and stopped.

The three turned and looked up the stairwell at him. Emilio had shaved and combed back his hair. A tall man with the look of an Aztec prince—in a terry cloth robe. He smiled at them. No one moved.

He took another step down, a hand casually resting on the polished banister. "Is there a problem?"

El Patrón crossed his arms, his mouth clamped in a grim smile.

"We have this report." The tall policeman held a clipboard with papers. He and his partner wore shorts to just above the knee and snug caps.

"I heard," said Emilio. "There may be some misunderstanding. You see, the fiesta. It was a good time. Probably too good, for me. I had a lot to drink and fell asleep outside." He shrugged "In a shed, I'm embarrassed to say. It happens."

His host was stone-faced. Not a hair, not a facial muscle moved. The arms stayed crossed, the feet planted far apart. He stared at his guest.

The policemen looked Emilio up and down. The short one said, "A locked shed?"

"Are you certain of that? I am standing here, after all."

"We are going to look around. Just the same. *¿Con permiso?*" He tipped his head slightly at El Patrón.

"Of course." El Patrón nonchalantly waved an arm and stepped back.

The policemen ascended the stairs to begin the search, from top to bottom, and Emilio moved aside. He and El Patrón locked eyes, both of them wary in the game.

It was well after midnight. Emilio and El Patrón sat in the drawing room, each of them nursing a brandy. Ana set a tray of cheese, meat, chiles, and a basket of fresh bread on the coffee table in front of Emilio. He was ravenous. He couldn't remember when he'd last eaten. But he only picked at the bread. He meant to practice calm, and discipline. *I need it.*

El Patrón had hardly said a word since the police left—empty-handed and blustering about "false alarms." They'd found the shed and the blanket, and a lock on the door. No trace of any kidnapping or other accusations.

"Thank you for your hospitality," said Emilio, a rueful smile on his lips. "I will be leaving in the morning."

"It is morning. A new day." He studied Emilio. "*Toma, toma.*" He shoved the tray closer to Emilio and sat back, took a sip of the brandy.

"Yes, a new day. And like I say, I will be leaving in the morning. *Pronto.*"

El Patrón tapped his fingertips. "Of course. I know where to find you."

Chapter Twenty-Nine

PILLOW TALK

BLANCHE AND HAASI SAT ON THE PATIO at the hotel, waiting for Cardenal to call about Emilio. They hadn't heard anything. The detective had said the local police would go immediately to El Patrón's hacienda. Blanche felt confident, but she could not sit for one more second.

No news is good news? Or is it the other way around? She wrung her hands and paced.

Haasi was reading Carmen Amato's *Hat Dance.* "Bang, you need to relax."

"I can't. Oh, I wish I'd sprung him when I had the chance."

"Well, you'd be chained up on that cot right along with him. Or worse."

Blanche threw herself on the chair next to Haasi. "They'll find him, don't you think?"

"Of course." But her voice was heavy with caution. "The way these people do business is frightening. We need to wrap it up and get out of here."

"But I love it here, except for the occasional glitch..."

"The occasional glitch? This place is Glitch City. Yes, most of it has been great and I love it, but I love you more. You keep going deeper into this mummy-art-theft-abduction hole, and I'm no help. Enough, already." Haasi tented the book on the table. "You've been down that road of terror, and you were lucky to get out. That was only last year when those thugs picked you up and dumped you in the desert. Jeez, that could have ended very badly. Bang, relax. Your blood pressure, your stress levels."

Blanche stared at Haasi. "Well, that was quite a… summation?"

Haasi went back to her reading. She loved a good detective story, but she didn't want to be in one. "This is real enough, Blanche." She waved the book at her.

"Well, this stuff we're dealing with is fur-ril." She pulled at the topknot. Curls tumbled down over her eyes.

"That's a good look. See no evil."

Blanche resumed pacing.

And then the door swung open from the lobby and there he was. Standing in front of her.

"Emilio!" She took a tentative step toward him and fell into his arms. He smelled of soap, and his cheek was smooth. She ran her fingers down the side of his face. She couldn't take her eyes off him.

He grinned. "I'm back. From hell. Where is the blonde Blanche? I liked that."

"Don't tease. Just take the old Blanche. OK?" Her head fell against his chest. They stood there and didn't move. A bird chittered, Haasi was chuckling.

He looked over at Haasi and smiled. "Hey."

"Hey, yourself. Welcome back."

"It's good to be." He took Blanche by her shoulders and kissed her forehead. "I have to go back to Tepequito today, but I needed to see you."

"Here I am. Waiting and worrying."

Haasi stood up. "I'll say. Enough with the crazies. You all right? Really?" She tilted her head one way, and then the other. Satisfied, she smiled. "Uh-huh. You look just fine. More than fine,

I'd say." With that, she picked up her book and her camera. "See ya, I'm headed to the Zocalo."

"What happened," Blanche took his hands, "since I found you there?" They collapsed on a loveseat under the ficus. The sun streaked across the patio, a few tiny brown birds flitted on the lower branches.

"When the police arrived, I was asleep in the main house, all cleaned up, and wearing a terry cloth robe. Breakfast on a silver tray."

"Well, now. I was worried, and you end up like you're at the Four Seasons."

Emilio shook his head. "Not exactly. El Patrón. He's, how you say, *slick.*"

"Well, that's an understatement." She still held his hands.

"*Señor* Detective Cardenal will not be happy when he gets complaints from his *compadres* in the Huehuetoca police detail. They didn't find anything."

"I'm just glad you're out of there, and they didn't hurt you." Her voice rose, she looked him up and down. "They didn't, did they?"

"I'm all right." He kissed her on the eyebrow.

"Emilio, what did they want? Why did they keep you locked up?"

"You were right. They want something, and I don't want any of that business."

"What?"

"Gangster doc?" The look on his face was so un-gangster that Blanche laughed.

"Oh, right. You're just the type."

"No, I'm serious, and El Patrón doesn't take no for an answer. He said he will find me. He knows where I am."

"Oh, great." She sat back her gaze still fastened on him. "What are you going to do?"

"Play with them. For now. I don't have many options. Besides, I think other things are happening. He mentioned a project. Such as, an art project. Sound familiar?"

"Yeah, and his lady friend might be just the one who knows all about that." Blanche had a faraway look in her eye, her thoughts drifting off to places where others had to run to catch up.

"Blanche, please. Just let it be. The *policía* will take care of it."

"Oh sure. That's worked so well 'til now." Her eyes snapped back to him. "Emilio, you look so tired."

"I am. I think I want to lie down." A half-grin played on his lips.

She smiled, a slow, loving, concerned—hungry?—smile. She kissed him gently, and one thing led to another. Escalation. Yes, she felt like she was on an escalator, going up up up. The loveseat wouldn't do. She took his hand. "Come on. I know just the place."

They hardly fit on that twin bed, but they didn't care since they were so tangled in the sheets and wrapped up together in one bundle, they couldn't fall off. "Do you feel like a mummy?" Blanche traced her finger over his aquiline nose. She loved that nose.

He laughed. "*Pues, sí*, I do. I could stay like this for a thousand years." He smiled a lazy smile at her. "Here we are, returned to the mummy thing."

"Not exactly like those poor people in the floor of the Palacio."

"No, nothing like that. I say you are very lively."

He kissed her again, and she responded. And then when their heads flopped against the one pillow, they lay like that, drifting.

She lost track of time, but then time caught up. She untangled herself and shot up in the bed. "Emilio! I need to pay that woman a visit."

"¿*Qué*?" He was half asleep. "Who, Blanche? Lie down, *por favor*. Do not go visiting that woman. Or anyone." His arm came out of the blanket and wrapped around her.

She turned and kissed him lightly on the forehead. Looked him in the eye. "You said El Patrón mentioned a project. The lab. Arts. Don't you see? It does get back to her. And him, this El Patrón."

"I suppose, but let it alone, Blanche. I'm back and safe, and so are you and Haasi. The authorities can solve the little problems."

"They're not solving anything." She was out of the bed and pulling on clothes. Emilio could see the heat rising in her like he was watching a thermometer. "Those people kidnapped you. And held Haasi and me. And they killed Amparo's daughter. There's more there."

"The daughter of Amparo?" He was half sitting, a look of confusion in his dark eyes.

"Yes, that one. Our new mummy. The Lady of the Pink Hair Clip. These people are crooked as hell. Listen, I want to get over to see Oleantha. Before she tries to clean up her act."

"Her act? This isn't some drama play, Blanche. You have to get out of it."

"I have to find out more about their project."

"*Por Dios*." He fell back on the pillow. "What am I going to do with you?"

"You have done quite enough with me already, *mi corazón*." She gave him a kiss on the temple. "I'm going to leave Haasi a note on the door, and I'll call you later. In the meantime, if your gracious host at the 'Four Seasons' hacienda contacts you, see what else you can find out."

"Ah, Blanche." He put an arm across his forehead. One eye peeking out at her. "*Mi Blanquita*. Be careful. Pay your visit and get out and come back. Call me."

She was fitting the blonde wig over the black curls. The cat-eye glasses. "How do I look?"

He smiled. "Why do you ask me that?" He started after her, the sheet wrapped around his middle, as he stumbled off the bed. She dodged, grabbed her bag, and headed toward the door. But not before she threw her arms around him and kissed his neck and squeezed. "I'll be seeing you."

Chapter Thirty

CROOKED BOOK

THE DOCTOR WORE A BLUE SILK WRAP DRESS with gold buckle, huge gold hoop earrings, and five-inch gold leather heels with wide T-straps. Everything about her seemed "golden." Blanche watched her through the window of the clinic as she moved around her desk and over to a wall of glass shelves. *One chic chick.* Blanche was no match for that. She pulled at her jean jacket, smoothed the leg of the slim-fit pants. At least the outfit was newish, secondhand designer, from the resale shop near the hotel. And the wig was top of the line…

Blanche pushed through the door of the clinic as the doctor lifted a bottle of pink liquid and lined it up with the others. She turned and smiled when she saw Blanche. "*¡Hola, chica! ¿Como estás?*" She descended on Blanche in a wave of heady fragrance. Sandalwood? Clove?

"Doctor Flórez, I just wanted to thank you for the wonderful fiesta. The food, the drinks, the music! It was all such fun. It was a wonderful party."

"Ah, it was our pleasure," she said.

"Yes, you and *Señor* de Avila. So gracious." Blanche swallowed. She was the worst at keeping a straight face.

"I do enjoy a good party." She clicked another bottle in place on the shelf and walked to her desk. "I could tell you enjoyed it. Your friend, Haasi, is it? She seemed so calm. And lovely. She talked quite a bit about your journalism and your life in Florida. It sounds so..." She stopped, looked at the ceiling, and waved her fingers in the air. "...idyllic."

Blanche did not want to talk about Florida; she wanted to talk about Mexico, specifically Doctor Oleantha. There was no question the doctor loved the subject.

"I'd say Mexico is idyllic in its own way. A different way than I've ever seen, and I'm enjoying every minute of it."

Oleantha folded her hands, the long fingers encumbered with many gold rings. An emerald here, an opal there. "I am glad you are enjoying yourself." Blanche saw a chink in the façade of heavy make-up. The typical warmth of most of the Mexicans she'd met did not shine through.

Blanche seated herself at the bench near the desk. "The fiesta. Tell me, how did you ever pull such an event together? All the flowers, the food. Everything. I'd love to know!"

"It was nothing. Just a bit of planning. And Rodrigo's money." She laughed, clicking her nails on the desktop. "And Haasi? Where is she today?"

"She's taking more pictures at the park. You know, we are actually working on a travel article. That's part of the reason I wanted to visit with you."

"A travel article? In the newspaper?" Oleantha glanced in the corner at a woman who had come in and was sifting through a basket of herbs. She leaned in toward Blanche. "Well, maybe just one photo. Or two."

"For our hometown newspaper, but sometimes they syndicate stories. Haasi would love to photograph you..."

At this, Oleantha actually patted her hair. Blanche was astounded at how far flattery could go with this woman. She had to take advantage.

"I'll check on that photo op," said Blanche. "And I have some questions for the article. You're so involved with the arts, and I'd love to get your perspective. You must have other projects in the works! Right? And it seems *Señor* de Avila is a bit of a patron." She was running at the mouth, Bang at her best.

Oleantha smiled, but it was plastic. Fake. "Yes, a patron, our Patrón." She appeared to be considering the statement. "He has been supportive, no doubt, and I've worked closely with him." She patted her hair again, twisted a ring. "Forgive me. Can I get you something?" She picked up an exquisite china cup on the desk. "Tea, perhaps?"

"Oh, no, thank you. I'm good." Blanche opened her notebook, shifting on the bench. She tried to relax. "About the arts. In general. Do you have a favorite period? Or artist?"

"Of course, you have seen the Mayan exhibit at the Palacio? *Fabuloso.* We have been so fortunate to have this collection. *Señor* de Avila has been instrumental in bringing it to us. But, I must say, he has relied on my expertise…"

The woman in the corner dropped a glass bottle, and the liquid spread across the tile, sending the aroma of herbs like cut grass into the air. Oleantha shot out of her chair. "¡*Idiota!*" She hissed under her breath. She glanced at Blanche. "That is off the record."

Blanche forced a smile.

Oleantha's high heels clicked across the floor. She thrust a box of tissues at the woman. It was clear that the doctor was not about to help with the cleanup.

Blanche was already swabbing at the spill. She shrugged her shoulders at the woman, but she didn't respond. Her face was cast on the floor, her features hidden under the cap. It was odd she didn't say a word… Oleantha watched from behind her desk, one golden shoe tapping. "*Bueno. ¿Ya?*"

Blanche was far from finished with the mess, and the interview. She leapt up and dropped the balls of tissue in a wastebasket.

The woman scooted out the door. Blanche watched her, a catch in her throat, and she didn't know why she felt like that. A wave of desperation swept over her. Things were happening around her, fast. Opportunity was slipping away. She was on the edge of discovery, and she couldn't jump away. Not yet.

"After all, I would love a bottle of water, if it wouldn't trouble you," said Blanche.

A tremor of irritation flit across Oleantha's face. "Certainly." She disappeared to the back of the clinic.

Blanche quickly lifted the corner of the ledger on the desk. Rows and rows of inventory. Herbs, lotions, treatments. She let the cover drop and scooted backward to the bench. She opened her notebook. Oleantha returned with a bottle of water. Blanche took a welcome swig, wishing it were tequila.

"Art? You were saying, doctor."

"Yes, the Mayans. *Muy interesante*, this collection. It will soon move to Paris, and the Palacio director is working on coordinating the showing."

"Is there a lot of interest in Mexican art in Europe?" Blanche took a moment to contain her expression. She cursed her inability to wear a poker face. *Is that where all this stuff is going?*

"*Claro*. Much interest. We have a large market…"

"A large market?"

Oleantha stood up. Blanche kept her eyes on her notebook. "Just wondering," she blurted. "Have you heard anything about art theft at the Palacio? And from other places around the city?"

Oleantha thrust her chin out and retreated, like she'd been swatted. Blanche was reminded of a small, cornered animal. "Why do you ask? What does that have to do with a travel article?"

Blanche mentally kicked herself in the head. She sucked in her breath. She had to slow down. She smiled. "I'm interested in art, studied it in college. Haasi and I went to the exhibit…" *Shut up, Blanche.*

"Yes, the exhibit," she said. Twitchy, in one eye. Her fingers tapping on the desktop.

Clearly, Blanche had reached the end of the interview. A door had slammed shut. She inclined her head as if to extract a line, a hint, a bit more information, but this one was done. Blanche glanced at the ledger before she could stop herself. She thought of a book she'd once read, and Oleantha was that book: She had a very fancy cover and the pages inside just didn't make any sense. Her work in the clinic did not seem to match her rumored expertise in patching up gangsters and making mummies.

"You might reach out to the director at the Palacio. I'm sure he'd be helpful," said Oleantha. She picked up her phone.

Blanche packed away her notebook. Before she entirely pissed off the exquisitely strange Doctor Flórez. She kept smiling. "*Gracias por todo.*"

"It was nice seeing you again, *Señorita* Blanche, and now I must get to work. *Señor* Blussberg, I believe, is coordinating the next phase of the Mayan exhibit. He has other details about *art*. Do call him."

Chapter Thirty-One

GONNA TAKE
A LITTLE TRIP

"Where are you?" Doctor Oleantha Flórez's voice stabbed at his eardrum, the sound of it like a hot steel poker. He held the phone away, and frowned. He sat up in the front seat and wished he were anywhere but in her vicinity.

"I'm in the truck, like most days, awaiting your orders, *Señora* Doctor." He settled his aggrieved stomach by answering as best he could. It would do no good to prolong this conversation. He liked talking to her as little as possible.

"You see her? The small blonde leaving the clinic? Cat-eye glasses, jean jacket? Follow her," Oleantha hissed. "Teach her a lesson. *El cuatro, no el primero. ¿Comprendes?*"

"*Sí.*" El Jefe heaved a sigh. He'd been looking forward to a peaceful afternoon, a nice late *comida*, an early retreat with Luisa Lu. And now this? It was a job, one which he was getting sick of, and if he tried to get out of it, it would be the last thing he ever did. He put the truck in gear, and drove it slowly while he followed the girl. She was walking at a pretty good clip, and he wanted to make his move at exactly the right moment.

The fourth lesson, not the first. Her call for a no-kill. Instead, a frightening shake-up. Sometimes that shake-up didn't work out so well. But he tried. He followed the damn orders and hoped he kept his head in the bargain.

It was a quiet, tree-lined street, not a lot of cars. Not a lot of people. He kept the pace at a discreet distance. Up ahead, he saw his opportunity. He swerved toward the curb, grabbed the sack in the back seat, and jumped out the door. The bag was over her head and she was on the floor of the truck in about five seconds. The man was on the heavy side but light on his feet. He was good at his job; he'd had a lot of practice.

The girl sat up on the floor of the truck. She hadn't said a word, but he could sense her wild fear when he grabbed her. She'd let out a yelp, but he'd jammed the sack into her mouth and told her to shut up. The sack was pretty worthless for anything except to muffle her scream and prevent witnesses from identifying her. Should there be any. He was careful there weren't. He wore a hat and dark glasses. The license on the truck was another matter, but he was sure he'd avoided that complication. In any event, there were people who were paid to take care of those slipups. That wasn't his worry. *Just pick her up and unload her.* Short and sweet.

He told her to shut up, again. He didn't know a lot of English, but he knew *Shut the hell up.* She was a smart girl. She didn't make a sound. At first.

Blanche was frozen in terror, and then the thaw began. She started kicking the back door of the truck, and the front seat. The back of the truck had been retrofitted. Dark glass all around, a partition between front and back, and no seats in the rear. She tried to stand, but he was driving so fast she couldn't get her bearings. It wouldn't do any good. She'd whipped the bag off her head first thing, but she couldn't see much of anything. The outlines of the streets of Mexico City were vanishing. She had a vague idea of where she was, and what good did that do? Didn't he stop at lights or stop signs? She'd noticed drivers did little of that. He seemed to be taking a lot of side streets, zigzagging, and she was about to vomit from his driving, if not from fear. She braced herself, rocketing along in a dark capsule, a demon of a vehicle. American-made, no doubt. Thank you, Mr. Dodge Ram.

She sat on the floor, teeth grinding, and dug into the carpet with her fingernails. Carpet! She raked some of the fibers off the floor and put them in her pocket. If she ever escaped, proof, and if she didn't make it out alive, maybe they'd find the fibers. She'd watched too many cop shows, but crimes had been solved on less. She sat still, deflated and desperate. She still had her brain. She listened hard to the road ahead. The sounds of traffic diminishing and thinning. She'd been in the truck at least an hour. It was hard to tell in the emotion of it, but it seemed they were out of the city and flying down a highway. Maybe on the way back to El Patrón's shed, and that awful cot. A dirt floor. It wasn't exactly the best accommodations. She thought of Emilio, and where would he be? Back in Tepequito? He'd be furious, and what good would that do?

What the hell good does any of this do?

Her only hope was Haasi. She'd left that note on the door when she left Emilio, that she was going to visit La Escandolera. To thank her for the lovely fiesta, and now this.

Thanks a lot, Doctor Dearest.

It had to be Oleantha who set up this little trip. She'd cooled off toward the end of their meeting, and she'd bridled at the questions. But abduction? Blanche's mind raced. She'd walked out, and the guy had been *right there*. Whammo. Blanche had been down this road before. Kidnapped in Florida by those drug-running goons. She was not inured to kidnapping, but this was serious, and she was scared. She didn't want to admit it, but she was. She had to focus on the positive if she wanted to get out of this. The good thing was, number one, she wasn't dead. Yet. And number two, if she used her wits she just might save herself. She sat cross-legged on the floor, wedged between the side door and the front seat, and she started thinking. And listening.

They were definitely on a highway. The road was smooth. The semi-trucks blared and the roar diminished to a point in the distance, and then another and another. The sound waves and the rocking back and forth worked on her nerves. Highway 57 ran out of the city. She and Haasi had taken that way to El Patrón's, and to Carmen and Eddie's. It hadn't taken long before the landscape changed dramatically from urban to rural, and the sounds outside the truck were eerily familiar. Oh, she missed Haasi. They were so good at digging themselves out of shit. But Blanche didn't want to dwell on it. She had to figure it out. She had to stay strong. *Well, I am strong. I would love to scratch that mother trucker's eyes out.*

The truck veered off the highway on to a small, bumpy road. Her panic spiked, and then she stopped herself. Panic was wasted energy. She let the anger take over, the fuel that would push her to survive.

She didn't have much time. The truck would stop, and he would open that door, and pull her out, and then she had no idea what would happen, but it wouldn't be good. She put the future out of her mind; she had to focus on the present.

Holy crap! She remembered. She was still wearing her purse, a small flat one that fit under her jacket, hidden from pickpockets, murderers, and kidnappers. She prayed she'd brought that cell phone. She fumbled inside. No such luck, and then…

A pen!

OMG. Thank you, God.

The pen is mightier than the sword.

It better be today.

She grasped the pen. It was a beautiful Cross, a sterling silver classic ballpoint, that Cap had given her when she got her first newspaper job. Reporter at Large. Which was pretty funny considering she weighed a hundred pounds and the newspaper had a circulation of less than five thousand. But she loved the job, and Cap. Oh, thank you, dear Cap, once again. He'd always looked out for her, especially after Gran died. He was a grandfather, mentor, cook, confidant, support, darling of her life. Now maybe he would save her life. She felt a surge of hope. It was better than nothing. It wasn't a flimsy, plastic version of a pen. This was a fine slim weapon of a pen. A good five inches of silver self-defense.

She held the pen point up. The idea of stabbing someone with it made her throat constrict. *But what's the alternative?* He was going to kill her, and if he didn't, she didn't want to think of what he might do before he dumped her in no-man's land. That had already happened one time too many. She'd been lucky once, but she wasn't counting on luck repeating itself.

She'd once practiced knife-throwing with Haasi—Haasi was a whiz with a knife. *Modern grip, point up. Medieval down— more for grappling.* Blanche was not in the mood to grapple. She wanted to end it quickly, and she would only have one chance. She'd have to be one very modern girl. *Point up, and done.* The pen was hardly a Bowie knife, but it was something, and it was all she had. She kept talking herself into it. Out loud, so she could hear herself think. Her heart was racing.

The truck stopped after a bumpy turn or two. Blanche couldn't imagine where they were. Not a sound. She figured her timing needed to be perfect; she had to move on the exact second, or she was toast. She focused like a madwoman, and she was plenty mad. She crouched on the floor of the truck, barefoot. She'd kicked the sandals off and once again cursed herself for her choice of footwear. When was she going to learn to wear combat boots, and like them?

She was small but strong as a coiled wire, and she was in a good position. She stared at the door in the dark, just a foot or two away, gauging, guessing when he'd open that door. She gathered her strength. Put the what-if's out of mind. She positioned her left fist under her right hand gripping the base of the pen and waited.

What the hell is he doing?

The extra seconds she waited sent adrenaline churning through her limbs, to her brain. She was ready.

The door popped open. It was dark outside, except for ambient light from the distant city. Or the moon. She could pick out his silhouette; she got a whiff of his greasy, mean presence. She never thought he'd have a weapon, and that was a good thing. Fear of that possibility didn't diminish her intent. He started to lean toward her, his bulk filling the opening, one hand on the roof of the truck.

"*¿Donde estás?*"

"*Estoy* right here." She let him lean in a bit more. He was off balance, and that was good; hers was perfect. She couldn't believe her good fortune. He was wide open. She sprang at him. At the soft part under his chin. It wasn't a clean hit, but the pen stuck. At least she thought it did. She felt the point stick him, like stabbing a piece of raw meat. He fell back, stunned, and screamed. He was writhing on the ground when she jumped out the door and into the front seat of the truck. He'd even left the motor running!

How convenient! Thank you, God, again!

She had no idea where she was, but she drove. She pushed the accelerator toward the moving dots of light, back over the bumpy road, and onto the highway. She was blessed with a sense of direction, but she hardly needed to guess which way to go. Mexico City shined like a rare pulsing jellyfish on the bottom of an ocean of stars in the black night. She drove and drove.

Chapter Thirty-Two

HOT SAUCE

Blanche used her sense of direction and good eyes. She eventually found her way to the Zocalo, and to the hotel, fueled by adrenaline, relief, and sweat. It was evening and traffic was light, and, fortunately, there were signs. She slammed into an alleyway near the hotel, and jumped out. She didn't care if she ever saw that truck again. Cardenal would have to deal with it. She dropped the keys, like they were on fire, into her bag, and bent over to catch her breath. She tried not to vomit. Her legs were like rubber; her sleeve was streaked with blood. But she was alive. She stood up, revived, and thankful. She wanted to scream and dance and announce to the world that she was still alive, but instead she ran. Through the hotel lobby and up to the hotel room. Haasi wasn't there.

Blanche found her on the patio, the phone pinned to her ear, pacing up and down. Blanche ran to her and threw her arms around her. Haasi dropped the phone. Blanche had never seen tears in Haasi's eyes, but she figured there was a first time for everything. Haasi didn't let go, sobs racked her. Blanche patted her back until they both calmed down.

"I'm back; I'm all right."

"Enough with the damn kidnapping," Haasi said. "We have to

figure out how to avoid this sort of thing. Once and for all."

Blanche held her by the shoulders and looked at her. "How did you know?"

"I got your note. I went over there. To that bitch's clinic. She was so vague, so sketchy. I knew something was up. She said you'd been there but wouldn't say when or *anything*."

Blanche pulled Haasi over to a bench and they collapsed. "She ordered that guy to pick me up and dump me off the highway, I'm sure of it. He grabbed me right outside the clinic."

"I know; I ran up and down that street asking if anyone had seen you. I finally found an old man. A man sitting in his doorway on a rickety chair. The neighborhood watcher, you'd call him. He saw it all. I called Cardenal, and we've been looking for you."

"I've got to call him. He needs to go pick up that thug. If they can find him. They'll have to get directions from Doctor Flórez. I'm sure she'll sing like a vulture."

They found El Jefe wandering down the grassy embankment of Highway 57, blood streaming down his shirt front. He'd live. He was in a hospital and in police custody, and he would remain there. With the old-man witness, and Blanche's testimony, and the truck that had evidence of her capture, the bag, her sandals, a few notes the kidnapper had scribbled about directions to the drop sight, Blanche was off the hook on grounds of self-defense. The Cross pen was never recovered.

Doctor Oleantha claimed she had no idea about any "apparent kidnapping."

"Well, what did you expect?" Blanche had barely come down from high anxiety after escaping her captor, and she wanted some answers.

Detective Cardenal stood on the patio, patting the top of his head when he wasn't shaking it. "We are relieved you are back, and you appear to be all right, but, *Señorita* Blanche, you should be in a hospital. Under observation. That is a terrible experience, and the repercussions could be devastating."

"I'm fine. My upbringing may've been simple, and peaceful, but my granny once lashed us to an upright during a hurricane. I guess I can weather this, too."

The detective's eyebrows shot up. "*¡Dios mío!* You *gringas*. You eat nails for breakfast."

"Well, no, that is not particularly appealing," said Haasi, who had tasted half of Mexico City. "Blanche is safe now, and that's all that matters."

"Yes, that, and getting those bastards," said Blanche. Haasi and the detective exchanged looks.

"At least this El Jefe won't be picking people up and riding them out of town. He's locked up until further notice," said Cardenal.

"Goody. Where does that leave us with this so-called doctor?"

"Blanche, we have nothing to connect her to your, er, detainment. She wouldn't even acknowledge she knew this El Jefe. She's clean."

"Like a garbage dump, or the bottom of a sewer."

"You could be right. We have our eye on her."

"I do, too."

Blanche and Haasi walked into the Cruz restaurant at the market and sat down at one of the tables covered in oilcloth. A bottle of Valentino hot sauce and plastic flowers in a foil-covered Coke bottle were tucked off to the side. Blanche scooted the white plastic chair closer. The place was packed, humming with the vitality of good eating and laughing and families.

"Rosabella at the tourist office said this place is good for fish," said Haasi. "Let's go fishing."

Most of the specials were written on a blackboard near the

door. The restaurant didn't have walls. A blue tarp overhead served as the ceiling, and the restaurant was open to the bustling market of stalls of vegetables, baskets, clothing, and herbs. Two indigenous women in brilliant skirts sat on the ground near the entrance cleaning the spines off cactus; a vendor had set up a dozen bird cages, and the singing was frantic and high-pitched, and so was the riot of color all around them.

"*Mojarra frita, por favor. Dos,*" said Blanche to the waiter, who smiled and quickly returned with two bottles of beer, a bowl of cut limes, and a huge basket of tortillas.

"Aw, don't you love this place?" said Haasi, her fingers tented under her chin. She had that contented expression when she was anywhere near food. "Fried fish, salad, and rice—for about three dollars!"

"Sounds better than thirty pesos," said Blanche, who sipped at the Tecate and smiled. "I thought you wanted to get out of here."

"Well, sometimes I do. First the new mummy and that business at the Palacio, and then you get kidnapped." Haasi grabbed Blanche's fingers. "Let's not do that again. Swear."

"Swear on thirty Bibles."

The fish arrived—whole fish with beady eyes and lovely, crusty fried coats on them—and Haasi and Blanche looked at each other and burst out laughing

"Gonna need more than a fishing pole," said Haasi.

"You're good with a knife."

They were poised for the attack with knife and fork when the waiter appeared. "*¿Con permiso?*" He slit the fish stem to stern and cut the head off in one swipe, lifted off the top filet, and extracted the skeleton of bones in one piece. He inclined his head and smiled.

"Did you see that? He bowed!" Blanche squeezed lime on the fish.

"So darn nice. Don't think we'd get that at the Peel 'n Eat."

"No kidding," said Blanche. "Mind the bones, Haas."

"Oh, I don't mind at all."

Haasi had already devoured one half of the top fillet. Blanche glanced quickly at her cousin happily savoring the fish. Blanche hesitated, gauging the best time to spring it on her. She knew Haasi was at her most approachable with food in front of her. They thought alike, but Haasi was more prudent, more inclined to keep a low profile, which never seemed to be the outcome between the two of them. It was always *something*.

"So." Blanche put down her fork, perhaps a bit too emphatically.

Haasi looked up.

"Now, don't get in a knot about this." A ridiculous notion since Haasi was one calm cookie, and Blanche was happy for that blessing.

"You're about to ruin my lunch."

"Nothing could ruin your lunch. Want a second helping?"

Haasi eyed Blanche's rice, and she shoved it toward her. Haasi doused it with hot sauce, rolled up a tortilla, and dug in. Blanche sighed. "Why don't you weigh two hundred pounds?"

"Dunno." She smiled. The tortilla suspended. "OK, let me have it. You have something on your mind. It's written all over your face."

"Well, good. Then you already know that I'm going to see Blussberg at the Palacio." Blanche finished the beer and waved and smiled for another.

"Bang. Does it never stop?"

"No, listen. It's all aboveboard. Oleantha told me to go see him."

"*What*? There's a red flag right there. We shouldn't have anything to do with any of them. Especially her!" Haasi splashed more hot sauce over everything. "Blussberg's probably as crooked as they come."

"But don't you see? Blussberg wasn't at that art fiesta. I think they're in cahoots to some extent but working separately on some of these projects, for their own nefarious reasons. This might be to our advantage. I don't think Blussberg knows all of the doctor's comings and goings, except for when he needs a mummy."

"I don't know what makes you say that, Bang."

"I don't either. Exactly."

"What about El Patrón?"

"He's at the top, but I think he's spreading it out, keeping distance between them. Divide and conquer, so to speak. He's putting money on this art project, no doubt. I just want to dig around a little." Blanche could see she was losing Haasi on this caper, so it was time to deflect. "I want to see who killed that poor woman. Amparo's daughter, Lalia."

"For Amparo?"

"Yes, for the mother of the young woman who became the new mummy. She must be out of her mind with misery." At this, Blanche shivered. She clenched her fist on the tabletop.

"Now that I think about it ..." Haasi frowned. Her face was scrunched into deep thought. "I guess there's no harm in interviewing Blussberg. In his office at the Palacio with people around. I don't think you'll get anywhere, but what the heck."

"Yeah, what the heck. And I have a perfectly legitimate reason to visit him. You see, I'm an art student and a journalist and I'm writing this travel article..."

Chapter Thirty-Three

PANIC IN THE PALACIO

SARLOFF BLUSSBERG SAT AT HIS DESK, his small hands folded, his bloated face plastered with a smile. His peculiar Elvis do looked especially brassy today; his eyes were puffy with blue bags under them. "Ah, so we meet again. I'm always happy to talk to the press, *Señorita* Blanche. What can I do for you?"

Blanche had so many ideas about what he could do for her. *In particular, lead me to the art theft and the creator of the fake mummy.*

Instead, she smiled demurely. She was definitely going to have to wing it—with Haasi's help and dramatic skills and trickery. Blanche was dressed to play her part. Professionally. Curls tamed, sensible shirtwaist dress from the secondhand shop. (She'd had to toss the daisy-dotted chambray.) Her heart was racing, but she stuffed it down and concentrated on the moment.

"I want to thank you so much for meeting me. The other day, I guess I should have told you about the purpose of our visit to Mexico City." She chuckled, deciding to avoid the details. "I know it's short notice, but I have some questions about this fabulous Mayan exhibit."

"Yes, you've seen it, and, ahem, I believe you've gotten some impressions."

They both danced around the unfortunate discovery of the "new" mummy and the demise of Lalia Solis Iglesia. She was sure Blussberg knew about the identification of the poor young woman. He should be on the hot seat for that one, but Cardenal had not made his move. The wheels of justice were creaky on this machine.

"Aracelli at the tourist office has been helpful. With background and such. I'm wondering about the future plans for the exhibit. It's going to Paris next? What's involved in moving such priceless treasure?"

A buzzer sounded on his desk. An intercom. Insistent and annoying.

Blanche was ecstatic. *Perfect. This just might work.*

She put on her most studious expression, pen poised. And she waited, the essence of patience, head tilted just so.

Blussberg pressed a button. "Yes, what is it? What?"

The voice boomed from the box on his desk: "Pick up the phone, please."

He grabbed the receiver and fifteen seconds later his face took on an unhealthy hue of exasperation. "Why can't you handle it? Yes, yes. I'll be right there." He stood up, half turned toward an adjacent office, its door open a crack. He called out. "*Señor* López? I have to go down to the floor. Will you help *Señorita* Blanche with the details of the exhibit?" No answer. "*Verdammt.* He's not here, but he'll be back soon, I'm sure. Will you excuse me for just a minute? Something is occurring on the exhibit floor, and they are calling me. I'll be right back."

Blanche nodded pleasantly, barely suppressing a smile.

Yes, it is working.

Haasi had to be talked into this one and fed amply—a couple of sugar buns from Alegría helped. But Blanche didn't have to do that much talking. The thing that got to Haasi was the death of that young woman, sacrificed to the god of mummies. It wasn't fair, and if Blanche had an idea about how to find out who did it, Haasi was game.

Before the interview with Blussberg, they had walked all over the city looking for a pet shop, and they found one near the market where they'd had lunch. The window of the shop was full of fish in bowls and tanks, two puppies in a cage curled up into a ball, and one striped cat who slept in a sunbeam. The place looked well-run. A family with two little boys was discussing the cat—or so Haasi and Blanche guessed. One of them kept crying, "*Sí, el gatito.*" And the papi was smiling.

"Where there is cat, there is mouse," said Haasi, not cracking a smile.

They browsed the shop and found what they were looking for. Mice. Half a dozen fat little mice. Haasi waffled, but Blanche said, "They'll love living in the Palacio! Who wouldn't want to live in a *palace?*"

Haasi had looked skeptical. "Well, I'm going to buy a bag of mouse food. Just in case."

"You're so humane, Haas. Or should I say, mouse-mane? I don't know."

Blanche watched Blussberg waddle out of his office. He was off to see "about the confusion on the exhibit floor." Blanche figured she had a good ten minutes, fifteen, if she was lucky. She zipped around his desk and peeked into López's office. Still out. She shut the door quietly. She poked at Blussberg's desk, lifting this, shoving that, but the man was a neat freak. A near-empty paper tray, blotter, pen in a holder, phone, a legal pad. She opened a drawer, same thing, all the accoutrements of running a business from the desk—more pads, paper clips, pens. She opened the narrow middle drawer, recessed under the desktop. It was empty except for a neat calendar agenda, the squares filled in with precise printing in German and English.

She almost missed it. At the top of the month of May were three words: *mumie, kunst, flug.* Blanche was not a student of German, but she recognized *mumie.* It made her stomach flip. The first two words were checked off; *flug* was not. She racked her brain. *Kunst? Flug* meant flight.

Under the calendar in the drawer was a silver key. She looked around for the lock that would fit the key, and under a table near the desk was a small metal cabinet. She hesitated, about one heartbeat. She grabbed the key, shut the drawer. She listened for footsteps, beads of sweat popping down her back. López had not returned. The offices, the corridor, were quiet except for her slamming and shuffling. She needed a break, for time to stand still.

The key fit the lock. Inside were stacks of euros, American dollars, and pesos arranged side by side, and sitting on top of the money, a travel folder for a plane ticket. Blanche couldn't resist. Her fingers burned to touch it. A round-trip flight to Frankfurt for Thursday. A note attached to the folder was written in blocky script: *Arrange for large cargo.*

It was as if someone hit her over the head.

She closed everything up, returned the key, and started toward the door. Blussberg would understand why she left. She'd "waited" at least ten minutes and neither Blussberg nor López had shown up. If he didn't understand, *so what?* She'd gotten what she came for. Information. She took one more look around, in a corner closet, the bookcase, and all of the drawers. Nothing. But that was all right. She'd hit paydirt, at least a small hill of it.

Haasi was outside the Palacio near the steps of the cathedral waiting for Blanche. She'd sought the shade of a vendor selling windshield wiper blades, rosaries, garbage bags, and gumballs.

She'd bought a rosary. "Just in case," she said, waving the string of beads and crucifix and kissing it as Blanche hurried toward her.

Blanche's face had that all-too-familiar look of anxiety mixed with news bulletin. She grabbed hold of Haasi, and the two of them scooted off away from the Zocalo. "Start praying."

"What happened? Everything OK with Blussberg and company?"

"I'll say, but more to the point, how'd it go down there in the exhibit?"

"You'd think they'd never seen a mouse before," said Haasi. "I let those little suckers go, one at a time, right near the mummy exhibit, and they scattered. Not a single bit of teamwork among them. The screams were so piercing I thought the mummies would wake up!"

"Oh, Haas. It worked! You bought time."

They'd been walking fast. They slipped into a café bar near Madero and prepared to fortify themselves with a couple of beers and a basket of Tacos Canasta, a chewy, delicious, steamed taco treat that had Haasi's eyes glowing despite the talk of mice. Blanche let her do the ordering: beef in adobo and pigskin. Haasi loaded them with cilantro, lime juice, hot sauce, and salsa verde. Blanche found a table and opened her notebook. Haasi landed across from her with the tacos. They both dug in.

"You speak taco so well," said Blanche. "How do you manage to get all that in your mouth?"

Haasi did not answer. Another taco disappeared.

Blanche drank off half her beer. "Keep eating. You're gonna love this, and I hope it doesn't curdle your salsa. He's got plane tickets, Haas. Blussberg is going to Frankfurt. *With a large cargo.*"

Uncharacteristically, an enormous chunk of onions and peppers fell out of Haasi's taco.

"No kidding." She slowly lowered the beef en adobo. "Well, I wonder what he's packing."

Chapter Thirty-Four

LOST ART

"WHAT DO YOU MEAN…HE'S 'INDISPOSED'?" said Sarloff Blussberg. He was back in his office after that ridiculous mouse chase all around the exhibit floor. Somehow, a visitor had smuggled mice into the Palacio, and one by one, the little critters created havoc. One of them had become so disoriented, it ran up a woman's leg and the result was an earthquaking scream. Blussberg had been beside himself trying to find the mouse-bearing culprit, but he and the frantic staff were unlucky. They later found mounds of particles in corners, suspected of being mouse food.

Blussberg got a hold of himself. He was flummoxed he'd had to explain a number of times that the Palacio was not "vermin infested." He had other business on his mind, and on the phone, now that the mouse incident was over. He held the receiver tightly. "I don't care how indisposed he is, I need him."

"He had a little accident," said Doctor Oleantha Flórez. She declined to give the details. Blussberg didn't know that Oleantha had tried to "teach" the little journalist a lesson, and that the plan had backfired. Oleantha had a habit of breezing over specifics when they talked. She'd never been one to dwell on missed opportunities and screw-ups, especially hers. He was grateful for the mummy she'd produced, and that's all that concerned him at the moment. And getting on that plane out of Mexico City. Now this.

"What kind of an accident? I need him Thursday. To get that cargo out to the airport. I've got a flight."

"It's an accident that prevents him from being at your disposal, and you'll have to handle this, Bluss."

"Do you have someone else?"

"I'm not your shipping clerk. And neither is he. I got the girl dried up for you to switch out of that exhibit, and I packed the ancient one nice and tight with all the art objects. You figure out the rest."

"You know how that plan turned out," said Blussberg. "The dead girl is in custody, and I'm down one mummy. I still have to account to the Convento for the *real* one we got on loan. Now that you've packed it with the art objects."

"Not my worry. I've done my end. You have to talk with El Patrón and finish the deal. Get the goods out of DF."

"Don't remind me. As long as he gets the money after the delivery… And, may I remind you, we are all in this together. I need help getting that cargo out to the airport."

It was always the same with this woman: She involved herself as little as possible, and she was never inclined to share the drama on her end. She didn't like to take orders, and she wouldn't have anyone breathing down her neck. She kept her pretty little neck to herself. She went where the money was and got out. After all, he could hardly blame her. They all understood El Patrón's methods. He paid, and the dealings were one-on-one. He didn't bring everyone into the mix. He kept them off-balance, just enough to manipulate the situation, and that was to be expected. They had to deal with the territory the way it was set up.

"What am I going to do? I can't bring any more people into this operation. I don't trust anyone at this point." His heavy breathing added an extra layer of disgust. "What about you, Oleantha? Will you drive me out there? I'll get a skycap to unload the baggage…"

Oleantha's laugh could be heard all over Mexico City. "That would be no. I'm certainly not a taxi driver. Ask that weird assistant of yours, López, to drive you."

Haasi and Blanche sat with Detective Cardenal in the police cafeteria. They drew looks, but that was not surprising. The two young women stood out in the milling group of hard-looking, holster-packing cops with few women among them. They casually stopped by their table and said "*hola*" to the detective and didn't listen to a thing he said while they stared at Haasi and Blanche.

Blanche seemed oblivious, except to say "*hola*" back. The police were gracious, and she wanted to avoid each and every one of them. Her eyes were blazing, focused on the detective. "This guy has something planned for Thursday. You need to check it out, either at the Palacio or the airport. Or both. You need to follow him."

"Now, just one momentito. Tell me, exactly, how do you know of a plan?"

Haasi and Blanche looked at each other. A little white lie was the order of the day. "I know," said Blanche. "Let's just say I saw the information. Didn't hear it. The only time I heard anything was that afternoon at the Palacio outside the restroom."

Cardenal leaned forward, his shirtsleeves rolled up, fingers clenched in huge fists. "You saw the information?"

Blanche sighed. "OK. I went over there to interview him. I saw it in his office. He was called away…" At that Haasi's hand shot to her mouth. To keep from laughing out loud. "The information was right there. Written down on a calendar: *mumie, kunst, flug*— mummy, art, flight. He's going to take the stuff out of the country on Thursday. Ten o'clock flight. I'm sure of it."

Cardenal sat back, studying Blanche. "Seems you know quite a bit about Blussberg's plans. Let me just say this: We've had our eye on him, and what you say fits."

"The exhibit is scheduled to move to Paris next month. There must be some connection between his Frankfurt trip and the opening." Blanche was insistent. She was not going to take no for an answer or be pushed aside on this one. "Between the exhibits and the art theft!"

Haasi's voice was low and steady. "Detective, we think he's smuggling art objects. Inside one of those *mumies.*"

"That's a big leap," he said.

But Blanche could tell he was considering it. "It's worth looking into. We've been working on all the angles. In the meantime, several paintings have been stolen from the Bellas Artes. They were rolled up in storage, and *boom*! Gone. Seems to be happening all over DF. No one noticed it for months, but after an inventory the missing pieces were unaccounted for. Blussberg has made several trips to Europe, but all under the guise of setting up exhibits. Paris next. We've been watching him. He's got all his permits and papers in order."

"Watching is not going to do it. You need to search the place."

"And where do you suggest we search? DF is a big place. Whoever is up to all this thievery and murder is covering his tracks. We're having trouble putting these pieces together."

"Did you search the Palacio?"

"¡*Claro*! After the Lalia Solis episode, what do you think we did? We still don't know who did that to the poor woman. Now that we've at least identified her, the mother has been after us almost daily to find the criminal who made a mummy out of her daughter." He was patting his head. "I am afraid I revealed my suspicions..."

"You told her about La Escandolera?"

"I didn't have to. Seems the rumor mill informed her."

"Did you check that lab? Really well?"

"Nothing. No hairs or tubes or bottles like you reported. Clean, maybe too clean. No mummy-making going on over there."

"Well, we saw it all," said Haasi. "The black hairs, the ledger, the cozy coffee corner. Someone was very busy in that lab. Had to be La Escandolera, the eminent Doctor Oleantha. The woman's a menace." Haasi was gritting her teeth, Blanche winced.

"As you say. The woman's a suspect, but there is nothing to pin on her," he said. "We know she's used the lab. The university verified that, but they were vague about permission to do so, and we need to look into it. Someone looked the other way or was paid off, no doubt. It happens. In any event, we didn't find a clue." He stopped, his eyebrows knit together.

Blanche suppressed a smile. "What are you thinking?"

"We did search there. But only the lab section. We didn't search storage areas and such."

"Don't you think you should? Where else would you store a *large cargo*?"

"Those museums have huge storage areas. And so, all those old buildings. Like that lab. There are closets and nooks everywhere."

"But he wants to be ready to go. Wouldn't you?" Blanche felt a little like she was extracting a tooth with a fork. "He's leaving Thursday! He needs to get out of there fast. And he's surely taking a passenger with him. One that's fully loaded and worth its weight in gold, or euros."

Chapter Thirty-Five
ARRIVAL

EMILIO LOOKED OUT THE DOOR OF THE CLINIC and saw a brand new Dodge Ram pulling in close to the plaza. It was completely out of place in the village of Santa Uriel de los Angeles de Tepequito.

He didn't have time to wonder about it now. He had a baby to deliver.

Emilio focused on the young mother-to-be, Abaya, measuring the trouble that was coming. The arrival of that shiny truck put a new spike in his nerves.

"It's too late now to get help." Emilio thought briefly of the new arrival of this truck but put it out of his mind. It wasn't anyone Abaya, or he, knew. He set his jaw in fury and in desperation. He had to focus on this, the birth of this child he was totally unprepared to handle in the dusty little clinic. Abaya was supposed to be at the hospital in Guanajuato, but her errant husband had failed her.

He glanced outside at a patch of earth and scrub where a group of children had started to gather. Maybe a game, or a chase, or kids being kids. There was very little to amuse them out there in the grubby little plaza.

Emilio went to Abaya. He carried a stack of clean linen and

hurried around, sliding to a stop on the soles of his well-worn boots. He usually had an assistant, but she was gone now, and she wasn't a medical assistant. She kept the clinic basically stocked and clean, and it was a daily battle with the dust. The shining glass doors of one cabinet held gauze and bandages, bottles of alcohol and iodine and soap. Emilio believed in soap, a simple thing but not so easy to put to use. The villagers didn't want to waste the water. It was already too hard to collect it and purify it. Why waste it on the outside when the inside needed it desperately?

Abaya had been dozing, and now she was fully awake. "Doctor Emilio?"

Emilio smoothed her forehead. He ran his fingers over Abaya's distended stomach. He may as well have been resting his hand on the moon. The baby was still transverse, a sort of breech, and this was not good. A foot, maybe a hand, protruded in a small bump, moving slowly, like a burrowing animal under the earth. I'm here, it said. Emilio looked with wonder, but his legs and stomach were weak. He hoped he didn't fail Abaya. *How the hell am I going to do this?* He'd only had that one rotation in the maternity ward, and even with all that staff, it didn't look easy. For anyone.

He needed a miracle.

Emilio said, "Abaya, rest for now. I'll give you some ice to wet your lips."

He dried his hands on a towel, bunching the linen in his fist.

He heard the yelling from a short distance away. He went to the door. A man was dropping peso notes on to a white plastic table across from the clinic. The children were running, old women were egging them on.

"*¿Donde está el medico?*" The man dropped a few more peso notes. He looked casually toward the clinic, but no one made a move. The man seemed to have all the time in the world. It made Emilio nervous.

Abaya screamed.

She leaned in Emilio's direction, anything to get away from the pain. She buried her face in his chest.

The commotion outside revolved around that plastic table and the shiny new truck. The noise rose and fell, the children yelling and laughing, the adults shouting. The man with the pesos had gone to the back of his truck and removed crates of avocados, oranges, and limes. Emilio could see it all outside the window of the clinic, but he looked away.

He steeled himself to focus on Abaya. He was sweating, coaxing the child to turn.

Then he felt it. The baby was no longer transverse. The silhouette of the child was north and south now, and the baby was crowning. Abaya gave one last scream, and a push, and he caught the child.

He cleaned the nose and ears and eyes of the new resident of Tepequito. Abaya's eyes were huge and shining as she took the baby boy in her arms. "Doctor Emilio. *Gracias.*"

He'd gotten a miracle. *How many can I hope for?*

Emilio didn't see the man approaching the door to the clinic, a gun on his hip. The doctor was attending to the new mother. The man walked over to Emilio and took his arm. "*Ven conmigo. Ahorita.*"

Chapter Thirty-Six

ALL TIED UP RIGHT NOW

HAASI AND BLANCHE WERE BACK AT THEIR HOTEL after their visit to Detective Cardenal at the police station. Blanche was determined to follow up with the surveillance of the lab, and Cardenal promised he'd be in touch. She didn't count on it anytime soon. In the meantime, she was plenty keyed up. For a whole bunch of reasons.

"Haasi, I can't get hold of Emilio."

Haasi was reviewing photos on her camera, and she looked up. "Did you call the clinic?"

"Yes, and my Spanish sucks, in case you didn't notice. Someone finally answered who hadn't been there all day. I got the idea that someone picked up Emilio after a delivery? Someone in a Dodge Ram?" Blanche was pacing in tighter and tighter circles.

"Dodge Ram? Why is that truck coming around again?" Haasi's voice had a hard edge, a reminder of Blanche's trip out of town, thanks to Doctor Oleantha.

"That's what I want to know. That goon who grabbed me is out of action, but apparently his truck is not. Someone got hold of his keys. Or there's a run on Dodge Rams."

"Don't sweat it, Bang."

Blanche stopped circling and stood in the middle of the patio. Her eyes focused on the fierce blue of another beautiful Mexico City sky. Some days were hazy, but they had been lucky with steady cool weather on the cusp of the rainy summer. *Where can he be?*

Haasi studied Blanche. "Now what? Sometimes I can hear your brain cells. Sort of like firecrackers going off."

"Blussberg is about to blow town! And now, this thing with Emilio. El Patrón knows where he is, and that's not good. I'm worried."

"You know that old ranchero is not going to hurt him. He wants to use him. Emilio'll figure it out."

Blanche flopped onto the loveseat, feeling the warmth of the sun and the memory of sitting there with Emilio. *I have to do something.*

"I'm gonna call El Patrón." She jumped up. "He wants Emilio to work for him. Be a kind of *gangster doc*."

"Oh great, I can see him doing that. And just what do you think you're going to accomplish calling that old *creep*."

"He's a creep, but he was courteous. I can play on his old-world manners."

"What a world!"

"Right. Gangster doc is not exactly Emilio's specialty. But he said he'd play along. See what he could find out," Blanche said. "In the meantime, *Señor* Rodrigo El Patrón owes me the rest of that interview."

"Be careful. Don't give yourself away. He doesn't know your connection to Emilio."

"True."

"*Señor* Rodrigo, thank you for taking my call. Wondering when we might finish that interview."

"Ah, *Señorita* Blanche. So good to hear from you. *Gracias.* But now is not a good time. I'm tied up…"

Emilio sat tied to a chair in a remote game room of the hacienda. He'd been held overnight and treated reasonably well. A clean bed in the servants' quarters, lock on the door, goon nearby. No hog shed this time. No gag on his mouth—who would hear him anyway? The place was deserted, except for those loyal to El Patrón. The man who had picked him up in Tepequito and brought him to the hacienda stood in the corner. Boots crossed at the ankle, a file scratching at a fingernail. He hummed a tune.

Emilio's eyes blazed at him. "How long?"

The man shrugged. "*No lo sé.*" He didn't look up.

"How long are you going to keep me here? I need to get out of here, get back to the clinic. I've got patients."

The goon looked up, raised his eyebrows. "You got patients? You need patience."

"*¿Donde está El Patrón?*"

"I don't know. Now, shut up, *cabrón.*" He shifted in the corner, let one boot drop. He changed his tone of voice. "I apologize," he said, pointing at the ropes on Emilio's wrists. "Precautions. Until El Patrón comes."

Emilio was furious, but he knew that would do little good. He took deep breaths and thought of what he'd say to his host. He'd gotten the royal treatment before, terry robe and brandy, after his detainment in the hog shed, and now this. The whole business was getting old. He'd keep his cool, get what information he could, and get the hell out of there.

He'd been glancing out the window, desperate to find a way to talk his way out of this mess. And now he couldn't believe what he saw. Had to be an apparition, a figment of his longing. But it was definitely her. Blonde hair, the sleeve of a T-shirt, peeking from behind low shrubs not twenty feet from the window.

Por Dios. The blonde Blanche! What is wrong with that chica? He fell in love all over again, and now he was even more desperate to get away before she did something even crazier. Like getting caught.

The man in the corner was still intent on filing his nails. El Patrón walked into the room, a large wood-paneled room with windows the length of one wall. Wildly, Emilio checked the window again, at the vast expanse of cactus and mesquite, a stark green and brown against a blazing blue sky. She'd disappeared from view. Maybe he'd been seeing things, seeing Blanche out of longing. But she needed to be gone from here. And so did he.

El Patrón smiled as he flipped absently through a sheaf of papers. When he saw ropes on Emilio's wrists, his eyebrows shot up. "¿Qué *pasa*?" He croaked. "Take away those ropes." He gave the handler a mean look. As if he'd been personally affronted that his guest was tied up, and he himself hadn't ordered it. The man in the corner slid the file in his back pocket, pushed off the wall, and untied the ropes.

"That's better," said El Patrón. He seated himself at a round table near Emilio and nodded for the man to go. He was as composed as a statue, and just about as unreadable. "I am truly sorry. That is no way to treat a valued employee."

Emilio was puzzled and barely able to keep a civil tone. "Valued employee? I'm not your employee."

"Ah, but you will be." He stood up and walked to the window, his back to Emilio.

Emilio's insides tightened; his mind raced. He had to get him away from that window. Desperately. "*Señor*, please sit and listen to me. ¿*Por favor*?"

El Patrón turned then. "I need you. I made the offer before, and you've had time to think about it. I'm sure you will agree it is an enticing offer. With many benefits." He paced the length of the room, a hitch in his gait. He couldn't see the look of disgust and exasperation in Emilio's eyes.

"I will not be accepting your offer," said Emilio. His voice was low and level, but the fear gripped him. He was afraid for himself, but worse, he was afraid for Blanche. She was out there, with Haasi, no doubt, and if they got caught, it wouldn't be pretty. He clenched his fists. He stood up. "I think we should conclude these arrangements."

El Patrón sat down slowly like an old machine that was creaking to a halt. "That is unfortunate. You will have much work to do here. All the medical necessities."

"Attending to your gangsters? I have other plans."

"I don't think so." He snapped his fingers. The handler goon in the dusty boots returned. Emilio kept his eyes on his host. The men looked at each other and let the tension hang between them.

Emilio couldn't think straight, but he grasped at what he could use as a lifeline. "I understand you have Doctor Oleantha at your disposal."

"Disposal is the appropriate word. She will not be working for us. Not in the future." His voice was a rusty knife cutting across his thoughts.

"What do you mean? What happened?"

"That is not your business what happens to her," he said. "What happens to you is all that need concern you. You will work for us *now*."

"Since you put it like that…," he said. He glanced out the window. He couldn't help himself. He saw an arm come out from behind the holly. He contained his expression, looked quickly from the window. "I will have to think about it."

What am I saying? He felt so rattled, he'd say anything to appease the man.

"Don't think too long. Take the offer. If I knew how to fix bullet wounds, I'd do it, or have one of these *idiotas* do it." He chuckled at his joke, inclined his head toward the goon who smirked behind his hand. "But that's not going to happen. I will make it worth your trouble, even possibly allowing you to work among those peasants you seem so devoted to. ¡*Basta*! You're the perfect candidate, and you're the best of the lot. Remember, I always get what I'm after."

"I need the toilet," Emilio said. He stood abruptly. "We'll resume our discussion shortly. Must be something I ate..."

"I have some work here. Take your time. Nando will show you, and then you come back here." His dark, empty gaze was unsettling.

"I will."

"...and we talk."

Chapter Thirty-Seven

THE SLIP

"Pssst! Emilio!" Blanche stuck her head around the archway to the patio.

"*Caramba*, Blanche, what are you doing here? You need to get away."

"No, it's fine. Trust me. Go back to him. Please." Her voice was just above a whisper, hoarse and pleading.

He turned his head and looked down the hallway toward the game room. "What are you talking about?"

"I'll be here. On the patio. Let's see where we can take this. Together." She gave him a thumb's up and ducked back through the door while he made his way to the bathroom. A look of confusion mixed with possibility playing across his face.

Ana was not afraid of Rodrigo Ortiz de Avila. Her family had cared for him and his family for decades. She was a trusted servant, but more than that, she ran the household. She had no qualms about interrupting him if she saw fit. Now, she entered the game room where El Patrón waited for Emilio to return. He was marking invoices and writing notes. When she appeared, he said, "Ana, I need to meet with you. Some orders I need for the vineyard and supplies…"

She inclined her head, hands knotted over her ample middle. "That will be fine. In the meantime, there is a *señorita* here, asking to see you. A *Señorita* Blanche."

"*¿Qué?* I have no meeting scheduled with the *señorita*. Tell her to go. I'm busy at the moment."

Ana cleared her throat. "Rodrigo, you are not busy. You can see her. She came a far distance."

El Patrón was not surprised at Ana's insistence, and she knew it. She'd nearly raised him though she was barely a dozen years older, and she had her place. It was high in the pantheon. The hacienda would not run without Ana.

"Tell her to wait then. I have this, er, interview with the young doctor to finish."

Ana pursed her lips. There were things that happened on the ranch that she did not approve of, things she didn't often see and hear. But she did not like coercion of any sort, and she believed in treating people well, especially feeding them. "Should I bring *antojitos* here, or to the patio?"

"No, no, *gracias*, Ana. I'll be there. Please tell her to wait."

Ana turned and started back down the hall to the patio to tell the girl he would see her. She didn't know why she was going along with this exactly. The girl had been acting peculiar the first time she visited the ranch, poking around in the kitchen. But she was persistent, and she was good to Bella. At the fiesta, she had been gracious, especially when the awful Doctor Flórez had embarrassed Ana in front of the staff, ordering her around rudely. And now the girl had brought chocolates. For Ana.

Ana entered the patio quietly. "*Señorita, Señor* Rodrigo will see you. *En un ratito.* He is in another interview at the moment. May I get you something?"

Blanche stood. She smiled at Ana's offer of hospitality.

She seemed happy as hell she'd gained entrance, and she had opportunity. "Oh, nothing, *Señora* Ana. *Muchas gracias.*"

"*De nada.*" She inclined her head and disappeared through the archway.

Emilio as yet had not returned from the bathroom. Nando was gone, and El Patrón decided to leave the game room. He'd finish with the doctor later. He got up, with difficulty, and impatiently, and hobbled down the corridor toward the patio. The hip and the old knees were acting up again. He wanted to take his medication and get a good rest. He would dispense with this *señorita* and her pesky business. He was in no mood for a chat.

She was sitting on the sofa, the notebook open on her knees. Bella was curled at her feet, and the girl scratched the dog's neck while she flipped through her pages. At that, El Patrón softened ever so slightly. The dog was not that good a judge of character, after all, but it was a lovely domestic sight to see the girl and the dog communing on his patio.

"*Señorita!*"

Blanche jumped to her feet. Bella made a low whine. "All right, girl," Blanche said, still rubbing and scratching the fur. "Oh, it's so good of you to see me, *señor*. I hope I didn't disturb you."

"Disturb? Why no. I was actually in an interview…"

"Really!" Blanche laughed. "Must be the day for interviews!"

El Patrón did not laugh. "I am quite busy. What can I do for you? What other questions?"

"Can we sit for just a few minutes?" She seemed anxious, all of a sudden, and then she made an effort to relax. She took a deep breath.

He moved slowly to a sofa opposite her. Bella resumed her position on Blanche's feet. "I see the dog has taken a liking to you."

"Yes, she's so sweet." Blanche bent down to the dog, petting, nurturing a cozy air. The fountain trilled, the birds in their white wicker cage sang, and she averted her face that belied the fact she was nervous. She hesitated. "I used to have a dog, a long time ago. She was a mix..."

They both turned toward the archway at the sound of a light knock. "Ah, *buenas*," Emilio said. "Here you are."

El Patrón stared. Blanche gazed at the doorway her expression visibly pale. Their host's manners did not fail him. "Please, do join us, doctor."

Emilio sat down, one sofa cushion away from Blanche. Casually, he crossed one leg over a knee.

"This is *Señorita* Blanche Murninghan, of the Florida newspaper, asking me about life on the hacienda. *Señorita*, Doctor Emilio Sierra Del Real."

"*Encantada*," said Blanche, her face a mask of smiles and guile.

"*Encantado*," said Emilio. He rose slightly and resumed his seat. The two stared at each other.

El Patrón folded his hand. "¡Qué *coincidencia*! Two interviews in one day. But, there are no coincidences." Just the hint of a smirk.

"*Sí*." Emilio and Blanche, in unison. Bella let out a contented sigh, but the tension could be cut with a knife. El Patrón frowned impatiently.

"*Señorita*, we will need to talk at another time. Doctor, Nando will show you back to our quarters so we can resume our meeting."

"You know, *Señor* Rodrigo, that won't be necessary. We can talk later. I must be going. Perhaps the *señorita* will give me a ride back into DF. Your hospitality has been charming, but I really need to be going." He was on his feet.

Blanche bowed her head to El Patrón, waved gallantly. She headed toward the door, moving quickly, Bella at her heels. The dog received one more pat on the head. "Oh, that would be fine. Great idea. I'd be glad to, Doctor Emilio. I didn't realize how late it's getting. I'll be in touch, *Señor* Rodrigo."

Emilio and Blanche raced down the gravel path before El Patrón could get his arthritic legs to pull himself up off the sofa.

They ran like their feet were on fire, holding hands, down the path under the laurels, to Blanche's car pulled off into a thicket of weeds. They didn't talk, they just ran.

They pulled out onto Highway 57, back to the city. "He'll come after me again. He wants me to be that doctor."

Blanche stole a look at him, hands ten and two on the wheel, speeding along the busy highway. She was still wearing the blonde wig and the cat-eye glasses. "Maybe not, maybe if El Patrón's out of the picture, things will simmer down. Besides, he has that *bruja*, Oleantha, to do his dirty work."

Emilio frowned. "That is another problem. I think she's gone. He spoke cryptically, but there wasn't anything puzzling about what he said. He spoke of 'disposal' like she was gone, or soon would be."

"Oh, great. He going to kill her?"

"I don't know. But it doesn't sound good for Doctor Flórez. I should warn her. Even after what she did, especially what she did to you." Emilio reached over and squeezed Blanche's arm. "Unforgivable. But murder? She might even offer help, or cooperate, if we tell her."

"You are kidding, of course."

He still had his hand on her arm, staring at her. "You know, I begin to like the blonde look, but the glasses? *Mi gatita.*"

"Now you're calling me a cat. I was pretty sneaky out there, wasn't I? Little cat's feet and all that?"

"You worry me. You shouldn't have done that, B. You don't

know what those people will do."

Blanche stared straight ahead at the road. It was a smooth ride, for now. "Couldn't let you sit out there, either in the hog shed or in your terry robe. Enough's enough with all this."

Emilio sighed. "*Eso espero*. I am going to have to maneuver to get out of this gangster doc business. How you say, do fancy steps. Now I am locked into social service, so unless El Patrón knows the president of Mexico, that is where I am going to be."

"Unless he can pay someone off. We need to talk to Cardenal. The law's on our side. It's creaky, but what else do we have here?"

"We need to warn Doctor Flórez."

"You're right. I can't help thinking if El Patrón doesn't get to her, the law's going to get her. She's going to slip up sooner or later."

"I think she already has. Do you know where to find her?"

"I think so. It's still early. We should go. Take that roundabout at the plaza ahead...."

Chapter Thirty-Eight
RED POOL

OLEANTHA WAS SITTING AT HER DESK. It had been a slow day, and she'd decided to close up early. She'd found a few gray hairs and chipped a nail, and so she made an appointment at La Mariposa Amarilla to get herself back in line with perfection. She looked around the clinic: It shined with a pastel light, the liquids in glass bottles, the baskets with pink and blue and yellow ribbons woven into the hemp, white marble floor and glass shelving...and that fabulous Veronica Ruiz de Velasco painting of ballerinas. Oleantha sighed. She had added such marvelous touches to the place. This brilliant shining cover for a pot of boiling evils. Well, she wouldn't think about that now.

There were certain things she had to do. Like getting rid of this customer. A slight person, dressed in black, with a hat pulled low. The doctor would have to answer one more heap of questions, maybe make a sale, and then she was out of there.

The customer stepped along the wall of shelves touching this and that and did not speak.

"*Buenas*," said Oleantha.

Nada, nothing.

She tried again. "I was just about to close up, but perhaps I can help you with something? An herb, or two? Oils? I have a new tincture of plumeria for skin conditions." It wasn't new at all; the Nahua used it a thousand years ago, and it was still a popular plant-based treatment.

Nothing.

The customer stopped touching the products, and, in fact, did not move. Oleantha frowned, and in a heartbeat, her radar zinged like she'd been stung. She'd learned early in life to be alert; an eye off the ball could prove to have drastic results. She sat up at her desk. Her phone was at the ready, but it might prove too late to use it. She was alone there. El Jefe wasn't nearby sitting in his truck, waiting at her beck and call—not since the little chica had stabbed him with a pen. What a pesky business this was getting to be.

Her hand went to the secret drawer, the place where she'd tucked her priceless dagger. She fingered its smooth blade, the stones on the hilt. It was small, but sharp. She knew a thing or two about a knife; well, she'd had a surgery rotation in med school. She knew where to cut. It was important to know where to cut, and it was important to be decisive. This was her strength, something she took pride in. She kicked off the high heels and waited and watched. Maybe this person would leave; she could lock up and go. And maybe she was just being paranoid. It wouldn't be the first time.

The customer stepped away from the shelves suddenly and turned toward the desk. Oleantha could not see the features under the hat, but she did see the gun. She hadn't planned on that eventuality. The person was small, and agile. Oleantha didn't think long before instinct kicked in.

The desk was one step up from the main floor. She hated to do this—to her beloved desk. She hated to make a mess of it, but she had no other choice. She needed a major weapon, and this was all she had. She needed to be ready to use it.

"What's this? A gun. So, you're going to shoot me here, in my shop."

"Yes."

"What do you want? Money? Here, I'll give you money, and then you can go." She sounded almost petulant. She started to reach for her bag.

"Don't"

"Are you sure? I have quite a lot. If you'll just take it and go." Her voice was cool but she started to shake so badly she had to grit her teeth and make her legs be still.

"No." The voice was quiet, low and menacing.

She'd have to do it. Oleantha put her hands on the underside of the desktop. She was small, but strong, and the mix of fear and adrenaline did the trick. She gave it a heartbeat for this person to come closer. Then she gave the heavy, marble-topped, wooden desk a savage push off the raised floor and it came crashing down at the black-clad figure. The gun went off. Oleantha fell back on the floor, and she lay still.

The shooter was quick, leaping away as the desk shot forward. Another round from the gun blasted the silence. The attacker quickly looked out the window for witnesses or passersby.

Doctor Oleantha didn't move. The white marble floor pooled red, the antique white-and-gold desk was a wreck, and the figure in black sauntered out the door of the clinic without looking back.

It wasn't hard to find a place to park near Doctor Oleantha's clinic, tucked among the boutiques and residences of the fashionable La Condesa. Blanche slid the rental into a spot on a tree-lined street. It was quiet.

Blanche turned to Emilio. "I am so glad to see you."

"Me, too."

They didn't talk. They just looked at each other. Blanche exhaled, finally, and was thankful they'd slipped El Patrón and were safe for now. Emilio took her hands and drew her toward him. They stayed locked together until Blanche broke away, completely out of breath. They sat forehead to forehead, Emilio tangling his fingers in her hair. "You have to go be Blondie again."

Blanche looked around for the wig and found it in the back seat. She pulled it over her head. "How do I look?"

"When will it be normal again?"

"What, you? Me? How?" She kissed him, hard and full.

"This feels very normal to me."

"I love the way you smell."

"What? Like fear and sweat? I delivered a baby yesterday. I must smell like the old hog shed."

"I'd say you're one sweet *cerdito*." It was hard to imagine they were in the middle of one of the largest cities in the world—and in the middle of such a mess. There wasn't a soul around. "I wish we could just stay like this. Not go in there. Just sit." She put her head on his shoulder.

"I know, I hear you. But let's do this and be done with them." He perched the cat-eye glassed on her nose and kissed it. "We will be one step closer to a resolution."

"Don't I wish. We can warn her. Tell her to go to El Patrón and talk her way back in so they'll leave you alone. It's worth a try. She's not stupid. She's got to figure this out, or she'll be dead. Seems like incentive enough."

Emilio and Blanche entered the clinic. Blanche gasped. The desk lay in smithereens on its side in the middle of floor, the marble top cracked in half and splinters of white- and gold-painted wood scattered about. The place was empty. "Doctor Flórez?" Then she saw her.

They crossed the slick floor to the back of the storefront. Oleantha lay in a heap, blood pooling under her head. She was barefoot, clasping a small dagger in her fist. Emilio bent over her, felt for a pulse. "She's been shot, looks like twice in the upper torso. But she's alive. We need an ambulance."

Blanche crouched next to Emilio, trying to hold the phone steady. She had Cardenal's number in her phone. She pressed it automatically and told the police operator to send an ambulance.

"Tell them to hurry, Blanche." He was loosening her top buttons, compressing the wounds to stop the bleeding. "She's lost much blood."

Oleantha's eyes popped open, but she didn't seem to be in there. She looked frantically from Emilio to Blanche. "Little *puta*," she said, and dropped off.

"Well, she'll probably be just fine," mumbled Blanche. "Her sense of recognition is just the same." She clutched the phone and ran to the window just as the wailing ambulance careened toward them.

Her eyes surveyed the broken desk, the legs and marble top cracked. Then she saw it. Next to a drawer that had shot out when the desk toppled. A large, old antique key. Shining in a sunbeam, like a pot at the end of the rainbow.

Chapter Thirty-Nine

MUMMY HAS A TICKET

"Do you know what day it is?" Blanche looked fairly ecstatic. She carried two paper cups of coffee and a bag of sugary buns, which Haasi sniffed out immediately. Blanche had been up since seven, out and about, and now she seemed raring to go.

"It's Thursday, Blanche. I mean, *jueves.*" Haasi sat cross-legged on her bed with notes and printouts spread out all around her.

"It's Museum Day!"

"Oh, jeez." Haasi bit into the bun, sugar flecking down the front of her light blue top. "Not that. I thought Cardenal was going to handle it."

"I'm sure. But he said he'd give us a heads-up. Don't you want to go over there? They're going to put a major dent in that museum theft ring today. I hope. Come on. Emilio is going to meet us."

"Blanche. Every day is museum day! For one, we've been over to the Palacio half a dozen times." Haasi waved a notebook. She was becoming something of a scholar on the fabulous pyramids and people of Teotihuacan, the ancient ruins thirty miles outside Mexico City. While Blanche was off visiting El Patrón and rescuing Emilio and finding the near-dead Oleantha Flórez, Haasi was climbing the ruins, absorbed in the mysterious history of the indigenous Nahua, Otomi, and Totonac, who came well before the Aztecs. She'd interviewed locals, brushed up on her Spanish, and read tracts and codices about central Mexico—even before it was called Mexico.

"Wow, Haas. What is all this stuff? Heck with the travel article. You ought to write a book."

"Now, I just might do that."

"You look like a regular Quetzalcoatl rising from the… papers?"

"Speaking of plumed serpents, I was thinking of visiting María again. Remember? The woman of the snake vibe?"

Blanche shivered. She flopped down on her bed. "Creepy. I picked up some anti-snake herbs from Oleantha the first time I went to see her. I like to carry it around."

"To keep the snakes away?"

"Apparently it's not working. We've run into a number of snakes."

A collective sigh.

"That woman, Oleantha, is a real snake," said Haasi. "They say she's going to pull through just fine. But we won't be here to see it."

Blanche put her hands between her knees, the corners of her mouth drooping. "I know. I think Cardenal is going to cut us loose, and we have to go. Eventually. I'm going to have to say goodbye to Emilio."

Haasi tossed her notebook aside, moved over next to Blanche, and put her arm around her cousin. "You know what they say here. *Adiós. Hasta la vista.* Not goodbye, not in Mexico."

"We'll see each other; I just know it. He's going for a fellowship at the University of Florida, but it'll be a while." She was smiling again. "For now, museum day, he's going to meet us over near the Palacio. You will come, won't you, Haas? Blussberg is supposed to take that flight later. Cardenal tells me they've been staking out the lab and the Palacio. They're figuring he's going to make a move to get that mummy out of there sometime today, and they want to catch them in the act."

"With La Escandolera out of the picture, and El Jefe, I'd say El Patrón is down a couple helpers." Haasi finished braiding her long hair. She was dressed in a short plaid skirt. She brushed the sugar off her light blue top. "How do you know all this—besides what you found out during your little escapade to Blussberg's office?"

"I've been bugging Cardenal, and he finally came around. He's been very vague but I got the basic scoop." Blanche already had her bag on her shoulder. "He kept saying he wouldn't be pressured, but I wouldn't give up."

"Oh, no kidding." Haasi was smiling. She reached for that last bite of pastry.

"Must have called him half a dozen times. I reminded him of the shooting and the mummy and I pulled at a couple of other threads that have been helpful to him and his investigation. I kept pulling until I got some action. He's a tough nut. But I think he likes us."

"Well, good for us. Ready?"

El Patrón had no desire to get his hands dirty on the transfer of the art-filled mummy from the lab to the airport. It was the job of his crew, but his crew was seriously depleted with El Jefe and Doctor Flórez out on "medical leave." Nando was on a mission. El Patrón didn't like to bring more than a couple of "assistants" into a project, and he already had enough people in the know. He liked to guard his secrets, and this project required the utmost secrecy. It had to be streamlined. Millions were riding on its success. The single-piece deliveries had gone well, but this was the big one. It was nerve-racking that he had to trust that bozo Blussberg and his ridiculous assistant López. He'd expected too much of them. Was his judgment slipping? They'd both turned out to be nearly brainless; when this was over, he was going to have to get rid of them and make some inroads with other contacts in the arts field. Blussberg and López had been in on the ground floor, and they'd have to finish it. The plan was crowded enough.

López was going to drive the SUV to the airport. They would have to move the box with the mummy in it out the back door of the lab and into the SUV. How hard could this be? The mummy itself couldn't weigh that many kilos, but with its burden of jewels, sculpture, and ancient weapons, the ancient one had taken on some heft. No matter. They could do this. Time to move the goods. He'd taken extra pain meds so he could ignore the piercing pain in his knees and hips. The thought of all that money helped.

El Patrón had gone into the lab through the courtyard. The lab was dim for midday, but they knew their business and they had to be quick about it. Blussberg fussed with the lock on a hidden closet, camouflaged in the paneling. He rolled out the gurney and on top sat the mummy in a box. El Patrón said, "Did you go over all this with Oleantha? You have the inventory? What if they check at the airport?"

"Hold on, Rodrigo. Oleantha gave me the inventory, and the papers. They are not going to bother me at the airport. I have credentials for the transfer of material from the Palacio, and that includes the Mayan exhibit to Paris. This is an extension of that little caper. If they open the box and see this mummy, I have proof I'm moving items for the exhibition."

"I hope they don't x-ray it," El Patrón mumbled.

"They won't. I have papers that say no x-rays or search are allowed because of the delicate nature of the contents. They are not to tamper with it. Thanks to Oleantha. I don't know how she did it, but it got done."

El Patrón pulled at his pointy beard. "Yes, she was good for some things. Now I'll have to cultivate others..."

"Why? I hear she's going to recover. You need someone, Rodrigo. She's served a purpose, an important one. Don't be a fool. We couldn't have done this if she hadn't cooked that mummy from the dead girl and switched out the exhibit. *And* helped with all this paperwork."

"She *served*. Operative word." He was becoming impatient. "She bungled the switch of the mummies. She left that pink clip, those hairs in the lab, the ledger open. Worst of all, she acts like the Duchess of Alba. She's too demanding, too expensive."

Blussberg sighed. He mumbled, "What's done is done."

El Patrón was busy looking over the contents of the box. Satisfied, he drew the lid closed and López nailed it shut.

"Let's get on with it," said Blussberg. "I have the permits to load it at the airport, and I've got the receiver lined up in Frankfurt. Once I meet Franz and deliver the box, funds will be transferred to the Swiss bank account. Per our deal. You can wire me my cut once you get confirmation."

"Tell Franz I'm working on a plan to move some items from the Bellas Artes and the Templo museum and maybe another. The paintings are newer, will bring less, but the volcanic sculpture and greenstone from the museums are priceless, thousands of years old. Should get millions for what I have lined up."

Blussberg was all smiles. He knew El Patrón was careful. He involved few people in the schemes, and those who were involved were paid off handsomely. "Spreading the joy of Mexico, one piece at a time." He wrung his hands, his lips wet at the thought of all that loot. And his impossible prospects with Oleantha. Now that he had money...

"I need to bring the SUV around to the door. I'll meet you out back," said López.

El Patrón turned to López, smirking at the scrawny look of him. López withered at the stare.

"*Bueno*. Go out through the courtyard. Drive up in the alley and come back up here. The three of us will lift it and get it out of here. ¡*Vámonos!*"

Chapter Forty

THE BUG BITES

BLANCHE, EMILIO, AND HAASI WAITED near the alleyway to the lab. They carried paper cups and appeared to be chatting. It was a bright spring afternoon, temperature in the low 70s, and flocks of Mexicans crossed the Zocalo headed back from the *comida* and toward late-day activities. Three sets of eyes scanned the building nearby, but they were nicely hidden in the crowd.

"We are not going to get in the way, believe me," said Blanche. "But we are here, and we earned the right to be here." She held the phone away from her ear so Emilio and Haasi could listen to the detective.

Cardenal chuckled. "You are—what is it you Americans say—a dog with a bone."

Haasi and Emilio nodded.

"Very funny," said Blanche. "You know we are going to stand here until this is done."

"*Mira.* This is tedious. We've been here for hours, and nothing is going on. This doesn't concern you, for now. I can't order you off the Zocalo, but you need to stay clear. I don't want you in the way, and I don't want you to get hurt."

"When will you know they're loading stuff? And how?"

"We know. We can hear."

Blanche was exhilarated to the tips of her toes. "Yes! You have a bug!"

"I didn't say that, Blanche. Now just stay clear. I have to go."

She slipped the phone into her pocket. Haasi and Emilio looked at her curiously. "It's going to work, I'm just sure. They're bugging the lab."

"He didn't really say that."

"Well, not exactly, but close enough."

They waited a half hour, then an hour. The flow of activity around the Zocalo was a regular parade, and they were hardly bored, especially hanging out together.

A black Escalade rounded the corner and headed toward the alleyway. It pulled up to the seemingly deserted building. The three lookie-loos crept closer to the building, sipping coffee nonchalantly. They snuck into a deep doorway recess not twenty feet from the entrance to the lab and waited.

"Kind of cozy here, just the three of us," Blanche said. But she was shaking, anticipating the heist, and another chapter in solving the case of the needless death of Lalia Solis. She wanted to get hold of Amparo and tell her they had done all they could to find the killer.

Emilio craned his neck to watch the car. Haasi linked arms with Blanche. "If this is our version of the three Musketeers, we could use a sword or two, or three."

"Who needs swords? We've brains, and brawn, and just plain stubbornness." He put his arm around Blanche. "I hope when this is over, we can calm down and enjoy the rest of this trip…"

López flipped open the back hatch of the SUV and ran back inside the building. In minutes he, Blussberg, and El Patrón emerged lugging a long box. They huffed and grunted and got the thing into the back. A door slammed. López started the car.

"Hey! They can't get away with that!" It was Blanche, and despite the noise of traffic and crowds in the busiest corner of the country, her voice carried down the alley like she was standing in an empty cave. She clapped a hand over her mouth.

"That's why we call her Bang," said Haasi.

Emilio was silent, standing in front of the two women, his arms out to the sides. "Get back," he whispered hoarsely. El Patrón stood next to the SUV and turned at once toward the sound of Blanche's voice. He pulled out a small silver pistol and shot. First high above the doorway, and then when he saw the three huddled under the stone arch, he aimed directly at Emilio. Blanche pulled him into a crouch, but it was too late. The gun went off again. Emilio went down.

Another door slammed, and the SUV took off.

Detective Cardenal got it all. Bugs had been set up in the lab with clearance from the medical facility, and in the Palacio for good measure, and the police were ready to move at his direction. Now this. A detail with screaming sirens shot off after the SUV as it sped down the alley.

The detective needed to attend to the shooting. He'd seen the commotion through binoculars, and even with the noise on the Zocalo, he couldn't mistake the sound of the shots. He prayed it wasn't bad, but there was nothing good about gunshots in a crowd.

He jumped out of the police van, a nondescript grey paneled vehicle parked near the lab. He ran toward the alley. "Blanche! I told you to stay clear. ¡*Carrajo!*" He held the radio in one hand, yelling into it for an ambulance all the while he yelled at Blanche. She and Haasi both looked like someone had hit them over the head.

Emilio sat up, one hand pressing his shoulder. "I'll be fine. It went right through the muscle." His face was pale.

Blanche was ripping the bottom of her T-shirt into raggedy

strips and holding them against his chest in an effort to staunch the blood. She kept looking in his eyes, and then to the spot near his shoulder that seeped red. He squeezed her with his free hand. "Bang. What a perfect name for you."

Blanche put her hand on his cheek. "Emilio, I'm sorry. Oh my God, I am so sorry!"

Haasi stood up. "What a sorry bunch of goons! Are the police picking them up, detective?"

Cardenal patted the top of his head. "We have them on the radar. We're heading them off."

They nabbed El Patrón, Blussberg, and López—and their ancient passenger stuffed with loot. The mummy was on its way back to the Convento from which it was borrowed to rest in peace. The recovered artifacts would be assembled and catalogued by the national arts alliances to be returned to the rightful collections. The perpetrators, including El Jefe, began to sing when it was clear they would all go to jail for complicity in art theft, murder, and kidnapping. They had myriad reasons, and a lot of time, to think it over while Cardenal and his team planned to piece together all the parts. Their culpability was all picked up on the bugs planted in the lab. In Mexico, Cardenal explained to Blanche in a rundown of the arrest and charges, one is guilty until proven innocent. They would all sit for quite a long time while authorities sorted things out and assigned blame.

Blanche and Cardenal sat in his office where he revealed some of the details. Blanche had calculated that it was a good time to produce another chink in the wall of chicanery and thievery. She handed over the key she'd found next to Oleantha's broken desk. "Maybe I shouldn't have picked this up at the scene, but I was afraid it would get lost."

"Well, you're right about that. How do we know where that key came from?" Cardenal wore a stern look.

"I'm telling you where it came from. I found it when we found her, and if we hadn't walked in when we did, she'd be dead. Come on, detective. You need to follow up with it. This key may open records, evidence, stuff she's into. You know?"

"*Sí*, Blanche. I know."

Emilio was recovering nicely. He did not require a hospital stay, but he needed time off from practicing his doctor duties. The medical academy had gotten him a room at the hotel near his caretakers so that he could rest. "Nurse" Blanche was in attendance while the three of them enjoyed a beer on the patio of her hotel.

Haasi breathed a sigh of relief and lifted her Modelo to the good news that the bad guys were locked up and they could get some peace in their final days in Mexico. She wondered out loud how the whole scene at the lab and Palacio would fit into a travel article. "You can't say this place isn't five-star in the action category, Bang. Let's see if we can just chill now."

Blanche and Emilio were sitting on the loveseat on the patio, holding hands. They raised them in one loving, entwined fist of solidarity. "We first and second that!" Emilio smiled. He appeared to be content; Blanche was calm. For the moment.

Cardenal requested that Blanche and Haasi come to police headquarters for a special ceremony. He wanted to celebrate "closing the books on a bad chapter," he said.

Blanche and Haasi were dressed in their best. Blanche was in yet another thrift-store find, a red paisley shift cinched at the waist with a silver belt. Haasi had opted for her black sheath. "I'd like to stay in the background on this one," Haasi said.

"*Imposible*. Especially when you look like Aztec royalty," said Blanche.

"Nahua. These days, I'm channeling Nahua."

A small group of police officers, María—who had introduced them to Detective Cardinal—Carmen and Eddie, and, of course, Emilio, with his arm in a sling, clustered around the detective. He held a document in a leather-bound folder. He cleared his throat. "It is with great pleasure that we present this *reconocimiento* to the *Señoritas* Blanche Murninghan and Haasi Hakla for their assistance in the pursuit of justice. And, may I add, their doggedness."

Blanche laughed. "The dog with the bone?"

"*Sí*," the detective said. He seemed to be in a particularly voluble mood, and added to that, there was a party of cake and bubbly set up on a long linen-covered table in the meeting room. Sun blazed through the wide windows, and Blanche could see the lovely treetops of the park across the street. It was a time for celebration, a victory over evildoers. "You saw something, and you said something. That is important." His eyes were serious now. He handed a copy of the *reconocimiento*, one to Blanche and one to Haasi. "We are grateful."

Eddie held his cane over his head. "*Let's dance!*"

"Oh, Eddie, sit down" said Carmen.

"Will you say a few words, Blanche?"

"Unaccustomed as I am to public speaking…" Haasi gave her poke in the ribs. "I just want to say, I love you all."

Haasi put her arm around Blanche's shoulders. Emilio squeezed her hand.

The *Tres-Leches* cake was delicious, and so was the Cava wine.

It was a recognition ceremony, but it was also a *hasta-la-vista* ceremony.

Cardenal pulled Blanche and Haasi off to the side. He was frowning now, completely switched from party to police mode.

"What's the matter? Are you sorry we're leaving?" Blanche was feeling the bubbly after all the toasting and celebration. Her cheeks were flushed red. She pushed away the melancholy that crept into her thoughts. It would be *hasta la vista* soon.

"*Pues, sí.* I hope you will return to Mexico one day and have, shall we say, a less eventful time of it. I want to thank you both."

Haasi was on a sugar high, working on a second piece of the white cake with strawberries, cream, and chocolate. "It has never been boring. It is delicious here, and you are all so kind and generous." She delivered this in a cool monotone, but her eyes were dancing with warmth.

"Not everyone," he said. "I am sorry for the trouble, especially the trouble with Doctor Flórez. The key you gave me, Blanche, it opened a closet in her apartment that was a treasure of books and records of all of her deeds. With names. We have enough evidence to put everyone in El Patrón's circle away, including him. Doctor Flórez was very culpable."

"Was? What do you mean *was*? Did she get out of this one, too?" Blanche was once again incredulous at how slippery the doctor could be.

"No, she did not get out of this one. She won't be causing anyone any more trouble. Ever again."

"Did you arrest her?"

"That is not possible. She is dead. She was murdered in her hospital bed. The killer got past the guard, smothered her in her sleep."

It was fortunate there was a chair behind Blanche. She melted backward and sat. Haasi's face was impassive as a dark sky, and for a heartbeat, Blanche wondered at her expression. Haasi's reaction to La Escandolera's kidnapping caper that put Blanche in grave danger, plus the doctor's other scandalous behavior—particularly the gruesome treatment of Lalia Solis—had been venomous, even vengeful.

Blanche recovered. She thrust her chin at the detective. "Why are you telling me this?"

"I thought you should know. Since you are the one who has helped so much. Pushed us to follow leads, look into all this trouble." He patted his head. "Feels like months ago. It's only been a few weeks."

"We were glad to help." Blanche linked her arm in Haasi's. But she was anxious. She'd gotten to know the detective, and she felt he was holding back. And then he didn't.

"Thought you should see this." He held out his enormous fist and opened it; in the middle of his palm was a pink hair clip. "We found this next to the body of Oleantha Flórez."

Chapter Forty-One

THE END IS SOMETIMES THE BEGINNING

BLANCHE TRIED TO RELAX, AND THIS WAS DIFFICULT despite the brilliant blue, sunny sky flying past her window. She was less bird and more fish. It was a six-hour flight, and she had to settle in. Haasi was rolled up in a ball, napping. Blanche got a whiff of a meat-like aroma wafting up the aisle and imagined tacos. Or beans and chiles. Something delicious, like in those swinging white boxes she saw every day at *comida* time.

She was "homesick" for Mexico already, and for Emilio. Carmen had insisted on driving them to the airport. They had huddled—more like cuddled—together in the huge hangar-like departure area. Emilio had nearly recovered his strength, and he did quite well with one "wing," which was draped around Blanche. She called him "Angelito"—one angel to another. He was free to finish his social service in peace, now that El Patrón and his crew were put away. Emilio had Bella to keep him company, and the plan was for the two of them to come to Florida as soon as he could get approval for a fellowship. He already had a "patron" at the university who would be happy and willing to facilitate Emilio's study of children's diseases and birth defects. The paperwork would be tedious, but it was possible. He'd picked a dire need, and his heart was in it. Blanche's own heart swelled with pride and hope for him. She missed him, and couldn't wait to see him again. And she would forever be sorry she'd opened her big mouth and gotten him shot.

The flight attendant plopped a tray down with beef in gravy, mashed potatoes, and cooked carrots, all wrapped in plastic. It was a strange selection for a flight from Mexico, and a bite of reality. She was headed home. Blanche longed for one of those juicy *tacos de chamorro* and fresh tortillas with roasted serranos and an orange Victoria on the side. But more than that, she longed for Emilio.

She pushed the food away. Her mind drifted back to Mexico City. The most fascinating place she'd ever been—outside of Santa Maria Island, Florida. Haasi wasn't thinking at all, curled up on two seats next to Blanche. Zonked out. She'd consumed two burritos and a pineapple-and-mango smoothie at the airport, so she was set for food, for now. Blanche knew she'd wake up ravenous. But then they'd be back in the land of McDonald's. Not that either one of them ate that stuff...

Back at the cabin on Santa Maria, Blanche walked in the door and the nostalgia of old cedar and memory rushed at her and wrapped her in welcome. Peace had settled, justice had been served. She was glad to be back on her island. She turned to look at the Gulf of Mexico, and her dreams flew faraway over the water. Over the stark white sand, over the turquoise Gulf. Under a bright pink sky—the color of Lalia Solis's hair clip.

ABOUT THE AUTHOR

Nancy Nau Sullivan began writing wavy lines at age six, thinking it was the beginning of her first novel. It wasn't. But she didn't stop writing: letters at first, then eight years of newspaper work in high school and college, in editorial posts at New York magazines, and for newspapers throughout the Midwest.

Nancy has a master's in journalism from Marquette University. She grew up outside Chicago but often visited Anna Maria Island, Florida. She returned there with her family and wrote an award-winning memoir *The Last Cadillac* (Walrus 2016) about the years she cared for her father while the kids were still at home, a harrowing adventure of travel, health issues, adolescent angst, with a hurricane thrown in for good measure.

The author has gone back to that setting for this first in her mystery series, *Saving Tuna Street*, creating the fictional Santa Maria Island home of Blanche "Bang" Murninghan. Blanche has feet of sand and will be off to Mexico, Ireland, and other parts for further mayhem in the series. But she always returns to Santa Maria Island.

Nancy, for the most part, lives in Northwest Indiana.

Follow Nancy:

www.nancynausullivan.com

@NauSullivan.